Double Exposure

Lori Roberts Herbst

Editor: Lisa Mathews, Kill Your Darlings Editing Services
Cover Designer: Molly Burton, Cozy Cover Designs

ISBN-13: 978-1-7362593-3-7
First printing: June 2021

Electronic edition:
ISBN-13: 978-1-7362593-2-0

For my parents.
I think they would be proud.

Also by Lori Roberts Herbst

SUITABLE FOR FRAMING
(Callie Cassidy Mysteries Book 1)

Acknowledgements

Many thanks to the following people:

My editor, Lisa Mathews at Kill Your Darlings Editing Services. Her thorough, thoughtful evaluations are slowly but surely sculpting me into the full-fledged author I aspire to be.

Cover designer Molly Burton of Cozy Cover Designs. What an amazingly talented and patient person she is.

My beta readers Lisa Nelson, Leslie Noyes, Barb Schlichting, Katie Shapiro, and Liz Tully. I so appreciate your time and input.

My brother-in-law David, who spotted a serious flaw in the book just in time for me to fix it.

My Sisters in Crime, especially the Guppies, who have been so generous sharing their time and resources.

My family. If you're a new writer, it certainly pays to have a large extended family. This wonderful group of people not only bought my first book, they read it, praised it, and mercilessly hawked it to their friends. Then they pressured me to write another one. How could I let them down?

Readers! What an honor to have people read my books, take the time to review them, sign up for my newsletter, and even send me the occasional email. I'm so grateful to all of you.

And finally, my husband Paul, who tirelessly proofreads every draft of every book, comments and critiques, encourages and applauds. Not only does he make me a better writer, he makes me a better person.

1

"Good news, Callie. You don't suck. At least, not today."

The voice offering such a lofty compliment belonged to Ethan McGregor, the business teacher at the local high school. I'd hired him this summer to promote my fledgling photography gallery, Sundance Studio. Now he stood in front of the shop, arm extended like a *Price is Right* model toward the spotless display windows and immaculate stoop.

Hands on my hips, I inspected every inch of the facade. "At least they left us alone last night," I said.

"Maybe the culprits are done for good. Bored with their stupid pranks." His blue eyes twinkled beneath short-cropped red hair, and his smile radiated through his scruffy beard and mustache. At twenty-eight, he was the definition of a Scottish ginger. Every time I looked at him, broad shouldered and stocky, I glanced down to check if he was sporting a kilt.

His grin was infectious, and I smiled back before I ran my finger across the inscription etched on the door's glass insert. *Sundance Studio, Callahan Cassidy, Photographer.* Sometimes I still had trouble believing I was back in my hometown, Rock Creek Village, and that this gallery belonged to me. The reflection of the Rocky Mountains shimmered in the glass. I turned to gaze at them, awash in the buttery early morning light. A soft breeze carried the scent of June wildflowers, and I drew it in before shifting my attention back to the window.

"I hope you're right," I said. "I don't know how much more of this I could take without going ballistic."

The vandalism had started on Monday, though I didn't realize at the time that's what it was. That morning, I'd arrived to find the iron bracket jutting from above the gallery's entrance securely in place, but the wooden Sundance Studio plaque that hung from it was missing. I'd discovered the sign propped against the shop's entrance and assumed it had simply fallen. The victim of a faulty screw, and a good Samaritan had moved it out of the path of pedestrians. I'd gotten my ladder, reattached the sign, and gone about my day.

On Tuesday, I'd been greeted with a mound of puckered tomatoes, peeled onions, and wilted lettuce littering my stoop, as if a passing zombie suddenly remembered he was a carnivore and disposed of his rotting salad at my door. A glance down Evergreen Way had confirmed that the salad shooter hadn't victimized any of the other shops. I'd experienced my first twinge of concern.

Yesterday, that twinge had blossomed into full-blown paranoia. A would-be graffiti artist had scrawled the B word in red spray paint across the studio's box window, followed by the poetic words: *You suck, Callie.* Now I knew it was personal.

Once I'd recovered from the jolt, and the wave of embarrassment that accompanied it, I snapped a few pictures to document the assault on my character and then filled a bucket with soapy water. After scrubbing the offensive words from the glass, I quizzed neighboring shop owners. No one had witnessed the event, nor had they experienced any vandalism at their own shops. My father Butch, the former Rock Creek Village police chief, had insisted I file a police report. I done as he instructed, but I knew the police couldn't do much about it. I just had to cross my fingers and hope the pranks didn't escalate.

Though my realistic—okay, cynical—nature warned me against premature relief, I was grateful that today provided, if not an end, a reprieve. It couldn't have come at a better time.

"Thank goodness," I said. "We have so much to do. No time to pick up garbage or clean windows." I flashed Ethan a grateful smile. "Thanks again for coming in so early."

"Will Alexis be deigning to join us?"

I glanced at my watch, ignoring his sarcasm. "She should be here any time." At twenty-two, Alexis Butler, the assistant I'd hired a month ago, hadn't developed Ethan's level of preoccupation with punctuality, but she'd proven reliable. She wouldn't let us down.

"Happy hour starts at five, right?" Ethan asked.

I nodded as I dug into my pocket, my nerves jangling almost as loudly as my keys. "We'll close the gallery at one to set up. Shouldn't take more than an hour to put out the tables and string the lights. Then we can all go home and change into our party clothes. I'll be back here at four so Sam can set up catering, but I won't need you and Alexis until four-thirty."

When I finally extracted the keys from my pocket, I fumbled them and watched as they clattered to the sidewalk. Ethan stooped to retrieve them. "Nervous much?" he asked.

"Is it obvious?"

"Shoulders up to your ears, ragged breath, can't hang onto a key. I'd say so." With a steady hand, he inserted the key into the lock and pushed the door open. "Take a breath. It's only a bunch of *Washington Sentinel* reporters coming to see your new digs. It's not like you're hosting Ironman and Thor."

That elicited an actual laugh, my first in days. Ethan was right. I was getting riled up trying to impress my former boss and some ex-colleagues, most of whom I hadn't even liked much.

"I'll try to relax," I said, taking one of those meditative breaths I'd learned down the street at Yoga Delight.

But I couldn't reach my inner Zen. My guests were fancy *Sentinel* journalists, after all, and I'd recently left their ranks to become a semi-obscure landscape photographer, catering mainly to tourists. I kept imagining those judgmental eyes scrutinizing my gallery with an air of superiority.

You would have been exactly the same way a year ago, I told myself.

Still, I yearned to impress my former colleagues. My mind raced with all the tasks I needed to accomplish before they arrived. Finish the photojournalism display, reorganize the portrait section, change out some of the winter landscapes to highlight summer shots. Only a few hours to complete those chores—all while dealing with what I hoped would be a steady flow of shoppers.

Ethan snapped his fingers in front of my face. "Earth to Callie. My friend, the best thing you can do to calm yourself is to scratch items off your to-do list. Let's get started."

I nodded and hurried into the studio, flicking on the light. Biting my lip, I paused to scan the walls, trying to see my photos as a newcomer might. First, my eye rested on the gallery's focal point: a huge panoramic shot of the majestic Rockies soaring heavenward from a meadow filled with wildflowers. This centerpiece was surrounded by a colorful array of wildlife photos—elk, mountain goats, deer, marmots, and chipmunks. Beside the door, a rack held postcard-sized prints of original Callie Cassidy landscape photos. Pride welled inside me. Even my snooty ex-coworkers would have to admit the studio was stunning.

Smiling to myself, I headed toward the sales counter. Then my nose twitched as I detected a foul odor wafting through the usually pine-scented space. The smell was unpleasant but familiar, pungent but organic—an odor I'd experienced a hundred times in my back yard. What was it doing inside my gallery?

Behind me, Ethan called out, his tone urgent. "Callie, stop. Watch your step."

I turned to look at him, my right foot hovering mid-air. But momentum partnered with gravity, and my beige canvas shoe descended with a squish.

Into a huge brown pile of poop.

I leapt backwards and squealed like a schoolgirl. I'd covered wars and murders and gruesome accidents. I'd seen more dead bodies than I cared to remember—people who'd been shot and bludgeoned and stabbed—including a resident of our own village just a few months ago. All those scenes I'd handled with fortitude.

But poop was my kryptonite.

How ironic that I had chosen two four-legged poop machines as my roommates.

Just then, the bell above the door jingled and Alexis entered, pulling her frizzy brown hair into a ponytail. She froze, and her brown eyes narrowed. "Ugh. What reeks?" Her eyes landed on my foot, hovering in place above the mess. "Eww," she said, wrinkling her nose. "Is that Woody's doing? Where's that bad dog hiding?"

If he had been privy to Alexis's comment, my golden retriever, who at this moment was likely snuggled up with his feline brother Carl at our new townhome, would have lifted his snout in haughty disdain. Since he wasn't here to defend himself, I did it for him. "Woody hasn't pooped inside since his puppy days. This was on the floor when Ethan and I walked in."

She pursed her lips. "Another visit from the vandals? And inside this time. That's a little scary. How did they get inside?"

"Good question," I said. "I'm certain I locked the doors before I left last night. At least, I think I did..." In truth, the memory was hazy. Yesterday had been a long and hectic day, and I'd been exhausted by the end of it.

"I just don't get it," Alexis said. "Who would go to all this trouble?"

"I know who gets my vote," Ethan said. "Those twits Braden and Banner Ratliff. Juvenile pranks are just their speed." He scowled and stalked off to the tiny kitchen that lay behind the back wall of the gallery.

"Tweedledee and Tweedledum." I murmured, using my private nickname for the boys. After the events that had occurred a few months ago, the twins had reason to hate me—at least in their own minds. They'd moved to Denver in February to escape village gossip but had returned to Rock Creek Village a couple of weeks ago, just before the incidents here at the gallery.

Alexis took a deep breath and followed it with a gagging noise. "Well, I'm not cleaning it up." She tiptoed around the poop and went behind the sales desk, a frown lining her face.

Ethan emerged from the back with a bucket of soapy water, a dustpan, and a plastic ruler he'd use for a scoop. "Don't worry, you delicate little flower," he said to Alexis. "Your knight in shining armor is here to take care of the mess. As usual."

She shot him an angry glare and lifted her hand, middle finger extended. I suppressed a smile. "Now, now. You two play nice. We have too much to do to indulge in faux sibling squabbles." I wrangled out of my soiled shoe and hobbled toward the front door. "Thanks for cleaning up, Ethan. Alexis, after he's done, please figure out how to get rid of the odor. I'd rather not open up with the smell of feces hanging in the air."

As I reached out to relock the door, I glanced through the glass in the door and did a quick double take.

Across the street, on a bench in front of the Peak Inn, two boys were laughing and elbowing one another. I leaned closer and peered out at them. They stared straight at me with smirks on their faces. One of them pinched his nose, while the other flapped his hand in front of his face, as if waving away a stench.

Yep. It was the Ratliff twins. I yanked open the door, but before I could cross the street to confront them, they jumped off the bench and took off down the street.

As I stood on the sidewalk and watched them sprint away, I pondered what other evil plots they had in store for me—and how I could put a stop to them.

2

Mellow jazz played softly through the gallery's speakers. A subtle scent of pine drifted through the air. After a deep sniff, I detected no trace of this morning's earlier odor.

Satisfied, I stood near the door and surveyed my little kingdom. From behind the sales counter, now serving as a bar, Ethan handed out bottles of Coors and refilled wine glasses with an award-winning Colorado pinot noir. Elyse, Sam's teenaged daughter whom I'd hired as a server tonight, paused to whisper something to Alexis. The two of them giggled. They threw a glance in my direction and hurriedly resumed their duties, carrying silver trays laden with finger foods.

Elyse made her way over to me, extending her tray. Since I'd already tasted the bacon-wrapped water chestnut and the crab-stuffed cucumber, I selected a pineapple chicken skewer and popped a bit into my mouth. "Your dad outdid himself," I said. Sam Petrie owned and operated Snow Plow Chow, in my opinion the best cafe in the Rockies. Perhaps I was a bit biased, since he was my…Was he my boyfriend, really? That sounded a bit adolescent. Lover? Too theatrical. I still hadn't discovered a way to characterize our current relationship, a reboot of our high school romance twenty-five years ago.

"He's showing off," Elyse said. "Probably wants to impress your fancy friends." She grinned and tossed her long blond ponytail. "You look great, by the way. Working that dress."

"Thanks." I blushed at the compliment, but it pleased me just the same. When her father had dropped off the food earlier, he'd said much the same thing, accompanying his words with a steamy embrace. Later, I'd studied myself in the mirror before the guests arrived, and even I had been content with what I'd seen. A fern-colored sheath, snug around my hips and waist, accentuated my figure, slimmer now thanks to a semi-regular yoga and jogging routine. My dark hair hung loose around my shoulders, and I felt pretty and feminine in a way I hadn't in a long time.

I was even wearing makeup and heels. Who was I? My former colleagues had hardly recognized me when they'd arrived.

"I'd better get back to work," Elyse said. "Gotta keep these big-city folks fed."

The big-city folks, as she put it, meandered around the periphery of the open room, studying the array of photo displays mounted on the walls. The first grouping was devoted to winter scenes: snow covered mountains gleaming in the sunshine, pine trees wearing lush white coats, icicles hanging from awnings of village shops. Next, I'd arranged a few spring landscape photos—meadows blanketed in wildflowers and miniature waterfalls created by the melting snow. A display of Rocky Mountains wildlife seemed to be generating positive attention. Broad-chested elk stood proudly in the middle of Evergreen Way. Bighorn sheep clambered up rocky crags. Marmots frolicked at the edge of Rock Creek. And, of course, my prize—a rarely sighted mountain lion, his face captured mid-yawn.

But the pièce de résistance, at least as far as my fellow journalists were concerned, was the collection of photos on a freestanding partition—ten of the best journalistic photos I'd taken over the course of my career. The photos represented a mixture of settings and moods, including a joyous celebration of a child's cancer-free diagnosis, an anxiety-laden election night shot, a young man kissing his withered grandmother goodbye as she lay in her coffin, a proud Great Dane winning Best of Show.

And in the center of it all, with a beam spotlighting it from overhead, hung the photo that won me the Felden Award for Excellence in Journalism.

In it, a young woman lay in a patch of grass, dandelions sprouting around her. Ebony hair fanned outward from an ivory-toned face. Her eyes were closed, and her lips curved slightly upward as if she were in the throes of a pleasant dream. But the syringe jutting from the crook of her arm told the true story.

Even now, five years later, the vision of the young overdose victim lying in a field alongside the highway still haunted me.

A touch at my elbow made me jump, and I pivoted to find my former boss, Preston Garrison, managing editor of *The Washington Sentinel*.

I swatted him on the arm. "You scared me."

His hazel eyes sparkled. "I have that effect on people." His salt-and-pepper hair was cut short above his ears, but long enough on top to sweep back in a lightly-gelled wave. Stylish, without coming across as overly suave. Tall and fit, he exuded athleticism, even in his early fifties. His tanned face carried just the right amount of cragginess, giving him the worldly handsomeness of a man who had seen it all and lived to tell about it. A face that said, *I'll protect you*, eyes that said, *You can trust me*, and a smile that said, *We could have some fun together…*

He did have an effect on people. Especially women.

I cleared my throat and gestured toward the gallery. "So, what do you think?"

"Stunning," he said, his eyes drifting from my face to my feet. "I've never seen you looking more relaxed or radiant."

Heat burned my cheeks. I took a step back and gave a

little curtsy. "Thank you, kind sir. But I was talking about the gallery. What do you think of Sundance Studio?"

He put his hands in his pockets and scanned the room. "Also stunning," he said. "Your landscapes are breathtaking, and your wildlife shots are among the best I've ever seen. *National Geographic* quality work, in fact. However…"

I held my breath. I hadn't realized how much his opinion meant to me.

"Your talents are being wasted here." He pointed toward my photojournalism display. "This is what you should be doing—what you were meant to do. You belong at *The Sentinel*. What do I have to do to lure you back? A raise? New title? Company car? Whatever it is, it's yours."

Aha. My suspicions were confirmed. As soon as I'd heard Preston planned to hold his team conference in Rock Creek Village, I'd known it was no coincidence.

Every summer, he arranged a three-day retreat for his investigative reporters, designed to reward them for their hard work—and also to prod them on to even greater achievements. I'd attended for the past eight years, traveling to Scottsdale, Hilton Head, Key West, and other desirable domestic locales.

And this year he just so happened to schedule the meeting in my hometown?

"I knew it," I said. "You're here with ulterior motives."

One side of his mouth turned up. "Now, Callie. This place is a worthy destination. A picturesque village in the foothills of the Rocky Mountains. And the Knotty Pine Resort more than meets our needs."

He had a point. The village was a nature lover's dream, and the lodge my parents owned and operated offered all the amenities. Still, I wasn't letting him off the hook. I stared at him until he gave a soft chuckle. "All right, you got me. Suffice it to say I may have dual agendas. Seriously, though, are you ready to come back to work?"

I tilted my head. "Preston, you know why I resigned. I

screwed up, big time. I can't go back."

He put a hand on my shoulder. "Callie, Jameson Jarrett was released months ago. It's over. Quit punishing yourself."

Despite myself, tears pricked my eyes. I thought I'd forgiven myself for the mistake I'd made, one that temporarily landed an innocent man in prison. When the source of my story recanted, I'd printed a retraction and done everything I could to get Jarrett out. His release marked the end of the saga, but apparently not the end of my guilt and self-recrimination.

I blinked the tears back. "I'll get there. Eventually. But really, that's not the point." I looked around the gallery, at the photos depicting the majesty of the mountains and the beauty of the wildflowers. "I'm happy here, Preston. I like what I'm doing." I gave him a wry smile. "Besides, what would Brie think if you brought me back?"

A cloud crossed his face at my mention of Brie Bohannan, the ruthless, ladder-climbing journalist who was my successor as lead investigative reporter on his team. "Don't worry about Brie. She won't be around much longer anyway, at the rate she's going."

I lifted my eyebrows, but he waved off my unspoken question. "I don't want to talk about her. I want to focus on you. I want you back. Plain and simple. I won't belabor the point right now, but as you may remember, I'm not a man who gives up easily. We'll talk again. Count on it."

He winked and walked toward the bar. Then, beer in hand, he headed to a table and sat next to his longtime assistant, Gary Padgett, who gave me a furtive glance as Preston started talking.

The conversation with my former boss had rattled me, and the tension went straight to my bladder. A quick scan of the room told me my guests were well-occupied, either exploring the photo arrays or clustering around tables to partake of Sam's delicacies. I wouldn't be missed if I took a quick bathroom break.

I walked through the gallery, stopping briefly to chat with three journalists examining my wildlife photos. Then I made my way down the short hallway toward the bathroom, which was tucked between the portrait studio and the darkroom.

As I reached out to turn the knob on the bathroom door, I heard two voices inside the tiny one-seat facility. My eyebrow lifted. What was this? A tryst in my tiny bathroom? I was glad I'd hired a cleaning crew before the gala. I'd certainly want them back to clean again tomorrow.

My sense of decorum told me to walk away and give the couple some privacy. But my curious nature held a differing opinion, and it won the debate. After all, what else could a nosy ex-journalist do? I leaned closer and eavesdropped.

"Why do you care where she is? She certainly couldn't care less about you. You're no better than a servant—just around to carry out her whims."

I didn't recognize the low but screechy female voice—one of the new reporters who'd been hired since I resigned, no doubt. But I pegged the irritated male voice that responded: Dev Joshi, a fellow photojournalist who'd been on the team for a year prior to my departure.

"Brie is my partner," he said. "If something is wrong with her, it's my responsibility to help."

Ah. No wonder the woman was so angry. If anyone could elicit such fury, it was Brie. I'd noted her absence from the happy hour, the only person at the retreat not to make an appearance. I assumed the snub was intentional. Brie had long considered me a rival, gleefully stepping into my role when I left.

Now that I had context, I deduced that the female voice belonged to Melanie Lewis, a young reporter I'd seen earlier, territorially looping her arm through Dev's. When she spoke again, her tone was edgy and tight. "You have no obligation to her. She's trying to get you fired."

"Nonsense. That's just a stupid rumor. She'd never do that to me. We're a team." He lowered his voice, and I pictured him leaning in, stroking Melanie's cheek. "You're sounding jealous, baby, but there's no need. It's strictly professional between Brie and me. You're the only one I want."

This romantic pronouncement was followed by rustling and the sound of wet slurping. Just as I began to suspect the tryst was going to happen after all, I heard Dev murmur, "Let's pick this up later in my cabin. I need to make sure Brie's all right."

"Then I'll come with you," Melanie said plaintively.

"No, you won't." He spoke with finality. "I don't need you tagging along to supervise me."

"But Dev—"

"I said no."

I heard movement, fingers turning the lock, and I scurried backwards. When Dev emerged through the door, I tried to appear as if I'd just entered the hallway. He stopped when he saw me, his face tinged pink. "I...we..." He cocked a thumb over his shoulder, and Melanie appeared, her eyes puffy.

She forced a weak smile. "Sorry, Callie. We just wanted a moment to ourselves."

I nodded as she brushed past me. Dev searched my eyes for a moment, and I looked as innocent as I could manage. "Still quite the charmer, I see."

"You know me." He grinned and ran a hand through his hair. "Callie, listen. It's been great seeing you. And this place, it's fantastic. I'm really happy for you. But I've got to run. Something I need to take care of."

I opened my mouth to respond, but before I could, he was gone.

3

That night, my physical and emotional reserves were depleted, and I fell into bed before nine p.m. When I woke up the next morning, Carl was curled around my head, and Woody's back pressed against my thigh. A queen-sized bed was barely big enough for the three of us.

Moving Carl's furry paw from my eyelids, I peeked at the clock. Just after six, two hours earlier than I usually got up. Apparently nine hours of sleep was enough, because I was wide awake. When I wriggled out from beneath the comforter, the creatures snuggled together into a two-headed ball of golden fur. *Be still my heart*, I thought, as I wrapped a quilt around my shoulders.

I tiptoed to the bedroom's French doors and stepped out onto the second-story balcony. The cool pre-dawn darkness enveloped me, and I slid into one of the sling chairs I'd bought cheap at a consignment store in Boulder. In the distance, the mountains materialized as dark silhouettes, stars twinkling above them like jewels in a crown.

My thoughts drifted to yesterday's happy hour. After Dev's abrupt departure, the evening had continued uneventfully. Melanie had donned an air of good cheer as she drank wine and chatted with her colleagues, but her troubled glances at the door and her phone screen belied her nonchalance.

Dev never returned, and Brie didn't make an appearance.

Preston ended the evening with a toast to my studio and a cryptic, "We've yet to see what the future holds for our Callahan Cassidy."

Despite my best intentions, I found his recruitment efforts flattering, and even a bit tempting. At the peak of my career, I'd been a cutting-edge convergence media specialist, paving the way in a relatively new field. I'd won a number of awards and had been widely recognized and admired. It was a heady and addictive feeling.

But it was also burdensome. Writing about and photographing a dark and angry world took its toll. In hindsight, I'd buried my idealism beneath a jaded layer of cynicism. An icy callus grew around my soul.

Then the events surrounding Jameson Jarrett's conviction culminated in my resignation, and I returned to the village of my youth with my tail between my legs.

It turned out to be the best decision I could have made. My parents provided me with a soft place to fall. I found friends, old and new, who welcomed me with open arms. I opened Sundance Studio, bought this townhome in the lower village, and reignited a relationship with the man I now believed might be the love of my life.

The icy callus began to thaw.

I breathed in the crisp, clean air and smiled. The eastern horizon gave birth to the sun, weaving pink tendrils through the clouds. In the meadow across the street, two mule deer grazed peacefully.

No, as alluring as Preston's offer might be, I didn't want that life anymore. This was my home, and I never wanted to leave here again.

My pets had spent most of yesterday on their own, so I decided they could accompany me to work today. They were gallery creatures, after all, perfectly at home in my office. After I tucked Carl into his backpack-style cat carrier and snapped a leash onto Woody's collar, we strolled out into the warm spring morning.

The trek to my studio took about thirty minutes, more than twice as long as it had when I resided in a tiny cabin on my parents' resort property. But I still walked most days, weather permitting.

Usually, the stroll down the pine tree-lined avenue, around the lake, and past the Knotty Pine Resort allowed me some quiet time to prepare my mind and spirit for the day ahead. Since the vandalism had begun, though, I'd grappled with a sense of foreboding that skittered spider-like up my spine. It was a feeling I hadn't experienced in several months, since the time I'd been involved in a murder investigation in the village. I brushed the feeling of dread away, electing to focus on optimism.

I was early today, but even at eight o'clock some of the neighboring shops were doing a brisk business. At Rocky Mountain High, the coffee house recently opened by my friend and self-appointed protector Mrs. Finney, a line formed inside. As I walked past The Fudge Factory, I caught the aroma of simmering chocolate. Down the street, I knew Sam was already serving breakfast at the Snow Plow Chow and Summer Simmons was torturing her enthusiasts at Yoga Delight.

But since the retail shops didn't open until ten, foot traffic along the avenue was still light. Approaching Sundance Studio, I steeled myself for evidence of vandals. At first glance, nothing appeared amiss. No vulgarities on the glass, no produce at the door. But yesterday, the little gift had been left inside the gallery, so I wasn't yet prepared to relax. I unlocked the door and stepped across the threshold, flicking on the lights. My eyes scanned the floor. Clean. I sniffed the air. A soft pine scent, nothing more. I inspected the walls for damage. Every photo was securely in its place.

I reached down and unhooked Woody's leash. He bounded across the floor toward my office, where the treats were kept. Carl squirmed and hissed in the carrier on my back. "Calm down, cat," I said. "Patience is a virtue."

Locking the door behind me, I followed Woody into the hallway and into the office. I squirmed out of the backpack and placed it on the desk. Carl glared at me from behind the netting. As soon as I unzipped the case, he darted from its confines and into the hallway, sputtering and yowling. I rolled my eyes. So temperamental.

I sat behind the desk and gave Woody a bone from the stash I kept in my bottom drawer. For a few minutes, I rearranged piles of invoices, sales receipts, and order forms, but I quickly realized I wasn't in the mood for paperwork. With a couple of hours to burn until I needed to flip the Closed sign to Open, I decided to do some darkroom work.

I shuffled through a stack on my desk and chose a sleeve of negatives, shots I'd selected for our Fireweed Festival booth. Ethan, marketing master extraordinaire, had suggested that matted landscape photos in a variety of small sizes would be our biggest sellers—easy for tourists to tote around and later tuck into their luggage. I'd already printed enough stock for the first day or two, but I wanted a surplus.

Stepping into the hall, I saw Carl poised on his back legs, scratching his claws against the revolving aluminum door. Woody scooted around me and trotted over to join him. When I reached them, I lifted the cat off the floor and tucked him into the crook of my arm. "You're in a mood today. Maybe I should have left you home."

Carl hissed in response, and Woody gave a yip. "What's gotten into you two? You know you're not permitted in the darkroom. Too many chemicals." I reached down and stroked Woody's soft fur, and my hand came away with at least a dozen coarse hairs. "And too much shedding."

I put the cat back on the floor and nudged the creatures back with my foot as I swiveled the door. Carl leapt over it and into the opening. I picked him up and placed him back in the hall. "Enough," I snapped. "Go take a nap. I'll be done in a while. Don't make me sorry I brought you."

The creatures looked at me mournfully. When I stepped

inside the door, I tried to shake off the nerves their behavior had awakened.

I turned the door, congratulating myself on the bargain I'd gotten when I bought it from a graphics company that had gone digital. Well worth the cost. Life was so much easier for a photographer when her darkroom was light tight.

Though I'd only had the place for a few months, I knew this darkroom space intimately and didn't bother to turn on the overhead fluorescents. I moved confidently through the pitch blackness toward the processing table at the back, where I would flip a switch to turn on the safelights and flood the room in a crimson glow.

One step. Two steps. Almost there…

I paused when I became aware of an unfamiliar scent. The darkroom always exuded a chemical odor, but this was more like perfume—and it wasn't mine. When I took another step, my knee bumped hard against something—an object out of place in the middle of the room. I reached out a hand, and my fingers made contact with a firm yet silky surface. A yielding texture. Almost like—

Skin.

With a squeal, I shuffled back toward the door. I flipped the switch, bathing the room in white light.

It took me a moment to make sense of what I was seeing. A rolling chair, the one we kept in the gallery behind the sales counter, sat in the center of the darkroom. A woman's body was slouched in the seat. My eyes first fell to her hands, which had been tied to the armrests. Then I noticed her face, tilted limply toward her left shoulder.

It was Brie Bohannan, and a camera strap was tied tightly around her neck.

4

My hand flew to my mouth, stifling a cry. Woody's bark echoed from the hall outside, accompanied by a single yowl from Carl. I shut my eyes, as if the scene before me was a hallucination I could banish. But when I looked again, Brie was still sprawled motionless in the chair.

I shook off my daze and squatted beside her, wedging my finger beneath the strap to locate her jugular. I knew I wouldn't find a pulse, but I had to be sure.

When I confirmed she was dead, I took a moment to study her. Slender and fair in life, her face now appeared bloated and purple. Her eyes were open and bulging. The blue irises were filmy, the whites tinged yellow. Her swollen tongue protruded through thin, blue lips.

I took a step back. My heart rate had slowed, and my breath came in long, even rhythms—a response to crisis I'd cultivated over decades as a journalist. The barking and yowling from the creatures had ceased, replaced by an occasional scrape of claws against the aluminum door. "I'm all right, guys," I called. "Go to the office and lie down. I'll be there in a few minutes." I doubted they understood my directive, but at least the scratching stopped.

I took my phone from my pocket and dialed 9-1-1. When the dispatcher answered, I reported finding a dead woman in my darkroom. A split second's pause on the other end indicated this wasn't a common occurrence in her world, but she rebounded quickly and told me she'd summoned emergency workers.

I disconnected before she could instruct me to stay on the line, and considered calling Raul Sanchez. Though a murder investigation last January got us off to a tumultuous start, the detective and I had now forged a mutual respect and even, dare I say, a budding friendship. My finger hovered above his number on my speed dial, but I hesitated. I knew he'd order me out of the darkroom. I also knew I'd refuse. Better to ask forgiveness than permission, I decided. At any rate, the dispatcher had likely notified him by now.

Meaning I had precious little time to investigate the scene before I'd be banished.

I paused for a moment, as I always did, to pay my respects to the departed. It was a ritual I'd clung to over the course of my career. I never wanted to lose sight of the fact that the person I was seeing—or photographing, back then—was someone's daughter, sister, friend. No matter how the person had ended up this way, she was deserving of compassion.

Ritual complete, I began my examination. Though I'd already put my finger against her neck, I was careful not to touch her again. I inspected the camera strap looped around her neck, its ends trailing down her back. The strap was a blend of nylon and leather, with a distinctive diamond pattern. I recognized it right away as one of my own. Then I noticed that my accessory drawer was open. I knew I hadn't left it that way. Was this a crime of opportunity, then, or had someone with knowledge of my darkroom's layout purposely chosen my strap as a murder weapon?

I looked at Brie's face again. Strands of smooth platinum blond hair jutted from beneath the strap, giving her the appearance of a scarecrow wearing heavy makeup. A second scan of her face revealed only one detail I hadn't noticed earlier. Above her upper lip, I saw a long, thin crease, the kind I always got from sleeping on my face. I made a mental note.

Then my eyes swept across Brie's body. From the neck down, little seemed out of place. She wore black-and-white-striped linen crop pants, belted at the waist, and a white button-down blouse sheer enough to show off a lacy camisole. Her graceful fingers displayed a sedate French manicure. Leaning closer, I noticed the nails were acrylic, likely an expensive professional job. A Tahitian black pearl set in sterling silver and surrounded by tiny diamonds sparkled on her right ring finger. I spotted a broken nail on her right index finger. That was the only anomaly—no other abrasions that would indicate a struggle.

I took a step back and continued my observations. One toned, tanned leg ended in a black espadrille wedge, but the other foot was bare. The errant shoe lay on its side several feet away.

Journalistic instinct tugged at my fingers, and muscle memory had me reaching for a camera, but I resisted the impulse. I wasn't an investigative reporter anymore, and I could only imagine the expression on Raul's face if he discovered me documenting the scene.

Still, I couldn't be blamed for poking around. It was my darkroom, after all. Who better to notice anything out of place?

In addition to the dead body, of course.

A question flashed in my mind. How had a killer—or Brie herself, for that matter—gotten inside my darkroom? After yesterday's poop incident, I'd been doubly careful to lock the studio doors when I left last night. Yet someone had gained access to my gallery.

It occurred to me that this was the first time I'd been inside the darkroom since yesterday morning—and that Brie had been a no-show at last night's happy hour. Was it possible she had been dead in my darkroom during the party? I shuddered at the thought, but I had no way of knowing. Though I'd seen my share of dead bodies, I wasn't an expert in forensics and didn't know enough about lividity and rigidity to determine how long she'd been here.

Conscious that I was running short on time, I conducted a quick study of my surroundings. I frowned when I noticed the file cabinet in the corner. The top two drawers gaped open, and a few files were strewn about.

Since my office was small and storage space limited, I kept a four-drawer cabinet in the darkroom, filled with remnants of my life as a journalist—awards I'd won, old negatives, notes on stories I'd covered. I rarely opened it, so I knew I hadn't simply forgotten to close the drawers. Someone had been searching through the contents. Brie, I wondered?

I looked again at Brie's shoe near the chair. How had she lost that shoe? Had it flown from her foot as she bucked against her killer? Other than the broken nail, nothing indicated a struggle had occurred. Perhaps the shoe had fallen from her foot as someone dragged her across the floor to the chair.

When I trailed my eyes along the path from Brie's bare foot to the shoe, I noticed a few dusty shoe prints, clearly not made by Brie's espadrille. No, these were the prints of a running shoe. I dangled my own foot above one of the prints and noted that my size seven foot was dwarfed by it. Had to be a man, I concluded. Then I thought of Mrs. Finney, whose six-foot frame was buttressed by large feet, and I amended my deduction. Women could have big feet, too. Still, I was leaning toward a masculine intruder.

I made my way gingerly across the darkroom, tracking the prints to what I assumed was their origin—the wooden door on the far wall. The traditional-style door was required by fire code as an emergency exit, and I also used it as a means of moving large items—such as a rolling chair—in and out.

A scene began to play in my mind's eye. A vague, faceless figure, sizable and strong, situated Brie in the chair and bound her wrists to the armrests. He stood behind her, coiling the strap ends around his muscular hands. Then he wound the strap across Brie's exposed throat. His biceps bulged as he took a step back, using his strength to compress her carotid arteries until her life ebbed away.

But something in my vision wasn't quite right. I knew from homicide scenes I'd covered that strangulation wouldn't cause unconsciousness for at least ten seconds, usually longer. In the meantime, wouldn't the victim be wrestling against the ligature? Wouldn't she be fighting ferociously to stay alive? But Brie's shirt was snugly tucked into her pants. Her makeup was nearly flawless, not even a smear of lipstick out of place. Aside from the few strands captured beneath the tightened strap, her hair was neatly styled. In fact, except for the displaced shoe and the single broken nail, her appearance was that of a Barbie doll in a box.

The killer must have somehow incapacitated Brie before he strangled her. But how? I didn't see any blood on her scalp. Drugs, perhaps?

Or maybe *he* was *they*—two, or more—killers working together.

I revised my vision. Now, my mind's eye watched as one person grasped Brie around the waist, pinning her in the chair, while the other secured her wrists and wrapped the strap around her neck.

All pure speculation, of course, but it made sense.

Assuming my theory explained the how, it still didn't answer the who, the why, or the when.

And how on earth had this crowd of people gained access to my darkroom?

The wailing of sirens halted my investigation. After one last look around, I hurried through the revolving door, wondering when I'd next be allowed inside my own darkroom.

I did my best to reassure Woody and Carl that I was fine before shutting them in the office. Then I went to the front entrance and peered through the window as a police car pulled to the curb and two uniformed officers got out. One was Kevin Tollison, an experienced officer I recognized from my last encounter with law enforcement. He was accompanied by a female officer who appeared to be twelve years old—a new recruit, no doubt. This would probably be her first death scene.

Tollison tipped his cap as I ushered them inside. "This is patrol officer Vicky Hardesty," he said, hiking a thumb in the woman's direction. "EMTs are on their way. Coupla minutes."

I led the officers through the gallery, down the hallway, and into the darkroom, using the wooden door. Tollison approached Brie's body without hesitation, crouching to examine her. Hardesty stiffened but quickly shook off her momentary paralysis. Tollison began reciting his observations, then paused and shot a pointed look at Hardesty, who scrambled for her little notebook and began jotting down his words.

I stood just inside the doorway, observing quietly. After a few minutes, footsteps thundered down the hallway, solid and steady, and I figured paramedics had arrived. But then I heard a familiar deep voice.

"Callie Cassidy. Why does all the trouble in this village seem to land at your doorstep?"

I took a deep breath and held back a snarky retort. *Stay calm*, I told myself. *Don't let him exasperate you.*

Then I turned to face one of the few people I knew who held the power to rile me up: Detective Raul Sanchez.

5

Dressed in brown pleated slacks, a beige dress shirt, and chocolate-colored paisley tie, Raul presented the picture of professionalism. His black hair curled around his ears, and the usual scruff on his face had grown thicker. The beginnings of a beard? I envisioned it fully grown and decided it would suit him.

His dark eyes glinted, and his mouth was set in a grim line. I braced myself for a lecture, but his voice was gentle. "Are you all right, Callie?"

I nodded. "All I did was find her. The killer is long gone."

He studied me for a moment before brushing past me into the darkroom. I felt like a puppy trailing at his heels. Raul moved to Hardesty's side and spent a moment examining Brie's body. Then he addressed the rookie cop. "Impressions?"

The young officer's eyes widened, and her partner suppressed a grin. Two experienced cops tossing the newbie into the ocean for her chance to swim—or sink.

After some momentary hemming and hawing, Hardesty found her voice. "She appears to be a victim of strangulation." Tollison rolled his eyes. Hardesty's gaze flicked from him to Raul. "What I mean is, there are no bullet wounds or other signs of trauma. No bleeding or lacerations."

Raul swirled a finger in a "go on" gesture, and Hardesty continued. "There's a broken fingernail, but otherwise, no signs of defensive wounds." She pointed at the open drawer. "I'm guessing the murder weapon came from there. Impulse killing. Crime of opportunity."

She stared at me pointedly, the implication clear. *Your* darkroom. *Your* camera strap. *Your* opportunity. From the corner of my eye, I saw Raul's mouth twitch.

I sighed. "I doubt it. I'm leaning toward premeditation."

All three sets of eyes turned toward me. I bit my lip, wishing too late that I'd stayed quiet. "For one thing, this chair doesn't belong in the darkroom. Someone brought it in here ahead of the murder." I pointed to the floor. "And see these shoe prints? They don't match Brie's shoes." I glared at Hardesty. "And they're much too big to be mine."

Raul shot me a stern look. "It seems you spent a little time poking around in here after you found the body. Even though, as you well know, protocol dictates that civilians vacate a crime scene immediately and leave it for the professionals."

And there it was. The tone. The one that filled me with the urge to recite my resume and remind Raul of all the crime scenes I'd covered during my career. "Listen, Detective, it's my darkroom. In my gallery. A woman I knew was killed here. I had every right to look around while I waited for your people to arrive. I didn't touch anything."

"Uh huh. Well, rights aside, *your* darkroom has become *my* crime scene. Please wait for me in the front room. I'll have questions when I'm through looking around for myself."

The paramedics hurried into the room then, and Raul turned to them without waiting for my response. I understood that I was being dismissed. Again. Just as he'd dismissed me before, the last time we'd both been involved in a murder case. It was infuriating.

When I returned to the gallery, I locked the front door,

pulled down the blinds, and checked that the sign in the window was still turned to Closed. I sighed, knowing the sign would probably remain that way the rest of the day.

A pang of guilt pierced me. Here I was worrying about my bottom line when a woman was dead down the hall.

Still, I needed to take care of business. I trudged over to the sales desk and climbed onto a stool, drumming my fingers on the granite countertop as I thought of all the obligations now in limbo. Today's schedule included an afternoon digital photography class, the second in a series I was teaching in the small classroom next to the darkroom. And I had a portrait session booked for later in the day— engagement photos of a young bride-to-be and her groom. Both could be rescheduled, but I'd need to get in touch with the participants right away.

As the computer booted up, I texted Alexis and Ethan and gave them a vague explanation, along with the promise of more details to come. I asked Alexis to call the bride and the students in the digital class. She agreed, and I promised to forward the contact information.

Business tasks completed, my thoughts turned back to the murder. *Why Brie?* I wondered. Maybe a peek at her social media would offer some answers. Before I could start my search, though, a banging at the door startled me. I scrambled to the door, and when I peeked through the blinds, a sense of calm swept over me.

The moment I unbolted the door, it whooshed open, and Sam pulled me into his arms. I melted into his embrace. After a moment, he pulled back and let his blue eyes travel over me. "Dan saw the police car and the ambulance out front. I was worried…But you look okay."

"Just okay? The romance evaporated from this relationship in a hurry." I reached up and moved a lock of dark blond hair off his forehead. Then I took his hand and led him to the sales counter. "All is well. For me, at least. Who's watching the restaurant?"

"Dan and Rodger have it under control."

Dan was Sam's assistant manager, a New York City transplant of whom I'd grown inexplicably fond. Rodger was the head chef, a likable, competent employee. I was sure they had things well in hand.

He sat on one of the stools. "What's up with the ambulance?"

"Sit down," I said. "I'll fill you in as best I can."

Like a good journalist, I summarized the facts, keeping the details succinct. A former colleague, death by strangulation, the mystery surrounding her presence in my darkroom.

He listened intently. When I finished the story, he ran his hands through his hair. "I can't believe this is happening. Again."

A commotion stirred in the hall, and the two of us turned toward the noise. Raul appeared first, his eyes taking in Sam's presence, then locking briefly with mine. The paramedics moved into the room behind him, pushing a stretcher. A black body bag rested on top, the words "County Coroner" stenciled on it in white letters.

Sam and I stood solemnly as Raul unlocked the front door and held it open. Once the paramedics had wheeled the stretcher away, Raul stepped back inside and relocked the door. He walked over to us and nodded to Sam, who shot him a thinly veiled glare. Since Sam's detainment in January on suspicion of murder, the two of them hadn't exactly been fast friends.

"Crime scene techs are on the way," Raul said. "We'll have to shut down the gallery for a while."

I nodded. "I've already asked Alexis to cancel today's schedule. Do I need to reschedule tomorrow too?"

"Today should be enough. Pretty sure you'll be able to reopen in the morning. In the meantime, though, I need to ask you a few questions." He shot a glance toward Sam. "In private."

Sam bristled. "I'm not going anywhere."

"Sam, it's fine." I patted his arm. "Go back to the cafe.

I'll call you as soon as I can."

He shook his head adamantly. "I'm staying right here."

I turned to Raul. "Can you give us a second?"

He walked across the gallery and pretended to examine a photo of the sun setting behind Mt. O'Connell. I watched Sam pace behind the counter. "Sit down," I said to him, hearing the edge in my voice.

He didn't sit. Instead, he planted his fists on the counter and stared at me. "I'm not leaving, Callie. You need someone here with you, and it's going to be me."

I counted to five before I spoke. "Sam. I'm a grown woman who has made it through my entire adult life without your protection. I reported from war zones. I walked through gang-infested streets. I even survived a gaggle of stage moms at a children's beauty pageant. I think I can deal with Raul asking me a few questions."

He stared at the countertop. Was he counting to five too? Finally, he straightened and crossed his arms. "Callie, not long ago I was in a pretty serious predicament. You did everything you could to protect me—even to the point of endangering your own life. Why is it okay for you and not for me?"

A solid point. Over the years, my pride convinced me I could—and should—handle everything on my own. But that self-sufficiency had ultimately left me isolated and lonely. Four months ago, I'd vowed to follow a different path. Perhaps now was the time to put some action behind that promise.

"You're right," I said finally. His eyes widened. "There, I said it. If you tell anyone, I'll deny it. But you can stay. In fact, I guess I'd like that."

Sam's warm smile made me think that maybe, just maybe, I could make a go of this relationship thing.

I waved Raul back over. "Sam stays," I said. Raul opened his mouth to object, but I cut him off. "He stays. If not, you'll just have to take me into custody to ask your questions."

I grinned tentatively and stretched out my arms.

Raul didn't reach for his cuffs.

He also didn't crack a smile at my theatrics. He was in I'm-a-tough-cop-not-your-friend mode. "Fine," he said, pulling his notebook from his jacket pocket. "Walk me through it."

He scribbled notes as I told my story—stepping into the darkroom, bumping into the chair, turning on the lights, seeing Brie's body.

"Brie Bohannan," he said, jotting down the name. "How do you know her?"

"We worked together at *The Sentinel.* Well, not exactly together. We were both part of the investigative team, but we never worked on the same assignments. The team came to Rock Creek Village this year for their annual retreat."

He nodded. "How many people on this team?"

"Twelve, including Brie. Staying at the Knotty Pine Resort. Arrived yesterday, departing tomorrow evening."

"Mm hmm," he said, as he documented the details. "What kind of relationship did you have with her?"

Relationship? Pretty sure that wasn't the word I'd choose. More like two alpha wolves sizing each other up from a distance. The world of investigative reporting could be cutthroat, and once upon a time, I was on top. When you're the lead dog, the rest of the pack mostly wants to take you down.

But Raul didn't need to hear about newsroom dynamics. "We were coworkers," I said evasively. "I hadn't even spoken to her since I left in December."

He raised a thick eyebrow, not letting me off the hook. "Elaborate."

"Please," I responded. Sam rolled his eyes.

Raul looked confused. "Please?"

"All right. Since you asked so nicely." I thought about how to explain. "It's like this. Brie was second string. I was the starter. She made no secret about wanting my job. I'm sure she considered us rivals. Except I wasn't competing. I really didn't pay much attention to her. When I resigned, she got promoted to my position. And that was that."

"Did you resent her for taking your job?"

I cocked my head. "Wait, am I a suspect here?"

"Should you be? Did you want this woman dead?"

The words rattled from my mouth like a bullet train. "No, I certainly did not want her dead. I didn't particularly like her, but I didn't resent her. She was promoted to a position I willingly vacated. More power to her." I paused, took a breath. "Besides, if I were going to kill someone, I wouldn't do it in my own darkroom. I'm not an idiot."

Raul's eyes twinkled, and I realized he'd been baiting me. "Relax," he said. "I left my handcuffs in the car. Anyway, you're not a suspect. I just needed to get the question out of the way."

I shot him a look, but he was lost in thought. "How did she end up in your darkroom? There are two doors into the gallery, right? Front and back? Were they both locked when you got here this morning?"

"I didn't check the back door when I arrived, but I'm absolutely certain I locked both doors when I left last night. I triple checked because of the poop incident."

Both Raul and Sam stared at me. It was Sam who broke the impasse. "The poop incident?"

"Oh, I forgot to tell you about that."

Raul's fingers clenched around his pen. Sam's brow furrowed. "You know about the vandalism," I said. They nodded. "Well, there was another incident yesterday." I told them about finding the huge pile of poop on the gallery floor. "Ruined my favorite pair of shoes," I muttered, before glancing in the direction of the darkroom. "But I suppose there are worse things."

Raul rubbed a hand across his stubble. "So someone already found a way to access your studio. Do you think the vandalism and the murder could be connected?"

The idea startled me. I'd pretty much settled on the Ratliff twins as the vandals. Were they vile enough to commit a murder in my gallery? "I can't see it," I said. "The vandalism began before the retreat. No one here knows Brie. It seems farfetched that whoever trashed the gallery would kill a stranger."

A knock at the door interrupted us. The crime scene techs had arrived, and Raul let them in. He called out to Hardesty, who hustled into the room and guided the two men and their equipment to the darkroom.

My phone vibrated. I glanced down to see a text from Tonya, my best friend and coincidentally the editor of *The Rock Creek Gazette*, the village's weekly newspaper.

What's going on over there? Rumor mill is abuzz.

I looked at Raul, who shook his head as if he'd telepathically read my text.

Can't talk now, I typed.

No sooner had I hit send than the phone rang in my hand. Dad, according to caller ID. I let it go to voicemail.

"Word's getting out," I murmured.

"So what's next?" Sam asked.

Raul tapped his pen on the counter. "I need to talk to the victim's coworkers." He turned to me. "You say they're staying at your parents' resort?"

"Yes. Dad told me they'd reserved the conference room for a morning meeting. They must be wondering why Brie isn't there."

"They'll all be in one place then." He wrinkled his nose as if he were about to bite into a lemon. "Callie, maybe you could join me for the interview—"

I jumped up, not even trying to conceal my enthusiasm. "Yes. Absolutely. Let me grab my bag."

Sam narrowed his eyes. "Is that a good idea, Sanchez? One of them might be a murderer. You could be putting Callie in the crosshairs."

My lips tightened, but I kept my tone even. "Sam…how do I say this diplomatically? It's not up to you. If I can help with this investigation, I'm going to."

Raul lifted a hand. "Hold up there, cowboy. This isn't an

invitation to participate in the investigation. I just figured a bunch of reporters would be more apt to open up if I came in with one of their own. You're a...a conduit. No questions. No comments. No interference."

I bit down a snide retort and nodded in feigned compliance. At this point, I'd take whatever I could get.

With a sidelong glance at Sam, Raul added, "If you'll give me your key, I'll have Tollison and Hardesty lock up and return it when the techs are done."

After I dug the key from my pocket and passed it over, Raul walked away. I guessed he sensed the tension and wanted to allow Sam and me a moment's privacy.

Sam scowled at Raul's back. I put a hand over his. "Sam, I appreciate your concern. It's very sweet. I know you want to protect me. But you need to acknowledge that I can take care of myself."

He sighed, and the shadow left his face. "My turn to say you're right. Sorry if I'm acting like a caveman. I need to remind myself every so often that your strong will is one of the things I love about you."

My heart skipped a beat, then went into full gallop mode. *Love?* Had Sam just used the four-letter word I'd avoided most of my life? We'd only been seeing each other again for a few months. How could we possibly be ready for that word? I was forty-three years old and hadn't experienced anything I'd characterize as love since...

Well, since high school. With this very same man.

I'd have to give this some thought. But not now. I couldn't afford to be distracted by romance and relationships. For the time being, I needed to focus on murder.

6

Hardesty locked the door of Sundance Studio behind the three of us. Sam kissed my cheek and headed toward the cafe.

Raul stepped toward the black Ford Expedition parked at the curb. "I have to make a stop at the station first," he said. "Won't take long. You can wait in the car."

I lifted my eyes to the sky, azure blue, and inhaled the aroma of wildflowers mixed with the ever-present scent of chocolate wafting over from the Fudge Factory. "I'll meet you there. The walk will do my brain some good." I touched the camera hanging around my neck. "Maybe I'll even snap a few photos on the way."

Raul glanced down the sidewalk and leaned toward me. "Are you sure? Looks like you'd have to run the gauntlet."

I followed his eyes to a gaggle of neighbors watching us with overt curiosity: Tabitha from Tabitha's Treasures, Pamela from The Fudge Factory, and Willie, the realtor who'd leased me the studio space and helped me purchase my townhome. Fran from Quicker Liquor scurried down the block to join them. One thing I'd been reminded of when I returned to Rock Creek Village last winter was that news traveled at warp speed here.

"We can't have you discussing what happened," he said.

I threw back my shoulders. "I can handle them."

His expression was skeptical. "I mean it, Callie. Not a word to anyone."

"Yes sir!" I offered up a mock salute. He heaved a sigh and got in his car.

As Raul pulled away, David Parisi walked out of his shop. I bit my lip. Now I'd have to be really tight-lipped.

A couple of months ago, David opened his bookshop, A Likely Story, in the space next door to Sundance Studio, once occupied by V&K's Fine Fashions. In his forties, David was tall and lean with a physique that could serve as the model for da Vinci's Vitruvian Man. His olive skin and Italian accent only increased his allure. The villagers were entranced.

Especially my best friend, Tonya. The two of them had already become an item. Anything I said in David's presence would likely travel straight from my lips to her ears—then straight to the front page of her newspaper. I personally didn't mind, but Raul would have my hide.

Careful, Callie, I told myself, tightening my grip on Woody's leash.

The business owners moved toward me, drawn like ants to a dollop of honey.

"What's going on in your gallery, Callie?" asked Tabitha.

"Was that a body on the stretcher? Who was it?" Pamela asked.

"You might as well tell us," Fran added. "We'll find out soon enough anyway."

David watched with a disinterested expression, but his eyes shimmered with curiosity. He reminded me of Carl.

"Listen, guys," I said, using a tone I'd heard countless times from sources who wanted me to go away. "I can't talk about it right now. As soon as the police give the green light, you'll be the first to know."

Fran pressed her lips together. "Another murder. I wonder how this will affect Fireweed Festival attendance."

"It could kill it all together," Willie said, oblivious to his poor choice of words.

Tabitha tsked. "Two murders in five months. Such things never happened in this town until…"

A flush warmed my cheeks. I knew how she'd meant to finish that sentence. *Until Callie moved back.*

Woody nudged in close to me. Carl yowled from the backpack. I opened my mouth, but no words emerged. Tears threatened, and I blinked them back. My goal had been to fit in with the villagers, to become one of them again. But now…

I felt a hand on my elbow then and looked back to see the petite frame of Jessica Fannon, Rock Creek Village High School's journalism teacher—and my warrior.

Despite her tiny figure and unassuming pixie face, Jessica carried herself like a giant. "What is wrong with you people? This is your friend. Your neighbor. You should be comforting and consoling her, not gathering around like a pack of hyenas. I'm very disappointed in you."

She sounded like the teacher she was, and her scolding had the desired effect.

"You're right," Pamela said, hanging her head. "I'm sorry, Callie."

"Si, scusi," David added with a flourish of his hand.

The others nodded in unison, though I didn't entirely trust their sincerity. Still, they were making an effort. So would I.

"It's okay, you guys. I understand your concerns. I promise I'll tell you what I can when the police allow it."

The group dispersed and walked back to their shops. Jessica looped her arm through mine. "Let's go. I'm on my way to that silly park yoga thing of Summer's, and she'll rip me a new one if I'm late."

I smiled. Jessica's wife, Summer Simmons, owned Yoga Delight and held regular Yoga in the Park sessions. The two of them had quickly become my close friends.

"Thank you for rescuing me," I said. "They seem to think I'm a trespasser with the sole purpose of sabotaging their village."

She waved dismissively. "So not true. They're just a bunch of busybodies with a nose for gossip. They're probably riveted by *Sophie's Scoop* and hope to be the ones to give her, well, the scoop. You can't let them get under your skin."

Jessica's supportive words made me feel lighter. But then her face scrunched up. "Do you really think whatever happened in your studio will hurt the Fireweed Festival, though?"

My gut clenched as my moment of peace ended. "I hope not," I said through gritted teeth. "We need it."

The Fireweed Festival was an annual street fair scheduled for the last weekend of June. Evergreen Way closed to vehicle traffic, and businesses displayed and sold their wares beneath open air canopies lined up on the cobblestone street. The town offered interactive events and contests each day—watermelon seed spitting, alpine yodeling, a pet pageant, a baking contest. The celebration attracted not only out-of-towners but residents of neighboring villages.

The annual fair was celebrating ten years of existence, so I'd never been part of it before. But I'd been told that the long weekend generated more income than the rest of the summer combined. The business owners relied on the festival, and I didn't want to be blamed for any hit to their pocketbooks.

I reminded myself of the words I'd learned from my therapist: *Control what you can and let go of the rest.* I took a meditative breath, then another, and felt my heart rate drop back to normal. Jessica and I walked in companionable silence, and I turned my attention to our surroundings. Tourists ambled across the cobblestone street and down the sidewalk, peeking through the box windows of the quaint village shops before stepping inside for a piece of fudge or a souvenir.

Lifting my eyes to the heavens, I watched wispy clouds float across the sky like dandelion fluff. Beneath them, the Rocky Mountains stood sentinel, like Greek Titans watching over their flock. The sun bathed the scene from above. Perfect lighting. Irresistible, in fact.

I stopped in my tracks. "You go on ahead," I told Jessica. "I'm going to take some pictures."

She smiled and squeezed my arm one last time before heading toward the park. I lifted my Nikon DSLR, flipped the aperture setting, and aimed the lens at the mountains, clicking the shutter repeatedly. Woody sat patiently at my heel, accustomed to my unscheduled photo pitstops. I turned the camera to the row of shops, the awnings, the tourists. These images would make great postcards, capturing the village in vacation mode.

I walked in the direction of the resort, stopping occasionally for more photos—a copse of dappled pine trees, a shiny red scooter leaning against a wall. Eventually, I found myself in front of the Knotty Pine Lodge, a three-story Swiss-style chalet magnificent in the shadow of Mt. O'Connell. The resort was fully booked this week, as I'd heard from Dad, but at the moment, the portico was devoid of guests. I'd already taken so many photos of the lodge that these would be redundant, but I couldn't help myself. I dropped to my knees and aimed my lens upward, an angle that imbued a sense of dominance and grandeur.

Raul's car wasn't yet in the lot, so I strolled over to the base of Mt. O'Connell and the line of people waiting for the ski lifts. Though the snow had long since melted, the lifts rose in a steady procession to the top of the mountain, thanks to a decision made by the Chamber of Commerce several years ago. They'd commissioned the installation of two alpine slides, making Mt. O'Connell—and Rock Creek Village—into a year-round destination. Customers rode up on the ski lift, climbed into a two-person cart, and sped down the mountain through a series of twists and turns. I'd tried it myself a few times. Exhilarating without being terrifying, fun for children and adults.

A little girl squealed as a chipmunk scurried past her, hunting for a dropped peanut or a kernel of popcorn.

Woody bounced on his paws, hoping for a play date. I wound his leash tightly around my wrist. "Not gonna happen, big fella," I said. "You'd terrify that little guy."

Behind me, a horn beeped, and I turned to see Raul's car pulling into the parking lot. Woody tugged at the leash, and I turned off my camera and trotted after him.

We joined Raul at the resort entrance and walked through the glass doors. My mother, Maggie, jumped up from her stool and darted around the registration counter. "Let that poor cat out of his cell," she said, reaching for my backpack.

I shrugged the carrier off my shoulders and handed it over. "He likes it, Mom. The vet said it makes him feel safe, and he gets included in the fun."

"Pish," Mom said. She set the carrier on the counter, unzipped it, and removed the golden tabby, giving him a few strokes before setting him on the floor beside his canine brother. Woody graced Mom with a sloppy kiss, and she laughed.

But when she rose to her feet, she was all business. Hands on hips, she gave me a stern look. "Callahan Maureen Cassidy, what have you gotten yourself into now?"

I saw Raul stifling a smile. Then she turned on him. "As for you, Raul Sanchez, how dare you involve my daughter in another murder?"

My mother had taught English to Raul and his classmates back in the day, several years after I'd graduated, and the authority she exerted had apparently never diminished. I saw him cower beneath her glare. I felt as if we were both about to be assigned detention.

Dad came to the rescue, sliding an arm around Mom's shoulders. He extended his hand to Raul in a peacemaking gesture.

Raul grasped it gratefully. "Chief," he said. Most villagers still addressed my father that way, and I expected they always would. Over the course of thirty years on the job, he'd left his legacy. "I guess you heard?"

Dad nodded. "I got a call from…well, that doesn't matter. But yes, we heard. Figured you'd be coming to speak with the victim's colleagues." He looked into my eyes. "You okay, Sundance? I tried calling…"

People had started calling my father, Charlie Cassidy, "Butch" when Paul Newman had made the outlaw's name famous back in the late sixties. It was only natural that he'd given me the Sundance moniker. I didn't mind—not anymore, anyway. In fact, it was the reason I'd named my gallery Sundance Studio.

"I'm fine, Dad. But I have to admit, it was a shock finding Brie like that, with the strap—"

Raul cleared his throat. Dad smiled gently at me. "Best not to share too many details, sweetheart," he said. He turned back to Raul. "Obviously, we haven't said anything to our guests."

"Callie's friends are in the second-floor conference room," Mom said, like we were a group of sixth grade girls at a sleepover. I rolled my eyes.

Dad lowered his voice. "One of them called down earlier, saying Ms. Bohannan was AWOL. Asked if I'd check her room. I went up and knocked. No answer, but the Do Not Disturb sign was hanging on the knob. And when I came back to the desk, I got the call from…" He trailed off, unwilling to throw his source under the bus. "Do you have any idea who might be responsible? If we have a killer staying at the lodge, I'd rather know sooner than later."

"No suspects yet." Raul shifted his gaze to the landing at the top of the stairs. "But hopefully very soon."

7

I left Woody and Carl in Mom's care and led the way up the grand staircase. Its wide planks, bracketed by thick cedar log handrails, offered a stunning focal point for the lodge. As we crested the top step, I glanced over the railing into the lobby, marveling yet again at the renovations my parents had made. An oversized fireplace in a river rock hearth stretched three stories from the wide pine plank floor to the wood beam ceiling. Surrounding the hearth, leather couches and armchairs invited guests to sit and sip hot chocolate and mulled wine in the winter or iced tea and Sangria in the summer.

But my favorite feature? The artwork, of course. Mom and Dad had lined the walls with breathtaking landscape shots, courtesy of a local photographer, who so happened to be their daughter.

Raul touched my elbow. "Remember, you're just here to introduce me and then observe. No questions. No comments."

"If you say so." I crossed the landing and knocked on the conference room door.

"Come in," a voice called.

I entered the conference room, with Raul behind me. Inside, ten people surrounded a massive table. Manila folders, papers, and reporters' notebooks littered the polished wood, along with coffee cups and the remnants of pastries.

One seat was empty. One unused coffee mug. One untouched folder.

Brie Bohannan's.

I tore my eyes from the empty chair and took a moment to collect myself by gazing out the window wall at the side of the room. The Rocky Mountains rose proud and majestic in the midday sunshine. I'd observed the panorama dozens of times, and it still took my breath away. How on earth did any work get accomplished in the shadows of that view?

Still, the man who stood at the head of the table had managed to capture the team's attention. If anyone could distract them from the beauty outside, it was Preston Garrison.

Today, he'd gone casual in stonewashed jeans, a white button-down shirt, open at the collar, and a beige linen sports coat. As always, he managed to pull off the approachable-yet-fully-in-charge look. When he saw me, his chiseled face creased into a smile. But a quick glance at Raul wiped the grin from his face and the twinkle from his eye. Seeing his reaction, the others turned their eyes to me, then to the detective. I could feel the atmosphere charge with anticipation.

Journalists sensed impending disaster like a wolf sensed a wounded elk.

Preston cocked his head. "Callie…?"

I quickly gestured toward Raul. "Preston, allow me to introduce Detective Raul Sanchez. Detective Sanchez, this is Preston Garrison, *The Sentinel's* managing editor."

The two of them shook hands, but Preston frowned. "Is this about Brie? Has something happened?"

"I'm afraid—" I started, but Raul cut me off.

"Mr. Garrison, if you could have a seat, I'll explain why we're here."

Preston opened his mouth, then closed it, a man not accustomed to taking orders. But he returned to his chair, resting his elbows on the table. I moved to the back of the room to better observe everyone's reaction to the news.

"There's no easy way to say this," Raul began, mimicking every death announcement I'd ever heard. "Your colleague, Brie Bohannan, was found deceased this morning."

Electricity buzzed through the group. They turned to one another with wide eyes and lifted brows. Surprise—real or feigned, I wasn't yet sure.

Then the faces began to rearrange themselves into a facsimile of grief, and I knew what I was seeing wasn't anguish. It was hunger.

I was ashamed to admit I recognized the expression because it was familiar. I'd worn it myself all too often as I chased a story. Here sat ten journalists, each calculating how this event could shape their own careers—and how they could keep the others from stealing the spotlight.

Preston alone wore a look I interpreted as true sorrow. Or was it fear?

Suddenly, his face turned hard as he shifted into inquisition mode. "What details can you give us?"

Hands moved toward notebooks, and Dev wrapped his fingers around his camera. Though no one wanted to be the first to shatter the pretense of caring, they all coveted the role of first vulture to the carnage.

"I can't tell you much," Raul responded. "We've just begun the investigation."

"Was it an accident?" Preston asked.

"I can't say—"

Preston turned to the window, thinking things through. "No, not an accident. If she'd been hit by a car or fallen down the side of the mountain, you'd be free to tell us. Some sort of foul play, then." He looked at me. "Callie, you found her, didn't you?"

All eyes turned to me. I tried to play clueless. "Why do you ask?"

Preston cocked his head toward Raul. "He wouldn't have brought you into this otherwise. Plus, I know you, Callie."

I glanced at Raul for direction. He gave a little shake of his head, so I clamped my lips together. Preston leaned back in his chair and watched Raul, waiting with the steady patience he'd perfected as a journalist.

Raul knew how to play the game, too, but he had no time for that. "The death was suspicious," he said. "That's all I can tell you right now. We'll be calling each of you to the station this afternoon to answer some questions. In the meantime, please stay close to the resort."

"Can't you just ask your questions now? Where we're already all assembled?" Preston asked.

"No, we need to do this by the book," Raul said. The team began to pepper him with questions, and he held up a hand. "Listen, folks, I get the whole freedom of the press thing. I know I can't stop you from doing your jobs. But I would ask that you not make this story public. Not yet, while it might interfere with our investigation. Besides, you won't get any information from either of us."

He looked in my direction. I nodded in a show of unity and followed him to the door. As soon as Raul turned his back on them, the reporters began scribbling. Dev leaned back in his chair and stared at the ceiling. Melanie looked frightened.

When I glanced at Preston, his expression was inscrutable.

He'd said he could read me. Unfortunately, the opposite wasn't true.

In the hallway, Raul put a finger to his lips and leaned an ear toward the closed door. I tapped my foot impatiently. Did he really believe seasoned investigative journalists would suddenly belch up usable information? Did he expect to hear a confession?

After a moment, he headed downstairs. I followed, spent a minute collecting my pets, and pretended to listen to my mother warn me against taking "foolish chances." Raul had offered me a lift, so I trailed him to his car.

Once I'd tucked Woody into the backseat, with Carl's carrier nestled beside him, Raul and I buckled up. "Any impressions?" he asked.

"Not really," I said.

"These are your people. Did any of their reactions seem odd?"

I shook my head. "Just the usual for journalists. Stone cold calculation hidden beneath a thin pretense of compassion. Remember, though, I've never even met some of them. And the ones I worked with I didn't know all that well."

He put the car into reverse, glanced over his shoulder, and pulled out of the parking space. "You know Preston Garrison, though," Raul said. "Pretty well, from the looks of it."

I felt the blush crawling up my neck. Only Tonya and Sam were privy to the details of my personal relationship with Preston. How had Raul guessed?

"He was my boss," I said, my voice defensive. "We worked together for over ten years—a big chunk of my career."

"Calm down, Callie. It wasn't an attack on your character. I just wondered if there's a chance he could be involved in Ms. Bohannan's death."

"You think he might've murdered his own employee?"

He tapped the brake as a skateboarder bolted into the road. She lifted her hand in an apologetic wave. "I suspect just about everyone right now. But Garrison seemed...I don't know...off somehow."

I mentally replayed Preston's reaction to the news of Brie's death. The reaction I'd seen wasn't a guilty one. It reflected his meticulous nature. I supposed it might have come across as emotionless. But a killer?

"I don't buy it," I said. "I've never seen any signs of violence in the man, nothing even approaching rage. And what would be his motive? He wouldn't benefit from the death of his top investigative reporter. Besides, how would he have gotten into the gallery?"

"Well, maybe you left the door unlocked—"

"I'm telling you, I didn't. After the—"

"Poop incident, I know. You triple checked. Then there must be a key unaccounted for." He paused to mull it over. "I still think the poop droppers might have done this."

Was that possible? I'd pretty well convinced myself that the Ratliff twins were responsible for the defacement and damage. Even so, would they really murder a stranger just to…what? Make me look bad? It seemed improbable. "It's a big leap from vandalism to murder."

He rubbed a hand across the stubble on his cheek. "All right. Let's think logically. Who has copies of your key?"

"Mom and Dad. And I keep a spare at home. But that's it."

"Ethan? Alexis?"

"No, I just lend them one of mine if the need arises. Like I did with your officers this morning."

His mouth turned down in a frown. "One of them could have made a copy."

"So now you suspect my employees? No way."

"How much do you know about them?" he asked.

I crossed my arms and stared out the window. Turned out, the answer was not much. I knew Ethan had moved to Rock Creek Village a couple of years ago to take a teaching position at the high school. His family lived in the Midwest somewhere, if I remembered correctly. And he was single. That was the extent of my knowledge.

The data I'd collected on Alexis was even skimpier. She'd come to Colorado for college from…what, Virginia?…but had dropped out this semester for reasons she hadn't chosen to share. She'd taken a weekend trip to the village, saw my Now Hiring sign in the window, and impulsively applied. Ethan and I had been running ragged, I remembered, and I'd hired her on the spot.

I grimaced as I realized how little I'd learned about the two people I worked with every day. Perhaps I could ascribe it to my goal of learning to trust again. But more likely, my journalistic skills were rusting with disuse.

One way or another, the idea of either of them luring Brie into the gallery and killing her was ludicrous, and I told Raul as much. He shrugged.

I snapped my fingers. "Wait. Here's something you should know. During the happy hour party, I overheard an argument about Brie between Dev, who's a photographer, and one of the reporters, Melanie. I guess they've been dating, because she was in a huff when he told her he was going out to look for Brie. From what I heard through the bathroom door, things got pretty heated."

He lifted a quizzical brow. "The bathroom door?"

I waved off his question and began summarizing the conversation I'd overheard. Then I threw out a worry I'd had since the beginning. "Raul, you don't think… Could Brie have been there—her body, that is—the entire time I was hosting my happy hour? Before this morning, I hadn't been in the darkroom since Wednesday afternoon."

Raul shook his head. "From what I could see, she hadn't been there that long. The autopsy will tell us for sure, but I don't think she'd been dead more than a few hours."

I hoped he was right. The idea that we'd had a party, a celebration, with Brie's dead body in an adjacent room filled me with despair.

Raul pulled to the curb in front of my house and put the car in park. On the porch, I noticed a figure curled into the rocking chair I kept there. Tonya. My best friend. But more importantly, in this moment, the editor of Rock Creek Village's newspaper.

She waved, and Raul immediately frowned.

"Raul, this was hardly going to remain a secret," I said. "You just informed a room full of professional journalists that their colleague was killed. Besides, you know how fast news travels here. Ninety percent of the people in town already know who died, where she died, and how she died."

He narrowed his eyes. "But they won't be getting details

from you. Understand? I do not want to see your name as anyone's source."

I made a zip-my-lips motion.

Before he could continue the lecture, I grabbed my purse and camera bag and jumped out of the car. Then I opened the back door and rescued my creatures. "Thanks for the ride," I said across the front seat. "Keep me posted."

He shook his head like he was dealing with a five year old, but as he pulled away, I saw him smile.

8

As always, Tonya looked as if she'd stepped off the pages of a fashion magazine. Today, she wore a gauzy, butter-yellow sleeveless blouse and a flared skirt. Her strappy sandals, complete with four-inch heels, would have incapacitated me. Thick hair fell loose around her shoulders, and her signature red lipstick complemented her brown skin. Tonya was darn near perfect. I always felt tousled around her, as if she'd been freshly ironed and I'd been sitting in the dryer for two days.

Tucking an errant wisp of my own hair into the high ponytail from which it had escaped, I looked down at my outfit—taupe linen drawstring pants and running shoes.

At least they were my dressy running shoes.

Woody whined, and when I unclasped his leash, he sprinted up the sidewalk to greet Tonya. She crouched to give him a hug, then rose and planted a kiss on my cheek. "Good morning, cream cake," she said.

Tonya's passion for calling me by pet names dated back to middle school, but this one I'd not heard before. "What's cream cake?" I asked. "Did you mean to say cream puff? Or babycakes?"

She laughed, and I swore her white teeth glittered. Despite my grouchy mood, I felt my own lips turn up in response. But just for a moment. "So, why are you here?"

"Silly girl. You must know what brings me to your little castle."

"Hmph. If you've come for a story, you're in the wrong place. Raul would skewer me."

"You underestimate my reporting skills. I'm already privy to all the dirty details. Maybe even more than you, my friend."

I pursed my lips. "Well, you can't quote me. I'm not your source."

"Oh my. Someone is out of sorts today. Luckily, I brought lunch. Let's go inside and feed the beast." She lifted a plastic bag, and my stomach rumbled. Whatever crisis was going on in my life, it never affected my appetite.

I unlocked the door and led Tonya and Woody into the kitchen, filled with natural light and oyster-colored quartz countertops. Once again, I experienced a swell of pleasure. This place belonged to me. I was home. It was nice to be putting down roots.

Releasing Carl from captivity, I lowered him to the floor. Woody nuzzled him, and the two of them scampered into the living room, chasing each other in circles around the couch. Tonya set her satchel on the small dining table in the nook and carried the bag of food to the counter, where she began unloading take-out bowls and plastic silverware.

"That looks like salad," I said, frowning.

"A little healthy eating won't kill you, girlfriend. Besides…" She gave me a wink. "I'm anticipating a nice, rare filet mignon at Pearly's tonight. I need to keep lunch light."

My eyebrows lifted. "Pearly's, huh? Am I to assume you have another hot date with David?"

"You assume correctly."

She smiled to herself, and I studied her. She and David had only been dating a few weeks, but she already appeared uncharacteristically smitten. "This seems to be getting serious," I said cautiously.

She pulled two ceramic bowls from the cabinet and began

shifting greens and veggies into them. "Too early to tell. Don't get carried away."

"I could say the same to you."

She shot me a warning look, and I decided to let it go. For now.

I poured lemonade, and we carried our lunches to the back patio, settling into padded wicker chairs at a round glass table, all of which I'd gotten secondhand. I let my eyes wander across the tiny yard. A soft breeze blew through the potentilla shrubs. I had plans for a lush wildflower garden and a cedar pergola, but right now, I could afford to either pay my employees or upgrade my backyard. Come to find out, adults sometimes had to forgo instant gratification.

Carl darted through the pet door, with Woody on his heels. The two of them stretched out in a beam of sunshine for afternoon naps.

I speared a wedge of Romaine lettuce. The tangy Italian salad dressing helped alleviate the knowledge that I was grazing on green stuff. Tonya and I made small talk as we contented ourselves with eating. Finally, she dabbed her lips with a napkin and stood, gathering her dishes. "Okay, friend, let's get down to business. Despite your skeptical nature, I'm not here to pilfer your secrets. I'm here to help you figure out who did this."

Her tone brooked no argument, so I followed her inside. After we stacked dishes in the sink, she sat at the table and booted up her laptop as I gathered legal pads, pens, and my own computer. When we'd set up our makeshift office, I chewed the cap of my pen.

"My first instinct would be to make a list of suspects," I said. "But I just don't have enough information. No one stands out."

She shot me a smirk. "You mean you didn't scan faces in the conference room and have a eureka moment? You're slipping."

"Ha ha. If you ever decide to give up your day job, I envision a future as a stand-up comic."

She drummed crimson fingernails on the table. "Okay, let's start with the obvious: Banner and Braden Ratliff. You told me you think they're responsible for the vandalism of your studio. Could they have taken it a step further?"

"Raul asked the same thing. My gut says no. Then again, my gut has been wrong before." I jotted their names on my legal pad. "I'll put them on the list, but unless the police turn up fingerprints or other incriminating evidence, I can't even prove they sabotaged the gallery, much less committed murder." I considered our next move. "Maybe we should start by researching Brie. Let's see what dirty secrets she might have been hiding. I'm sure we'll uncover someone with a motive to kill the woman."

"Sounds like a plan," Tonya said, pulling her laptop closer. "*The Gazette* subscribes to several nationwide databases, so I'll look into her background. And I'll skim through stories she's published lately for anything that might have triggered rage-induced revenge."

"While you're doing that, I'll explore her social media presence. If we're in the market for rage, social media is usually the perfect place to find it."

We hunkered down in front of our laptops. For the next half hour, the tapping of keys and the soft snoring of pets filled the room. I started on Facebook, quickly determining it hadn't been Brie's platform of choice. Her site yielded a few photos of birthday celebrations in which she'd been tagged by friends, but nothing scandalous.

Likewise, Brie's Twitter account revealed little of interest. Whenever she published a story in *The Sentinel*, she shared the link and garnered a handful of likes. But I found no controversial or incendiary responses.

Frustrated, I grabbed our empty glasses and headed to the refrigerator for more lemonade. "I'm coming up empty. What about you?"

She leaned back in her chair and stretched her arms. "Mostly mundane biographical data. Brie grew up in Nebraska. Went to college in Lincoln, editor of the university's newspaper her senior year. After that, she worked at a small daily in Omaha for a couple of years." She scratched her nose. "I did discover one item that might be of interest."

I set our glasses on the table and peered over her shoulder at a court filing, with Brie named as defendant. "It looks like the case was dismissed. What was it about?"

Tonya took a sip of lemonade. "Someone sued Brie for libel ten years ago, well before her tenure at *The Sentinel* began. Much of the information was redacted when the court dismissed the case. I haven't been able to ferret out the plaintiff's name or any details regarding the case, but I can use my contacts to dig it up if you think it might be relevant."

I went back to my chair. "A libel suit isn't unusual for a journalist. I have two in my own history. And ten years would be a long time to hold a grudge that culminated in hunting Brie down at a retreat in Rock Creek Village and then murdering her."

"It happens, though. We have recent experience."

I cringed at her reference to a murder in the village a few months ago. "Still, it seems improbable."

She nodded. "I'll keep going."

While she pecked away at the keyboard, I pulled up Brie's Instagram account. At first glance, my pulse accelerated. I'd clearly stumbled across Brie's social media outlet of choice. She'd posted photos torrentially—sometimes three or four a day. In them, she posed in evening gowns, bikinis, workout attire. She danced and drank. She climbed mountains and swam and rode a horse on the beach— always in the company of friends.

And most of those "friends" were men.

One photo drew my immediate attention. In it, Brie rode piggyback atop a strapping young man. Laughing, she held her hand in the air as if she were maneuvering a bucking bronco. The man grasped her thighs and twisted to look at her with an expression that could be described as lustful.

It was Dev Joshi.

When I enlarged the photo on the screen, I saw Melanie Lewis looking on from the background, her face contorted.

I turned my computer to face Tonya. "Look what we have here." As she examined the photo, I filled her in on the argument I'd heard between Dev and Melanie in the gallery bathroom.

Her eyebrows lifted. "Oooh, a love triangle. My favorite motive. They definitely go on the list."

I scribbled Melanie's name, followed by Dev's. Tonya and I went back to our computers. After a moment, she murmured, "You didn't tell me Brie covered the Jameson Jarrett story after you left *The Sentinel*."

My chest tightened at the mention of Jarrett's name. "There wasn't much more to it by then. Just housekeeping, as far as I know. I tried to avoid obsessing about it— therapist's orders—so I didn't read Brie's stories. Why, did you find something?"

She chewed her lip and read silently for a moment. "This story says Jarrett considered filing a lawsuit against *The Sentinel*, but was advised against it by his lawyers. First Amendment and all. And here's a sidebar…Oh, my."

I braced myself.

She looked at me, her face lined with concern. "That young man who gave you the original story—the one who later recanted…"

I took a deep breath. "He committed suicide. Preston called me when it happened."

"Oh, Callie. That must have been awful for you. Why didn't you say anything?"

I blinked back the inevitable tears that always accompanied memories of the biggest mistake I'd ever made. "Like I said, my counselor advised me not to dwell on what I can't control."

Tonya rose and moved behind me, wrapping her arms around my shoulders. I allowed a few tears to trickle down my cheeks. After a moment, I patted my friend's arm.

"Okay, enough," I said. "This isn't getting us anywhere."

"But this might." She pointed at my screen, to a photo in the middle of the collage.

In it, Brie smiled at the camera, standing tall in a tight-fitting, low-cut white dress. Her blond hair flowed past her shoulders, and her blue eyes shone bright between thick lashes. Her arm was looped through that of a tuxedo-clad man, who gazed at her with a predatory expression.

I'd seen that look directed at me once upon a time, from that same man. Preston Garrison.

"He looks ravenous," Tonya said.

I studied the photo again. The date stamp showed it was taken in April. Standing beside Brie, Preston appeared tall and fit. No surprise. An avid triathlon competitor, Preston worked hard to maintain his edge, both physical and mental, and it showed.

I considered the photo's ramifications. Preston had been a stellar boss, savvy in the ways of the journalistic world, supportive of my efforts. A great mentor as I honed my craft. But his reputation as a ladies' man was not unfounded, as evidenced by this photo. I hadn't been the first of his employees to succumb to his charms, nor was I likely to have been the last.

Maybe my job wasn't the only thing Brie Bohannan had taken over.

Tonya placed a hand gently on my shoulder. "Callie, if the two of them were engaged in an affair, he's a suspect."

Much as it pained me to admit, she was right. I picked up my pen and added his name to the list.

Tonya's phone beeped, and she peered at the screen. The secret smile crossed her face again, and I knew it must be a message from David. She sent a few words back and gazed at the phone for a moment. When she looked back at me, she was starry-eyed.

"Time for this girl to hit the road," she said, packing up her computer. "I only have a couple of hours to make myself alluring."

"Far be it for me to stand in the way of true lust." I pouted. "Who knew you'd turn into one of those women who would dump her best friend for a guy?"

"A girl's gotta do what a girl's gotta do," she said, patting me on the cheek. "Listen, sweet potato. Call it a day. Watch some TV or go for a hike. Something besides obsessing about murder." She waggled a finger. "Tomorrow is another day, and I don't want you solving this without me."

9

With Tonya primping for a date, Sam working, and Sundance Studio closed for business, I was at loose ends. I tried to use the time to teach the creatures a trick for the pet pageant, but neither of them were having it. Carl screeched *ack ack ack* and darted up the stairs, while Woody gave me an apologetic look and bounded up after him.

I could clean house, I supposed, and do a load of laundry. But then I spotted the book I'd been reading on the coffee table. Ah, yes. A much more productive use of time.

An hour later, with the detective on the verge of revealing the killer's identity and me gnawing on a cuticle as I turned the pages, a sudden knock at the door caused me to jerk so hard I nearly knocked over the half-filled glass of lemonade on the table. Woody and Carl bounded downstairs, yipping and yowling, and quiet time ended. I glanced longingly at the book as I placed it facedown on the couch. My curiosity would have to wait.

When I unlocked the front door and pulled it open, Sam strolled in bearing two insulated food containers and a reusable grocery bag. The aroma of beef and garlic followed him like a heavenly cloud. My mouth instantly watered. The salad I'd had for lunch had clearly not quelled my gluttony. Woody, too, sniffed the air. Carl glanced at Sam with feigned disinterest and sauntered back up the stairs. I knew he'd return soon. He adored Sam, but also enjoyed playing hard to get.

"You brought dinner," I said.

"Proving once again what a crack investigative journalist you were." He headed into the kitchen and placed the containers on the island.

I unzipped one of the thermal bags. "A little presumptuous, don't you think? What if I'd spent all afternoon slaving over a hot stove?"

He burst into laughter. "If that were the case," he said, "you'd have to call the paramedics, because I'd be flat on my back in shock. When was the last time you actually cooked a meal?"

"Hey!" I pouted in mock indignation. "I made myself dinner just last night. No, wait. It must have been Wednesday. Or maybe Tuesday."

"I'm talking about something that doesn't go straight from freezer to microwave."

"You don't know everything there is to know about me. I've got moves in the kitchen you've never seen."

He wrapped his arms around me. "I'd love to get a glimpse of them."

I lifted my lips to his. "Mmm," I said when we parted. "If dinner is anything like that, I'll take seconds."

He moved a strand of my hair aside and brushed my ear with his lips. "Wait'll you see what I brought for dessert."

Woody's patience ebbed, and he nudged our thighs. Sam reached down to scratch between his ears. "Message received, pup. But I'm afraid this isn't for you anyway. Too spicy."

I opened the fridge and chose a bottle of cabernet franc I'd picked up at the Long's Peak Winery. Now that I'd cut back on my intake, I could afford something in a bottle instead of a box.

As I poured us each a glass of wine, Sam ladled food onto two plates—bite-sized chunks of steak, medium rare, doused in a buttery garlic sauce, complete with red pepper flakes and parsley. From another container, he scooped out creamy herbed mashed potatoes, along with a helping of green bean amandine. Pearly's Steak and Chop House couldn't compete.

I dipped a finger into the sauce and stuck it in my mouth. "Intriguing. New recipe?"

He nodded and carried the plates to the table. "You're my official taste tester. If it passes muster, I'll add it to the official Snow Plow Chow menu."

I picked up a fork, speared a cube of steak, and bit into it, conscious that Sam's hopeful gaze followed my every move.

"Oh my," I said with a moan. "My tongue is doing a happy dance. This one is definitely a winner."

He grinned and picked up his fork. "Rodger and I both liked it, but three's the charm. Now you have to name it. Something clever. Mountain-village themed."

"You know I'm terrible at that game. If it were left to me, it would be called Steak in Garlic Sauce, or some equally riveting title."

He chuckled, and we both spent a few minutes simply enjoying the meal. Then I told him about Tonya's date and my concerns about her whirlwind romance with David. "Want me to have a word with him?" Sam asked.

I smirked. "I can only imagine how that would go over with Tonya."

He tilted his head toward the legal pads I'd moved to the window seat. "Looks like you talked about more than Tonya's love life. Are the two of you hot on the trail of a prime suspect?"

Though I'd promised Raul I wouldn't go public with the details of the case, I had no hesitation about sharing information with Sam. There was no one I trusted more. I walked him through the whole day and everything Tonya and I had discovered.

He leaned back in his chair and locked his hands across

his stomach. "Sounds like you've ruled out the twins."

I patted my napkin against my lips. "Not exactly, but they're not at the top of the list. I just don't see them exercising the discipline or, I don't know…sophistication. And why Brie? There's no connection. It's much more likely to be someone she worked with. I'd bet on someone here at the retreat."

"As long as we're betting, my money's on Preston Garrison."

My eyebrows rose. A couple of months ago, Sam and I had decided to take the commitment plunge. Or rather, a cautious dip of the toes. As part of that, we had agreed to divulge everything of significance regarding the twenty-five years between the end of our high-school relationship and the beginning of this one. No secrets, fresh start. He'd synopsized his brief and ill-fated marriage to Elyse's mother, Kimberly Wainwright, now Kimberly Lyon. After the divorce, he'd dated occasionally, but nothing serious. Too busy raising his daughter—and pining for me, according to Tonya.

In turn, I'd revealed everything there was to know about my own nearly nonexistent romantic life—a couple of semi-serious relationships that quickly fizzled, mostly due to my devotion to my career.

I'd also mentioned Preston. I'd described my dalliance with him as no big deal, expedient and convenient. Sam had blanched at my cavalier tone but took it in stride.

At least, that's what I'd thought at the time. I wondered now if I was seeing a green-eyed monster peep out from behind those baby blue eyes.

"Think you might be a little biased?" I asked.

"I think you might be a little biased in his favor," he responded. "You shouldn't try to protect him, Callie. If you know something about him, you're obliged to tell Raul. You can't let your past…friendship…get in the way of doing what's right."

I stood so abruptly I nearly toppled my chair. "Are you

actually suggesting that I would conceal information relevant to a murder investigation in order to protect my old boss? Is that what you think of me?"

He opened his mouth to respond, but I held up a palm. "Or is this more about your own insecurity?"

Sam's jaw tightened. "You're overreacting—"

"Stop right there." I could feel my face get red. "When a man tells a woman she's overreacting, it's the same as saying, 'Simmer down, little lady. Don't get your panties in a wad.' Don't you dare say I'm overreacting."

The air between us crackled with tension. The creatures scampered into the room. Carl wound between my ankles, and Woody rested his head in Sam's lap. The kids didn't like it when Mom and Dad fought.

After a moment of stroking Woody's head, Sam spoke softly. "You're right. I'm sorry. Maybe I am jealous. But I know you'll always do what's right. I was wrong to imply otherwise."

I clamped my lips tight. Sam had apologized, and I knew I should let it go. But he'd said it too fast. My anger still boiled beneath the surface, and like a petulant teenager, I wanted to wallow in it. Silently, I began clearing the table. Sam sighed and started packing leftovers into Tupperware, loading the containers into the refrigerator. We worked together in silence, me rinsing dishes and Sam arranging them in the dishwasher.

By the time we'd finished, I was ready to mend fences. Or, more accurately, tear them down. I put a hand on his arm. "Dinner was delicious," I said. "I'm sorry if I spoiled it."

He took me in his arms. "I've heard love means never having to say you're sorry."

I froze. There was that L word again—twice in one day. Was it simply a turn of phrase? Or did he mean it? And if he did, was I ready to hear it?

But then Sam nuzzled my neck, and I decided I'd worry about all that another time.

10

S am and I moved to the couch. I was once again behaving like a teenager, but this time, not a petulant one. So when Woody barked sharply and a knock came at the door, I jumped from the couch as if my parents had walked into the room. Sam laughed. "Expecting someone?"

"No." I ran my fingers through my hair and straightened my blouse.

Sam draped an arm across the back of the couch and watched me. "You look fine. Beautiful, in fact. The picture of innocence. No one would ever suspect you of making out in the living room."

"Stop it." I grinned as I headed to the door.

I opened the door to find Raul on my porch. He had turned away, though, focused on the western sky. I followed his gaze to the horizon, where the sun lazed low, painting the clouds red and orange around the mountains. Photographers called this the golden hour, and the soft lighting called to us like a siren song. A gleaming halo encircled Raul's head, and I fought the urge to run for my camera and shoot his portrait.

He sighed. "That just never gets old."

"No, it really doesn't." I smiled. I rarely saw this side of

Raul, and I found it endearing.

He turned back to me and shook a little, as if he'd wakened from a dream. Then he was all business once again. "Sorry to show up without calling. Just wanted to drop off your studio key and fill you in on the status of the investigation." His eyes traveled across me, and he cocked an eyebrow. "Unless you're busy."

I felt myself blush. "Of course not. I mean, of course." I snatched the key from his fingers. "Come in."

Sam appeared behind me, and the two of them shook hands. "Ah," Raul said. "Now I understand why the place smells so good."

I rolled my eyes. "Why doesn't anyone believe I can cook?"

The men shared a knowing look, apparently bonding over my lack of prowess in the kitchen. Sam said, "There's plenty of food left. I'd be glad to make you a plate."

Raul lifted his eyebrows. Did I hear his stomach rumble? "That'd be great," he said. "If you're sure it's no trouble."

Sam retrieved the Tupperware from the refrigerator and piled food onto a plate, settling it into the microwave and pressing a few buttons.

"You're off duty, right?" I asked, holding up the wine bottle.

He nodded gratefully, and I poured us all a glass, handing his over as I took a seat across from him. "You look tired," I said.

"Long day. We interviewed everyone at the retreat…" He paused, shooting a glance toward Sam.

"You can talk in front of Sam. I've already gotten him up to speed anyway."

Raul started to scowl, but then Sam set a steaming plate of beef and potatoes in front of him. He scarfed down a few bites, wiped his mouth, took a sip of wine, and began the routine again. I waited, amused. "Delicious," he said between bites.

When he finally paused for a breath, I pounced. "You

were going to tell us about the interviews?"

He scraped up the last few morsels, shoved them into his mouth, then leaned back in his chair. "That hit the spot. Thank you, Sam. Can't tell you how long it's been since I've had such a good meal."

Sam smiled. "If you can come up with a good name for it, I'll serve it to you free for a year at the cafe."

I rotated my hand in a get-on-with-it gesture. Raul bent his head sideways until his neck cracked. "First, let me tell you about the crime scene."

"My darkroom," I said wistfully. Would I forever forward think of it as a crime scene?

"The techs collected fingerprint samples from Ethan and Alexis. Already had yours on file from the last case. Every print in the darkroom is accounted for by the three of you. Our killer must have worn gloves."

"Just as we'd assumed."

"Yes, but we always have to try. As far as the shoe prints, nothing unusual there, either. Run-of-the-mill Nikes, men's size nine, or possibly women's size eleven. Could have been purchased in any of a thousand shoe stores."

I nodded. I hadn't expected anything else, but I still felt a surge of disappointment. This case wouldn't be easily solved.

"As for the doors, no sign of forced entry."

"I guess someone did have a key," I murmured.

"About that…" Raul pulled out his phone and scrolled. When he found what he was looking for, he turned the screen to me. It was a photo of a key resting in the palm of a latex-gloved hand. "Someone had a key all right. Brie herself. The coroner found it in her pocket. Do you recognize it?"

"What? How did she get a key to Sundance Studio?" I leaned in and studied the picture. It was a typical bronze key, nothing special, except…

"All the copies I have are blue." I rummaged in my pocket and pulled out the key he'd just returned, holding it out for his inspection.

"Huh," he said, considering. "You told me earlier you lent your key to Ethan or Alexis when necessary. It would have been pretty easy for one of them to make a copy. We need to check the number, see if we can figure out where this key was cut." He pulled out his notebook and began writing.

A wave of irritation surged through me. "You can't seriously believe one of my employees murdered Brie Bohannan in my darkroom. There's no conceivable reason. They'd never even met the woman."

"As far as you know."

I bristled, but he shrugged. "Let's just assume you're right. But we'll interview them for their whereabouts anyway. Trust but verify, as they say. Let's move on."

He swiped his phone screen again and faced it toward me. "We found this under the rolling chair where the body was positioned."

I leaned in and examined what looked like a clear rubber hose. "What is it?"

Sam peered at the photo over my shoulder. "Looks like the vinyl tubing we use in our soft drink dispenser."

My brow furrowed. "Why would something like that be in my darkroom? I have no use for vinyl tubing. I've never seen it before." Raul tucked his phone in his pocket, and I asked, "What else did you find?"

"It's not so much what we found, but what we didn't find," he said. "No sign of Brie's phone. Not on her person, not in the darkroom, not in her room at the lodge."

"Hmm," I said. "Have you tried tracing it?"

"We're working on it, but it's more complicated than you might think." He flipped through his notebook. "Anyway, let me give you a summary of the interviews. The coroner estimates time of death between eight p.m. and midnight. During that window, five of your journalist buddies were hanging out in the lobby of the lodge playing pool and cards. Jamal vouched for them."

I nodded. Jamal, who'd managed the Knotty Pine on evening shifts for over a year now, was a completely reliable witness. "What about the rest of the team?"

"Two others said they were in their cabin playing an online, on-camera video game. We've confirmed that with the gaming company. The seven of them have been cleared, and they've already booked a flight to D.C. for tomorrow morning."

He flipped a page. "Dev Joshi and Melanie Lewis told us they were together in Dev's cabin all night."

"Not an airtight alibi," I said. "Did you ask Dev whether he'd located Brie after he left the gallery?"

"He says he didn't. Jamal said Dev came into the lobby and asked him to ring Ms. Bohannan's room. There was no answer. Jamal didn't see Dev again, and that never saw Ms. Bohannan all evening."

I put my fingers to my lips. "It feels a little fortuitous that Dev so happened to establish his whereabouts by asking for Brie."

"True," Raul said. "Also, Dev is booked into one of the cabins, out of sight of the front desk."

So Dev could have met up with Brie in his cabin. And there was really no way to confirm the alibi Melanie gave him—or the alibi Dev provided for Melanie. One of them could be covering for the other. Or the two of them might have been working together.

Raul shifted in his chair and turned another page. "Then we have Gary Padgett, who said he went to his cabin and watched TV. Fell asleep before nine and slept until six the next morning. No one to vouch for him."

I pictured Gary, tall and thin with a receding hairline. He'd been Preston's administrative assistant forever. And he was in his late sixties.

"I've known him since I started working at *The Sentinel*. I wouldn't say we were friends or anything, but he's a nice enough guy. Is he a suspect?"

"During the course of the interview, he admitted that he

hated the victim and that she went out of her way to make his life miserable. Granted, it's not a great motive, but given his lack of substantive alibi, we decided to keep him in town."

I pursed my lips. "You can't possibly believe he killed Brie. Have you seen him? He's too old, too scrawny. No way he could have subdued her long enough to get the strap around her neck."

"Probably not. But as you already noted, the murder could have been committed by more than one person. Maybe he left the grunt work to someone more suited to it, someone in top physical form. Someone like our next suspect…"

My gut clenched. All three of us knew who Raul was referring to, but he said the name anyway.

"Preston Garrison."

11

I heard Woody in the distance but couldn't see him through the shroud of fog. His bark sounded agitated, alert. Frightened, even. My heart pounded as I raced along the tree-lined trail. I needed to get to him.

I halted at the mouth of a cave. Woody's growl echoed from within. I moved through the opening and into the damp darkness without hesitation, stepping cautiously toward the rumble of his voice. My knee bumped against something. I reached out, and my hand grazed something soft. I knew suddenly what it was. Brie's face. She was there in the cave, tied to a chair, barely discernible in the gloom. I opened my mouth to scream…

Carl's paw batted against my teeth. "Pppt," I said, using my tongue to push out the furry appendage. I pried my eyes open and emerged from the dream. Given my exhaustion, the trauma of the day's events, and the three glasses of wine I'd imbibed, it came as no surprise that I'd been sleeping hard. The red numbers on my digital alarm clock read 3:15.

"What the heck are you doing?" I pried Carl off my head and lifted myself up on my elbows. Moonlight wove through the window sheers, illuminating Woody's silhouette. His low growl morphed into an angry snarl.

I scrambled out of bed and crouched next to him, pulling back the curtain to get a look at whatever had him in a tizzy.

A hooded figure—whether male or female, I couldn't tell—meandered down the sidewalk in front of my house, face obscured in the darkness. The person's hands were tucked in pants pockets, the shoulders slumped. I buried my fingers in Woody's fur, trying to calm his nerves. And mine. "Just a passerby," I murmured. "A neighbor, maybe. Someone out for a stroll. In the middle of the night." Woody nestled against me, and Carl squeezed between us.

Then the figure pivoted. Though I still couldn't make out any features, I was sure of one thing.

The person was staring straight up at my window.

When morning dawned on another beautiful Colorado day, webs of exhaustion clouded my appreciation of it. The stranger in front of my house had seen to it that I wouldn't drift back into dreamland.

Still, a girl had to make a living, so off I trudged, past the lake, the mountain, the lodge. The creatures had chosen not to accompany me today, preferring to fill their day with napping, eating, and more napping. Just as well. Besides Saturday's usual steady flow of customers, Alexis had rescheduled my digital class for eleven o'clock. After that, I'd tend to the uncompleted darkroom work from yesterday.

And, of course, there was a murder to solve.

I stopped in front of Rocky Mountain High, Mrs. Finney's coffee shop. A boost of caffeine—and a brief visit with the former CIA agent and current contemporaneous philosopher—would provide just the jumpstart I needed.

Despite its name, which conjured images of a different type of now-legal substance in Colorado, the shop had been an immediate success. And no wonder. Turned out Mrs. Finney was a wizard at the coffee urn, and almost as talented a baker as my mother. The moment I walked through the door, olfactory overload greeted me—deep, nutty, smoky aromas with an undercurrent of fruity pastries.

A smattering of customers sipped coffee and chatted at round bistro tables against pine paneled walls lined with original Callahan Cassidy photos. From her spot behind the tiled counter, the proprietor beamed at me with motherly affection.

"Good morning, dear," she trilled in the faux British accent she'd maintained since her appearance in the village five months ago.

Today, she was dressed from head to toe in shades of purple, her usual color scheme. She scooted her lilac-framed glasses to the top of her head and wiped her hands across a violet apron that covered a lavender pantsuit. Then she flipped up a hinged portion of the countertop and bustled through, placing her large hands on my cheeks and giving them a pinch. "I've been quite concerned over the ghastly occurrences at Sundance Studio, my dear." She gave my cheeks one last pat. "But we'll get to that in a moment. First, I have a special treat for you."

She scooted back behind the counter, and I settled onto a stool, observing as she lifted the dome off a glass container. She used silver tongs to remove a pastry and placed it gently on a plate, presenting it to me as if she were bestowing a priceless gem. "Lunettes aux Abricots," she said proudly. "Just out of the oven. My unique version of the French apricot croissant. You'll be the first to try it."

I studied the work of art before me. Puff pastry cradled two shiny golden ovals of fruit, lathered in warm apricot jam. It certainly didn't look low-cal. With the way everyone kept feeding me, the ten pounds I'd lost over the past few months were certain to reappear.

But life was short, right? I lifted the pastry and tore off a piece with my teeth, letting the flaky pastry, the rich cream, and the tart apricots glide across my tongue. My eyes closed as I chewed.

"Divine," I said.

"Truly, dear?"

"Absolutely. Your best creation so far. You need to enter this in the Fireweed Festival baking contest."

She gave me a modest smile. "You're a flatterer."

"I'm an ex-journalist, Mrs. Finney. Only capable of telling the truth. This deserves a blue ribbon."

She turned serious then, leaning her elbows on the counter and narrowing her eyes. "Speaking of your former career, I understand you've been involved in yet another murder."

I tittered nervously under her stern gaze. "Mrs. Finney, you make it sound like I committed the deed myself. I simply discovered the body."

"An out-of-town acquaintance," she said. "Inside your gallery. You simply can't ignore your danger."

I understood she was worried about me. I felt a swell of affection, along with a surge of irritation. Since I'd moved back to Rock Creek Village, it seemed everyone wanted to take care of me. I was appreciative—usually, anyway—but after twenty-five years of total self-sufficiency, I occasionally found the abundance of concern smothering.

Still, I pushed that knee-jerk reaction aside and focused on my new life goals—trust, intimacy, belonging. "It was a shock," I admitted.

She tipped her head even closer and lowered her voice. "And I've heard rumors Preston Garrison is a suspect. Tsk, tsk. Honestly, I can't fathom that he might've been involved."

Preston and Mrs. Finney had been acquainted professionally some time ago. In her capacity as a one-time CIA agent, Mrs. Finney had guest lectured on occasion in a class Preston taught at Georgetown titled Journalist and Law Enforcement Relations. In fact, she'd first come to Rock Creek Village at Preston's behest—to keep me safe.

"I feel certain he'll be exonerated," I said. "The police have this under control."

"You're referring to that Raul Sanchez," she said, sniffing. "He's an adorable young man, yes, but is he up to the task?"

I guffawed, picturing Raul's response to her dismissive depiction of him. "He's a top-tier detective, Mrs. Finney.

Getting better every day, in fact. I have every confidence in him, as does my father."

She cocked an eyebrow. "Perhaps you're right, my dear. However, I observe that he hasn't yet managed to apprehend your studio vandals. Those nasty Ratliff twins, I'd say. If your detective doesn't deal with them soon, I will be forced to give them a piece of my mind, along with a swift kick in the nether regions."

I stifled a laugh as I envisioned the scene. "I share your suspicions, Mrs. Finney, and I'd love nothing more. But there's no proof, so I'd urge you to leave the boys' nether regions intact. In the meantime, I need to get to work. Would you mind pouring me a coffee to go?"

"Of course," she said, her expression softening. "I think you'll enjoy the new cup."

Mrs. Finney's gimmick, which set Rocky Mountain High apart from the chain shops, was her paper cup design. On one side, the shop's name was emblazoned in royal purple above her logo, a simple silhouette of our own Mt. O'Connell. The motto beneath read, "Nature. Knowledge. Caffeine." But the masterwork lay on the opposite side— one of Mrs. Finney's mysterious adages, a new one unveiled periodically.

Lifting a silver carafe, Mrs. Finney poured a cupful of steaming liquid and added a squirt of vanilla and a pinch of cinnamon, just the way I liked it. She popped a plastic lid on top and slid the cup in front of me. I lifted it and read the words of wisdom.

If you stand too long in a shadow, your own light fades.

I smiled. "I love this."

"Yes, dear," she said. "I'm delighted that you've emerged from your shadow. Your light burns so brightly these days."

I reached across the counter and squeezed her hand.

12

C offee in hand and sugar already careening through my veins, I headed toward the exit of Rocky Mountain High. As I reached for the knob, the door flew open, and I jumped back to keep from getting trampled.

Sophie Demler bustled into the shop. I cringed, wondering if I could pretend I hadn't seen her. Then I took a look at the woman accompanying Sophie. My exasperation transformed into intrigue.

Melanie Lewis appeared disheveled with her dark hair pulled into a messy bun and eyes red-rimmed and swollen.

Sophie spotted me then, and her eyes sparkled. "Callahan Cassidy. What a coincidence. You're just the person I wanted to see."

Wearing a self-satisfied expression, she dragged Melanie to a corner table and waved me over. I considered my options. Since she'd quit writing for *The Gazette* to pursue her own blog version of *Sophie's Scoop*, a glorified gossip column that advertised itself as investigative journalism, the woman chased stories with a maniacal—and unethical fervor. I still held old-school ideals when it came to journalism, and I didn't have any use for Sophie's brand of it. The prospect of associating with her made me feel a little dirty.

Then I looked again at Melanie's face, and the tug of curiosity overwhelmed me. I took a seat at their table, hoping no one else I knew would come inside and see us together.

Sophie looked toward the counter and snapped her fingers. "Mrs. Finney, bring us each an espresso. And whatever pastry you have on hand. So long as it's fresh."

My shoulders tensed as I anticipated Mrs. Finney's response to Sophie's haughty tone. I predicted the older woman would launch herself over the counter and settle a roundhouse karate kick into Sophie's solar plexus. Or perhaps her nether regions. But behind me, all was silent.

I sneaked a peek over my shoulder and saw Mrs. Finney polishing the counter, studiously ignoring Sophie's request. When I looked back at Sophie, she reddened and then shot an embarrassed glance at Melanie. "Poor old thing. Must be a little hard of hearing."

Shifting in my seat, I called out to my friend. "Mrs. Finney, if it's no trouble, would you mind bringing over two espressos and some of your heavenly apricot pastries? When it's convenient."

Mrs. Finney flashed a dazzling smile. "Why of course, my dear. I'll bring it over in a jiffy."

I turned back and gave Sophie a smug look. She shifted in her chair, then said, "Callahan, I found this downtrodden creature sitting on a bench across the street, just as sad as can be. Naturally, I took her under my wing. That's my nature, as you know. We've already become friends, haven't we, Melanie?"

Melanie stared at her hands, clasped in her lap, and didn't respond. Sophie waited a moment and then plucked at the short red curls framing her round face. "Anyway," she continued, "the dear girl told me something I think you ought to hear." She lowered her voice conspiratorially. "You know, in light of the dead woman you found in your gallery."

Melanie inhaled sharply, and I bit back an angry retort.

Had the woman ever heard the word empathy? Mrs. Finney appeared then, placing coffee mugs and croissants on the table. She leaned toward my ear. "Just give me the signal if you need anything. Anything at all," she said with a wink, and I knew my friend wasn't talking about refills.

After Mrs. Finney strode back to the counter, I turned to Melanie, ignoring Sophie. "What is it, Melanie?" I asked. "Is this about Brie? Dev?"

She choked back a sob. Sophie straightened her shoulders and said, "Melanie is in love with Dev, but she believes he was in love with the Bohannan woman. On the other hand, Sanchez thinks Dev might be the killer. And now Melanie says Dev is acting strangely. Grief stricken, maybe." She lifted an eyebrow, and her voice rose. "Or guilty."

Melanie dropped her face into her hands. I shushed Sophie and motioned toward the other customers, now regarding us with interest. She swiveled her gaze to them. "Don't worry, people. You'll be able to read all the juicy details in the next edition of *Sophie's Scoop*. Tell your friends!" Then she leaned across the table. "Callahan, I'm doing you a courtesy here," she whispered fiercely. "You mustn't go public with any of this, not until I've published the story on my blog. Nothing to Tonya. Nothing to Sanchez."

My mouth gaped, but I quickly returned my attention to the frazzled woman across from me. "Melanie, look at me." She lifted her face, her gray eyes hazy with tears. "I want to help you. Just talk to me."

Her breath hitched. "There's really nothing to talk about. Dev didn't kill that horrible woman. He wouldn't."

"Raul—Detective Sanchez—said the two of you were together Thursday night. That you had alibied each other."

Sophie snorted. "She fell asleep early. Dev could easily have—"

"Hush," I said. "I need to hear this from Melanie." Sophie pursed her lips but thankfully remained quiet. "Melanie," I continued, "were the two of you together

Thursday night? All night?"

Her eyes flicked upward and to the left, a sure sign the next words out of her mouth were going to be a lie. "Yes," she said, not making eye contact. "I'm a light sleeper. I would have known if he'd left."

I nodded and shot a sideways glance at Sophie, who gave her head a little shake. She didn't believe Melanie either.

I rubbed my earlobe as I thought. "When Dev left the happy hour at the gallery the other night—"

Melanie's jaw clenched. "He went to the lodge to check on Brie. That's all. She was his partner, and he was concerned. But she wasn't there. He never found her." She glared at me. "In fact, you're the one who found her. Why isn't everyone interrogating you instead of us?"

The vitriol startled me, and I raised my hands as if to ward off an attack. "Hey, I'm not accusing anyone of anything. I only want to help."

Her eyes continued to flash. "Well, you might not be accusing him, but that detective is. Why would he target Dev, anyway? He's one of the few people who halfway liked Brie. He's actually sorry she's dead."

My eyebrows lifted. Such venom. "I assume you're not sorry, then?"

No flicking of the eyes this time. Just downright daggers. "I hate to say it, but no, I'm not. That woman collected dirt on everyone she knew and cheerfully used it against them. It's no secret she slept her way into her job. And she stole assignments that should have gone to me. Sorry she's gone? Ha. I'll be dancing on her grave." Suddenly, Melanie seemed to realize she'd spoken the words aloud. She looked from Sophie to me, her face ashen. "I didn't kill her, though, and neither did Dev. And we don't know who did."

I paused, recalling the Instagram photo I'd seen yesterday on Brie's site. "You say Brie slept her way to the top. Are you referring to a…relationship…with Preston Garrison?"

Melanie pulled her lips into her mouth. Then she stood abruptly, her chair rocking as it scooted backwards. "I've said too much." She looked at Sophie. "You can't use anything I've told you. I don't give you permission."

Sophie grinned. "Darling, you're a journalist. Why, you're even employed by the esteemed *Sentinel*. You should know how this works. I identified myself to you as a journalist, and you never once said the words 'off the record.'"

Melanie glared at Sophie for a long moment, then rose and marched toward the door.

Sophie called after her. "Rest assured, I'll treat you fairly, darling. We're friends, remember?"

13

A s I walked down Evergreen Way, my mind spun. Melanie's anger and hatred toward Brie. Dev's weak alibi. Could the two of them have conspired to commit murder? Brie had somehow gotten her hands on a key—had Melanie and Dev followed her inside sometime that night and killed her? But why? Any motives I could come up with felt feeble.

As I neared Sundance Studio, I noticed Alexis standing with her back to the wall, one foot propped against the bricks, tapping away at her phone. When she glanced up and saw me approach, her lips pressed together in a tight line. I sighed. My young employee was angry. I'd already dealt with one emotional maelstrom this morning. I wasn't sure I was up for round two.

"Good morning, Sunshine," I said, keeping my voice cheerful. "Fingers crossed we won't step in any fecal matter this morning."

"Or find any dead bodies," she retorted.

Touché.

I unlocked the door and edged inside, flicking on the light. Alexis stepped in behind me. Tense, we both scanned the room. Then we relaxed. Except for the layers of fingerprint dust the techs had left behind, all seemed well.

Alexis trudged to the counter and tossed her bag down,

heaving a sigh.

"What's got you in such a huff this morning?" I asked.

"Oh, nothing much. Just being fingerprinted and interrogated as if I were a stone-cold killer. No big deal."

I winced. "I'm sorry about that. I told Raul it wasn't necessary, that I trust you and Ethan completely, but he's covering all the bases."

She forced a smile. "I know. He's doing his job. It was just unsettling. I'm a private person."

"Really? I hadn't noticed." I grinned.

Her eyes settled on the entrance to the hallway, and her expression was grim. I realized she was thinking of the darkroom and what had happened there. "It's weird," she said. "We're opening up this morning as if everything is normal. And just yesterday…" She shuddered. "Anyway, do the police know who did it?"

Melanie and Dev flashed into my mind, followed by Gary and Preston. But I knew better than to share Raul's information. "I'm not at liberty to talk about suspects."

She sighed. "I figured."

"I wish I could, but it's an ongoing investigation. I've been sworn to silence."

"No biggie." She climbed off the stool and tossed her hair. "I'll get started cleaning up. Don't forget, you have a digital class at eleven." She pulled out her phone and swiped at the screen as she walked away.

I watched her go, thinking about Raul's question: *How well do you know them?* I had to admit, not terribly well. As Alexis had alluded, she was a private person, and I'd respected that. In leaving behind my role as an investigative photojournalist, I'd made a promise to myself to trust more, to stop interrogating everyone I met as if they might be a source. As such, I realized I might have traveled too far in the opposite direction. I hadn't learned much about Alexis's personal life, or Ethan's. Maybe it was time to remedy that.

When she came back in the room carrying a feather duster, I cleared my throat. "So, I noticed you were texting.

Is it a boyfriend?"

She eyed me suspiciously. "It was Elyse. We're setting up a coffee date. Why?"

"Just a friendly question," I said, stacking some papers so I'd appear nonchalant. "I don't feel like I've gotten to know you as well as I should."

She threw up her hands. "So now *you* suspect me too."

"No, that's not what I meant—"

The bell above the door jingled and Ethan hurried inside, looking frazzled. Since I'd never known him to be prone to melodrama, I felt a swell of concern. "Ethan, what's wrong?"

He went behind the sales counter and pressed a button on the computer. "I have to show you something." He tapped a foot impatiently while it booted up, then maneuvered the mouse and made a few clicks. "Here, have a look at this."

He pointed at the screen. I sat on a stool in front of the computer. Ethan peered over my shoulder, and Alexis moved in behind us. I quickly understood I was looking at an Instagram post. The main photo was slightly blurry and not well lit, so it took me a second to recognize it as the interior of Sundance Studio. A red circle highlighted a focal point in the center of the floor. I leaned in closer and then sat bolt upright. It was the pile of poop that had sullied the gallery floor two days ago. The vandals had documented their deed.

Ethan reached across me and grasped the mouse, opening a library of photos. He selected the next one, pulling up a picture of the graffiti painted on my front window. Then a third, which showed the rotten produce strewn outside. Finally, he clicked another image, and this one took my breath away. It was a stretcher being wheeled out of my studio. On it lay the black bag that contained Brie's body.

I looked up at Ethan. "Who posted these pictures?"

"Let me slide back in there," he said, gesturing for the

stool. I rose, and he took my place, guiding the cursor across the screen. "It's a fake account. The only content is those pictures. Look at the name on the site."

He leaned back, and I looked over his shoulder. The site's name read Sundancestudio, with the associated blurb of "Picture this. A photo gallery that develops death."

All very bleak, but it was the small, round profile picture that caused me to tremble: an illustration of a camera strap wrapped around a faceless head.

"Well, this isn't good," Alexis said.

"No kidding," Ethan said. "I'll notify Instagram and ask them to remove the account, but it'll probably take a few hours."

"Wait a second," I said. If this was the Ratliff twins' doing, as I suspected, we needed to stop them in their tracks. "Can you trace the origin of the account before you get it removed? Is there some way to prove who posted it?"

"I tried, but I can't get past the author name, where it says sundancestudio. I'm decent with technology, but I'm not a hacker. I'll never get past Instagram's firewalls."

I weighed our options. If we left the page intact, we might be able to locate someone with the necessary skills to uncover the site's creator. But that would mean...

My phone rang, and I dug it out of my bag. Tonya started talking as soon as I clicked accept. "Prepare yourself. There's this fake Instagram account—"

"We're looking at it right now," I said. "Call you later, okay?"

That settled that. We couldn't wait. If Tonya had seen it, any number of other people would too. Our online business was just gathering steam, and I couldn't afford potential buyers to associate this site with my gallery.

Plus, what would my Evergreen Way neighbors think? They'd already expressed concern that the murder might disrupt the Fireweed Festival and their businesses. This certainly wouldn't elevate my status in their eyes.

"Do what you have to do," I said. Ethan leaned over the

keyboard and began typing.

"One more thing," he said over his shoulder. "I think you need to get the locks changed. I'll be glad to handle it if you want me to."

Why hadn't I thought of that myself? And I couldn't believe Raul hadn't mentioned the idea. Or Sam. "Yes, good idea. Thank you." I checked the time and turned to Alexis. "Five minutes to opening, and I haven't even begun setting up for the digital class in an hour. Can you handle customers while Ethan deals with all this?"

She nodded. "Absolutely. Whatever you need. Just let me clean up that fingerprint dust really quick."

For a moment, I watched Ethan typing on the computer and Alexis swiping the feather duster across surfaces, both working feverishly on my behalf. I felt a wave of gratitude that these two were in my corner. Maybe I'd never learned their mothers' maiden names, but this told me all I needed to know.

14

C lass went well, all things considered. All six students scheduled showed up, and aside from a few sneaky glances at the darkroom door as they entered the classroom, no mention was made of the murder. I taught a few Photoshop techniques, critiqued their photos, and at the end of the hour, sent them on their way with a homework assignment.

In the meantime, Ethan had contacted Instagram. The account was flagged and would likely be permanently removed within a couple of hours. He'd also scheduled a lock change for the afternoon. Alexis reported a steady but manageable flow of customers, with only a few she'd characterize as looky loos hoping to gawk at a murder scene.

Everything seemed to be under control, so I decided to leave the two of them in charge while I headed over to the Knotty Pine. Paired with the photo I'd seen yesterday, Melanie's accusation of an inappropriate relationship between Brie and Preston had my former boss in my sights. I'd insisted to Raul and Sam that I didn't believe Preston could be guilty of murder, but now I found myself with a niggle of doubt.

I grabbed my purse and camera and stepped out the front door, allowing myself a moment to breathe in the warm, clean air. Nothing better than a soft mountain breeze to elevate the mood. I closed my eyes for a moment, pushing away negative thoughts and letting the sun warm my skin.

Alas, all good feelings must come to an end. I opened my eyes to see Tabitha peering at me over the top of her horn-rimmed glasses. "This murder of yours couldn't have come at a more inconvenient time," she said.

A sigh billowed in my chest. Nothing Tabitha said surprised me. I'd known her almost my whole life, had even worked in her souvenir shop, Tabitha's Treasures, for a summer during high school. Even then, she'd wielded a sharp tongue against villagers and tourists alike. Now, in her late seventies, any modicum of discretion had disintegrated.

"First of all, it's not my murder," I said.

"Well, it happened in your studio." Her gray curls bobbed as she shook her head. "Young people these days. Never want to take any responsibility."

"All right, I apologize for the terrible timing," I said. "But I really don't believe this will damage your bottom line."

If she'd had eyebrows, they would have risen to her hairline. "Guess you haven't heard. The idiots on the Chamber of Commerce are thinking about cancelling the Fireweed Festival. Worried about tourist safety, or some such rubbish." She gestured down the street with both hands. "If they cancel it, or if people decide to stay away due to this murder of yours, we'll all suffer the consequences. The whole village will take an economic hit, including you. So maybe you should start thinking about *your* bottom line."

The news stunned me. I knew there'd been concern, but cancelling the Fireweed Festival? I hadn't believed it might really happen.

Tabitha grasped my forearm. "You got to the bottom of a murder in our little town not so long ago. If you can do it again—and fast—we can get back to normal before the festival." She gave me a stern look before marching into her shop.

I watched her go, my brain reeling. Fireweed Festival cancelled? I pictured my mother's response—she'd enrolled in a cake decorating class just so she could enter the contest. More importantly, local business owners simply couldn't afford to lose the income. And if Tabitha was any indication, they'd all hold me responsible. This crime had to be solved fast. I set off with renewed vigor to talk with Preston.

Behind me, footsteps pounded down the stairs from the realty office above Sundance Studio. Willie Wright rushed by without sparing me a glance. I remembered that in addition to his job as a realtor, Willie served as the newest president of the Rock Creek Village Chamber of Commerce.

"Willie," I called. "I need to talk to you about the Fireweed Festival."

No response.

I called his name again, but he didn't acknowledge me at all. In fact, he may have even picked up his pace. Either the man was late for a showing, or he had no interest in talking to me. Did he, like Tabitha, blame me for the town's current troubles? I swiveled my head, glancing at all the businesses along the sidewalk.

Did everyone?

I arrived in the lobby of the Knotty Pine a little breathless. From behind the registration desk, Dad cocked his head. "New workout routine?"

"Hardy har har." I glanced toward the Great Room and saw a small group of resort guests hanging out there. From the game room, the smash of pool balls indicated a game in progress. The lodge seemed to be doing a brisk business. With a pang, I wondered if this murder would also hurt my parents' business. Or Sam's.

I walked behind the counter and climbed onto the stool next to Dad's.

"How're you holding up?" he asked.

From anyone else, that question always grated on my nerves. But from my father's lips, it translated into "I love you. I care about you. I'll do whatever I can to protect you."

I shrugged. "Oh, you know. Another day…"

"Another donut," he said, finishing the joke we'd shared since I was a kid. "Seriously, though, anything new with the investigation? Have you heard from Sanchez?"

I summarized the information I'd gotten from Raul, though I suspected Dad had already heard the same particulars from Frank Laramie, his old partner and Rock Creek Village's current Chief of Police. The two of them liked to pretend they weren't sharing classified information, but we all knew Frank told Dad everything—just like the old days.

I nodded and changed the subject from murder to business. "Dad, there's something else I'm worried about." He waited. "Tabitha told me this…incident…might throw a wrench into the Fireweed Festival. She said the Chamber is considering calling it off."

"I heard that rumor. It's never going to happen."

"She said they're worried tourists will stay away, that they won't feel safe."

"Ridiculous. First of all, the scene of a crime draws more people than it repels. You know how that works. If anything, it'll boost attendance. Second, the masses have short attention spans. I doubt anyone will be talking about this—outside of the village, that is—by the time the weekend is over. The Chamber will never cancel. Willie's like Sophie Demler—a drama queen. They both just like to stir up trouble."

I felt a little better, but I knew I wouldn't be able to completely let go of my anxiety until the murder was solved. I wrung my hands together, and Dad's lips tightened. "I know that look. You're here to investigate."

"Not exactly."

"Callahan Cassidy, you need to..." He shook his head. "It's no use. I should know that by now. You're going to do what you're going to do. Just be careful. And stay out of Sanchez's way."

"No problem," I said. "I'm actually here to chat with Preston. Doubt it will amount to anything, but do you know if he's in his room?"

"I've been at the desk most of the morning and haven't seen him leave. Room 301."

Of course. One of the two luxury suites. The other was on the opposite side of the third floor. "Let me guess," I said. "Brie was in 302."

He nodded, then squirmed on the stool. "Listen, Sundance, before you go up to question him—"

"I'm not questioning him. Just talking."

"Whatever. Before you go up there, would you pop in and see your mother? She's been in the middle of some major cake decorating project, and I'm afraid I didn't come off as very supportive. She's in a snit with me. Maybe a few kind words from you would improve her mood."

I grimaced. "Is it a disaster?"

"Well, I mean, I'm no expert…"

"So you want me to go upstairs and lie to her?"

He gave me a sheepish grin. "I'm sure you'll do whatever you think is best."

I rose and walked toward the entrance to their home. "If I'm not down in ten minutes, send up the troops."

When I stepped into the living room upstairs, the pleasant aroma of freshly baked cake wafted through the air, perfectly mouthwatering. *So far, so good*, I thought.

A quartz peninsula countertop separated the living room from the kitchen, and I found Mom hunched over her work, her back to me. The mild scowl on her face quickly transformed into a bright smile when she saw me. "It's you, Angelface. I'm so glad. I was afraid it was your father, coming to make amends."

All right, then. She obviously still carried a grudge. I remembered my argument with Sam last night and the way it took me a while to let go of my anger. Guess I knew where I got it.

A strand of silver hair fell across her forehead, and she blew it out of her eyes as she stepped back from the counter, holding a piping tube. "What do you think? Keep in mind that it's my first independent attempt."

I approached the counter and examined the cake. Three round tiers, each layer equal in circumference. Light blue frosting provided the base, and yellow swirls danced across the sides. She was in the process of adding buttercream flowers in purple, orange, and red. Her theme was apparent—blue sky and a meadow filled with wildflowers. Not bad. Very nice, in fact, especially for a rookie effort.

The real problem lay not in the decorations, but in the construction. Sad to say, but the cake leaned. A lot.

The angle reminded me of the Leaning Tower of Pisa, bent at least twenty degrees. I tilted my head to match. Had Mom not noticed the incline when she originally stacked the layers? Maybe too much time on her inversion table had affected her equilibrium.

I considered my words carefully. How could I provide constructive criticism without facing Dad's fate?

She sighed. "Ignore the incline, Callahan. I was experimenting with a three-dimensional approach, wondering if I could create a mountain slope effect. As your father somewhat candidly pointed out, it didn't create the desired effect. Try to look past that, at the artistic effort. What do you think of the decorations?"

My face lit up in a genuine smile. "Mom, I love it. The colors, the flowers, the overall aura—it's lovely. It makes me feel as if I've been transported to a meadow in the mountains."

She looked at the cake, appraising it through narrowed eyes. "It has promise, I think. With practice, I might be able to snag an honorable mention in the Fireweed Festival contest."

"Oh, I think you could do better than that. And you have five days to iron out the kinks. Or to straighten them, as the case may be."

She laid the piping bag on the counter and rolled her shoulders. "Anyway, sweetheart, I'm glad you're here. Even if I'm fairly certain you came at your father's behest."

I chuckled. "Now, Mom. Cut him some slack. He feels bad that he didn't come across as more supportive."

"Yes, well, the key to a long and happy marriage is learning to rise above perceived slights." She smiled slyly. "And knowing how to use such moments to your advantage. I predict a lovely dinner date in my immediate future, perhaps even flowers. But tell me, darling, how are you doing? Recent events must have thrown a bit of a wrench into your own Fireweed Festival preparations."

"Assuming there even is a Fireweed Festival." I explained Tabitha's worrisome conjecture.

She waved dismissively, sending a dollop of green frosting onto the floor. "Pish. Hot air, that's what I think. A few self-important buffoons getting everyone stirred up. Willie Wright and his cronies on the chamber will never cancel. Too many people depend on the revenue. They'd be voted out of office—or worse—before they signed the mandate. I advise you to continue preparing your photos for the market and your pets for the pageant."

"I have a pretty good stock of photos ready. Another afternoon or two in the darkroom should be sufficient." I clenched my teeth. "But Woody and Carl have refused to learn a single trick."

She smiled. "Well, at least they own a suitable wardrobe. You needn't worry about that."

I nodded. We lovingly referred to my mother as a hobby jumper, and prior to cake decorating, she'd spent time in a knitting phase. Net result: several suitable ensembles for each of my pets. No, I wasn't concerned about the costume portion of the pageant. I also held no qualms about presentation. Woody and Carl were naturally beautiful animals, if I did say so myself. A good bath and brushing would provide sufficient grooming—though I grimaced at the thought of the nail trims.

But the talent section gave me hives. Currently, Woody's main abilities centered on licking, smiling, and wagging. If friendliness were a talent, he'd win the gold cup. Carl, on the other hand, had "a very particular set of skills," but none that would translate well to a red carpet setting. Coaxing my cat into obedience mode didn't seem promising.

"Could I recruit you as their coach? I'd be willing to pay top dollar."

She threw her head back and laughed. "Not a chance. I'm too busy trying to get cakes not to fall over."

"Worth a try," I said. "Well, I'll let you get back to it. I'm off for a chat with Preston."

She frowned. "Please tell me you're not in the midst of conducting your own investigation."

I averted my eyes. "Just doing what I can to keep the festival in play and customers flowing into the gallery. And guests into your resort."

"Mm hmm. Well, you know the drill. I'd urge caution, but I expect all you'd hear was blah, blah, blah."

After she released me from a hug, I wiped errant bits of icing from my arm and traipsed downstairs. When I passed the front desk, Dad raised his eyebrows in a question. I gave him a thumbs up. "All is well. Just take her out for dinner. Flowers would be a nice extra touch." I snapped my fingers. "Oh, and don't order cake for dessert."

15

I plodded up the grand staircase, pausing on the second-floor landing to catch my breath. A few months ago, I'd vowed to get into better shape, but I obviously wasn't there yet. I forced myself upward to the third floor.

As I approached the top step, my peripheral vision caught a bit of movement near the only door on the right. I peeked between the balusters for a better view.

An unkempt, sock-footed man wearing wrinkled trousers and an untucked dress shirt stood in the hallway. With the air of a person sneaking out after a forbidden tryst, he glanced furtively down the hall before latching the door.

When he turned, I glimpsed his face, and my jaw dropped open. Stubble shadowed Preston Garrison's usually clean-shaven cheeks, and his hair looked like a rat's nest. His appearance was completely out of character. He was normally a male version of Tonya, well-groomed and fashionable.

Yet there he stood, scruffy and rumpled, creeping out of Suite 302, the room once booked to Brie Bohannan and now, as far as I knew, an off-limits crime scene.

I stomped up the last step, and Preston jumped in surprise. Guilt clouded his face, and he quickly replaced it with his usual expression of authority. "Good afternoon,

Callie. I wasn't expecting you."

"Clearly," I said. "What were you doing in Brie's room?"

"What? Oh, that. Just looking for this." He opened his hand to reveal a sliver of shiny metal. "My tie clip broke on the plane, and Brie put it in her pocket. I was hoping the police hadn't taken it into evidence—gift from my father, you know. Turns out they hadn't."

I scowled. Despite the evidence nestled in his palm, his story smelled fishy to me. "How did you get in?"

He arranged his face into a look of embarrassment. Contrived, I could tell. "Brie gave me one of her keys. When we traveled, we often exchanged keys. Sometimes we met after hours. For a drink or…something."

The innuendo caused warmth to spread across my cheeks. I stretched out my palm. "Hand it over." He looked at me blankly. "The key. That room is a crime scene. You know better than to go in there."

"Well, the police have come and gone, so I doubt I've committed any egregious offense. But here you go." He dropped the key into my hand, and I tucked it into my pocket. "What are you doing here, anyway?"

"I came to talk to you. Let's go to your room."

He opened his mouth to argue, but one glance at what probably resembled a thunderstorm on my face deterred him. Without a word, he walked down the hall to Suite 301, slid his keycard into the lock, and gestured me inside.

The suite was spacious and elegantly detailed, in a rustic, mountain-themed way. Picture windows overlooking the Rocky Mountains spanned the back wall. The sitting area was comprised of a plush couch and armchair, both facing a currently dormant fireplace. A bar was located to the side, and beneath it a small refrigerator, which Preston opened. He pulled out a mini bottle of whiskey and held it up. "Want something?"

I did, but it wasn't alcohol. I wanted relief from the suspicions currently gnawing at my gut.

Dropping into the armchair, I shook my head and

summoned my patience as Preston spent precious time plucking ice cubes from the insulated bucket, dropping them into a crystal highball glass, and pouring the whiskey. At long last, he sat on the couch. But the ritual apparently wasn't complete. He swirled the amber liquid in the glass and took a long sip. "You're here to lecture me, right?" He laid his head back and closed his eyes. "Go ahead and get it over with."

I studied him. Though he tried to conceal it, distress darkened his features. But why? Was it Brie's death, or his own culpability? I decided I'd play good cop. For now. "No lecture. I'm sure you realize you shouldn't have entered Brie's suite, but I'd probably have done the same. The techs have already completed their work. And my guess is your fingerprints were all over the room, anyway."

He opened one eye. "Jealous, are you?"

I smiled gently. "No, Preston. Those days have passed."

Both his eyes were on me now. He lifted his glass. "To better days then."

A beat of silence passed before I pressed forward. "Why were you really in Brie's room?"

He shifted his gaze to the ceiling, staying quiet so long I thought he might not respond. But after a deep sigh, he spoke. "All right. I'll 'fess up, as they say. A while back, Brie turned up some…information. Something that would, at the very least, prove embarrassing to me. At the most, it would be professionally damaging. She showed it to me the day we arrived. I went to her room hoping to retrieve it. But it's not there. Not that I could find, at any rate. Either the police confiscated it, or it's in the safe. Either way, there's no chance of keeping it private now."

My gut twinged in a familiar response. It was the spasm I'd always experienced when I knew a story was about to break. "Tell me."

He grunted. "Why not? I'm sure that detective of yours will fill you in soon enough."

He lifted his glass, drained the remainder of the whiskey,

and went to the refrigerator for another bottle. I waited, my nerves singing, as he went through the interminable process of refilling his glass.

When he returned to his seat, he spent a moment studying the glass in his hand. "The catalyst for Brie's little discovery is the news that Nicole Harrison-White is retiring soon—"

"*The Sentinel's* editor-in-chief?"

He shot me a sardonic look. "Do you know any other Nicole Harrison-Whites?"

Point taken. "I hadn't heard she was leaving."

"It's not public yet. She's won't make the announcement until her replacement can be chosen."

"Ah," I said, finally understanding the direction this was going. "The replacement is likely to be you."

"I'm on the short list, yes. Word is I might even be the top contender. For the moment, anyway."

"But Brie's little tidbit might hurt your chances."

"No might about it." He clinked the ice cubes against the glass. "I'll be out of the running. For that matter, I'll probably be out of a job."

My mind churned with possibilities. I didn't know what Brie had on him, but whatever it was, it sure sounded like it gave him motive. "Go on," I prompted. "Might help to talk about it."

"Confession is good for the soul, right?" He chugged the rest of his drink—his second in less than half an hour.

He started to get up—heading for another refill, no doubt—but I put a hand on his arm. "Maybe you should take it easy. I can tell you from experience that getting drunk won't make your problems disappear."

"I beg to differ. Problems no longer bother you when you've passed out." But he put his empty glass on the coffee table and stayed put, resting his head on the back of the couch. His eyelids drifted shut. He breathed in and out once, twice, a third time. Just as I began to suspect he'd actually fallen asleep, he stirred. "You're a good lady,

Callahan Cassidy. Best journalist I've ever known. Gritty, determined. Ethics on steroids. The newspaper hasn't been the same without you."

I smiled softly. "Much as I love a good compliment, you're stalling, Preston. Just tell me. Get it over with."

He sighed. "Those aforementioned ethics I attributed to you? Once you hear my little secret, you'll have to tell the police, I suppose."

"It depends." I paused, knowing I owed him the truth. "But probably."

He laced his hands behind his neck. "Well, they'll find out one way or the other. Probably already have." He dropped one ankle across his knee. "Brie dug up some old photos and correspondence between Nicole and me. Compromising stuff, you might say. Years old—long before your time at the paper—but that won't matter in the long run."

His revelation was a bit anticlimactic. Preston's reputation as a ladies' man wasn't exactly a secret and, as I could personally attest, it had been well earned. A romance with Nicole didn't rise to the level of earth-shattering news. "Where did she get this compromising stuff?"

"Where do you think? Brie was a regular…guest…in my home. She must have searched the contents of my desk when I was sleeping. Years ago, Nicole and I had engaged in a little…self-videoing, you might say. And I'd printed a few still shots for personal viewing. Kept them tucked away in a drawer, long since forgotten." He blew out a long breath. "What was I expecting? If you invite a viper into your home, you're likely to get bitten."

He was right about that. And I supposed if Brie had leaked the information, it could cause embarrassment, more to Nicole than Preston, I thought. She was married. But if it happened over a decade ago, so what? Seemed like old news.

Preston seemed to read my doubts. "It's a bigger issue than you might think. See, when Nicole and I began our affair, I was a lowly reporter. Not even a Felden Award to my name. Nicole was managing editor—"

Now I saw the gravity of the situation. "She was your immediate boss."

He nodded. "Then she was named editor-in-chief and had to choose her successor."

She'd named Preston. He'd been her secret lover. If news of their affair—ancient though it might be—spilled into the public forum now, people would say he'd slept his way to the top. Or worse, that he'd blackmailed Nicole the way Brie had blackmailed him.

"So Brie threatened to divulge her newfound knowledge, which would conceivably kill your chances at the promotion—" He winced at my word choice but didn't interrupt. "Did she want another promotion of her own?"

He pointed at me. "Bingo." He rose from the couch and headed to the bar again. This time I didn't try to stop him. "Brie was in no way qualified to be managing editor. I never even should have given her your vacated position. If I rose to the editor-in-chief job and slid her in as managing editor, I'd instigate a mutiny. So I've found myself between the proverbial rock and hard place."

"Unless Brie was suddenly out of the picture," I murmured.

He swiveled toward me, drink in hand, his jaw clenched. Then his expression softened. "You're right, of course. That is, if I'd been able to get my hands on the information she had. But now—"

"Her death only compounds the problem," I said. "Not only will your reputation be tarnished, but people might even believe you're a murderer."

He seemed to age twenty years right before my eyes. When he went to set his glass on the bar, it slid off the edge and tumbled to the floor. He stood frozen in place, so I jumped from my chair, grabbed a cloth, and dropped to my knees to sop up the whiskey. When I rose and moved to the sink, placing the glass inside and wringing out the wet cloth,

Preston watched, his shoulders slumped and arms limp at his sides.

"I'm sorry, Callie. So sorry."

I wasn't completely sure what he meant. Sorry about spilling his drink? About overindulging? Or was I hearing a confession?

"You've been under a lot of stress," I said. I rinsed my hands and dried them on a towel. "But I'm afraid things might get worse before they get better. And I think you'd do well to face the situation sober."

He dropped his eyes. "You're right. But the only thing I care about at this moment is that you believe me. I didn't kill her, Callie. I'd never—" He stopped, choking back his tipsy emotions.

I looked into his pleading eyes and decided to offer him the one bit of solace I could. He wasn't asking me to be his defense attorney, and anyway—I did believe him. "I don't think you killed her, Preston. I truly don't. And that's what I'll tell Detective Sanchez."

"You're going to see him now?"

I nodded. "If he's available."

"Should I come with you?"

I considered the idea, but decided against it. "I suggest you take a shower, try to sober up. Don't go anywhere. Let me talk to the police, forge the path, as it were. Maybe then we can avoid…"

"An arrest," he finished, his face turning pale.

"I can't guarantee that. Given everything you've told me, you'll likely be their top suspect. But I can promise you, Sanchez is a fair, honest cop. He'll dig as deep as necessary to uncover the truth."

"All right. Whatever you say, Callie. I trust you."

I walked to the door and put my hand on the knob. A thought occurred to me, and I turned back. "One more thing before I go. What about Gary Padgett? Did he have any problems with Brie?"

"You mean, something that would inspire murderous

rage?" He grunted. "Gary is sixty-eight, not a vicious bone in his body. I'd suspect you before I'd suspect Gary."

I didn't mention Sanchez's theory that Gary and Preston might have been in cahoots. He'd likely hear that news soon enough.

16

When I closed Preston's door behind me, I had every intention of borrowing Dad's car and driving straight to the police station to fill Raul in on the information my former boss had dished out. I even placed one foot on the top stair.

But then I felt a tingle in my pocket—a magnetic pull. I thought about the key Preston had relinquished, and it drew me to the door of Suite 302.

Hand on the banister, I tried to fight the relentless tug. But it was no use. I simply had to take a peek inside Brie's room. To do anything else would be to deny my essential nature.

Once the decision was made, the rationalization began. What harm could it do, anyway? The police search had concluded. Certainly they hadn't overlooked a critical piece of evidence. Even Preston had been inside the room. One more set of eyes—and hands—wouldn't make a difference.

Justification process complete, I tiptoed to the door and slipped the keycard into the locking device, flinching at the electronic beep I was sure had alerted Preston—or Dad— to my trespass. After a glance over my shoulder, I slid inside the room, closed the door softly, and took a breath to slow my heart rate.

Flipping on the light, I took a moment to examine the

setting. Fingerprint dust coated the nightstand, the bureau, and the coffee table. Half-opened drawers gave the room a sense of urgency, as if someone had departed in a hurry. The comforter and sheets had been stripped from the bed and lay in a heap on the floor. I thought of Felicia, the resort's chief housekeeper, and smiled ruefully. Her A-type personality was going to be in a snit.

It felt a little creepy entering the room where Brie had stayed—the last place she had ever slept. But the feeling quickly billowed into excitement. This room oozed the ambience of a treasure hunt. I strode toward the bureau and started scavenging.

I patted my hands along the rough wood interior, to no avail. Likewise, the desk drawers were empty. I got to my knees, clicked my phone's flashlight and aimed it under the bed. Not even a tiny dust bunny. I'd have to lobby Dad for a raise on Felicia's behalf. A search beneath the mattress also proved fruitless. Finally, I explored the bathroom, where I unearthed absolutely nothing of interest. The police had apparently bagged everything here, even Brie's toothbrush.

I wasn't prepared to give up, though. Brie had offered Preston her second keycard, meaning she'd known her suite wouldn't be completely safe from prying eyes. Anything she didn't want him to see had to be well camouflaged.

Standing in the center of the spacious main room, I pirouetted, letting my eyes flick across the suite. My gaze came to rest on the bureau again. All those empty drawers. My mind flashed with an *aha* moment. I hadn't searched every inch of that dresser after all.

I pulled out the top drawer and ran my hand across the wood above the chasm. Except for a tiny splinter, I came away empty-handed. Second drawer, same story.

Then I dropped into a crouch and yanked the bottom drawer off its slider. Setting it aside, I contorted my upper body and wedged an arm into the open space, twisting my head and shoving it into the opening as far as I could in order to get a glimpse.

Nothing.

Heaving a sigh, I sat back on my feet and slapped my hands against my knees. I reminded myself it had been a long shot and reached for the drawer, intending to slide it back in place. Then a thought crossed my mind—one last glimmer of hope.

When I turned the drawer over, I practically heard the trumpets of angels sounding in my ears.

There on the plywood, thick packing tape secured a legal-sized yellow envelope to the surface.

I grinned as if I were a pirate who'd just discovered a coffer of gold doubloons. Cross-legged, I used a thumbnail to pry off the tape and free the prize. I ran my hands across the envelope, detecting what I assumed was a short stack of papers. When I turned the envelope over, I found the flap sealed tightly with the same clear packing tape covering the clasp. I glanced around the room guiltily, as if I'd discovered something I shouldn't keep to myself. Which I supposed I had.

I knew I should take this envelope—unopened—to Raul. But if I did, I might never get a glimpse of the contents. And I really wanted that glimpse.

What to do? My inner angel perched on one shoulder and my inner devil on the other, both whispering furiously in my ears.

As always, the devil whispered louder.

I struggled to my feet and replaced the drawer on its sliders. Then I carefully folded the envelope in half and tucked it into my bag. I told myself I only wanted to save Raul some time. After all, knowing Brie as I had, I might be able to recognize clues he'd overlook.

Just a quick examination. Then I'd immediately hand it over.

At least, that's the story I gave my shoulder angel.

A glance at the bedside clock told me it was four o'clock. I'd abandoned Ethan and Alexis for almost half a day. The secrets would have to wait.

By the time I got home at six-thirty, Woody and Carl were apoplectic at being left alone for so long, so I spent a half hour on creature comfort. Then I filled their bowls with kibble and lumbered upstairs, where I wriggled out of my clothes—most importantly, my bra—and slid on pajama pants and an oversized t-shirt. Sleuthing worked best in comfy clothing. Back downstairs, I poured myself a glass of wine, spooned leftover garlic steak and mashed potatoes onto a plate, and popped it into the microwave. Thank God for Sam, or I'd only ever eat frozen TV dinners.

While my meal heated, I made a quick call to Preston, telling him I'd been unable to get in contact with Raul and would try again first thing in the morning. Just a tiny white lie, I assured that pesky shoulder angel, easily rectified tomorrow. After a brief call to Sam as I ate, reassuring him all was well, my evening's commitments were complete. I rinsed my dishes and settled onto the couch, smoothing Brie's envelope beneath my fingers in anticipation. I felt as if she were sending me a message from the great beyond— a well-protected message.

A few scissor snips freed the tape, and I wedged a fingertip beneath the flap.

I experienced a surge of adrenaline, a familiar response when I was about to break a story. What could possibly have been so important that Brie felt the need to hide it beneath a dresser drawer? Time to find out.

Woody jumped onto the couch and laid his head in my lap, covering the envelope and looking up at me with liquid brown eyes. Who could resist? I stroked his fur and cooed some words of affection before giving him a gentle nudge. "Okay, boy, move it. This crime ain't gonna solve itself."

He shot me a look of betrayal before shifting to the other end of the couch. Within seconds, he was asleep.

The cat, on the other hand, appeared unnervingly alert. He perched on the back of the couch, swishing his tail as he stared over my shoulder. "All right, partner," I said to him.

"Let's get to it."

I reached inside the envelope and retrieved the contents. Not sure what I'd been expecting, but the hidden treasure trove came down to a few sheets of paper. Very disappointing.

These pages had better be worth the effort.

A printout of an email topped the stack. Dated three weeks ago, it was addressed to Brie's personal account. The sender: Melanie Lewis.

The rambling letter started with a B word—and devolved from there. Laced with profanity that embarrassed even my worldly journalistic sensibilities, the note accused Brie of attempting to steal Dev away from her, of appropriating all the best story assignments, and of sleeping with anyone and everyone who could boost her career. Melanie blamed Brie for her own lack of advancement at work, for Dev's inability to get promoted, for every negative event in recent history. To hear Melanie tell it, Brie might somehow have been responsible for the extinction of the dinosaurs.

But the biggest eye-opener had to do with Melanie's family tree. It seemed Brie had somehow uncovered information on the mental health issues that plagued Melanie's bloodline—her mother's bipolar disorder, her brother's OCD, and her aunt's schizophrenia. From the content of the email, I couldn't work out Brie's nefarious intent. But Melanie rage was easy to deduce.

Interesting. If the first page was this incriminating, what damaging information would subsequent pages hold? Melanie had accused Brie of being a blackmailer. I realized now that I could be looking at her trove of secret weapons.

I turned to the second sheet, and it took me a few seconds to decipher what I was seeing. When I did, I felt a blush creep into my cheeks and instinctively averted my eyes. After a moment, I forced my gaze back to the grainy picture—a semi-risqué shot of Preston, maybe fifteen years younger. He was passionately kissing a bikini-clad woman, and one of his hands had disappeared into the bottom of her suit. The photo wasn't pornographic or anything—probably wouldn't merit more than a PG-13 rating—but ugh. I knew that every time I looked at Preston now, that image would pop into my mind.

I pushed away my discomfort and studied the photo. The woman's long, dusty blond hair fell to her shoulders in wet strands. I could only see her in profile, but there was no doubt it was Nicole Harrison-White.

Now that I'd seen this, I understood Preston's concern. If Brie had made this public, his chances at promotion would vanish.

Placing the paper on the coffee table—facedown—I read the accompanying letters. Steamy romance novel fodder. If this were a book, it would be banned in a dozen countries. Still, nothing earth-shattering, though I was certain Raul would find it all quite intriguing. And given Sam's feelings about Preston, I could only imagine his reaction.

I felt a flutter of chagrin over my own previous involvement with Preston. I swallowed it down with a sip of wine and turned my attention to the next page.

A collage of four photos filled the paper—none of them, thankfully, even slightly romantic in nature. They appeared to be war shots, modern times, though I couldn't make out the location. It was excellent photography—well-composed and emotionally riveting. Definitely professional. Beneath the photos, the name Phillip Sonder had been scrawled in black marker.

Frowning, I searched my memory, but the name didn't mean anything to me. I made a mental note to Google the man tomorrow.

I drained the last of the wine, holding it in my mouth for a moment to enjoy the sensation. When I looked at the last page in Brie's stash, I nearly choked. My eyes watered as the wine streamed into my sinuses, and I pinched the bridge of my nose. After I'd sufficiently recovered from the infusion of fermented pain, I held the paper closer, staring at an image I recognized well.

It was a copy of my own Felden Award-winning photo, the one I'd had on display at Thursday's happy hour.

Beneath the photo, a typewritten message read: *Behold this Callahan Cassidy photo. I'm here to inform you that it was STAGED. Evidence is available at Sundance Studio, stored in a file cabinet you'll find in the darkroom. Use this key to enter—if you dare.* A bit of torn paper indicated a spot where a key must have been taped.

A thump on my shoulder made me jump. Carl emitted a feral-sounding yowl, causing Woody to raise his head briefly before settling back into slumberland.

The cat dropped to my side and arched his back. I nodded at him. "Agreed. This solves the mystery of why Brie was in my darkroom in the first place. She was hot on the trail of a scandalous story." Carl meowed. "It also answers the question of how she got the key. So we know the why and the how, but not the who. Who wrote this note? Who gave Brie a key?"

I put the sheet of paper on the coffee table and pulled Carl into my lap. "It's not true, you know. That photo was not staged. I didn't do anything to alter its integrity. I never would." The cat glanced up at me, and I swear he rolled his eyes. "Don't mind me," I said, running a finger down his spine. "Just feeling defensive, I suppose. That photo represents the pinnacle of my career, and for someone to suggest…"

Carl raked a claw lightly across my thigh, and I smirked at him. "You're right. Not the point."

But what was the point? My thoughts tumbled around in my brain like marbles, and I couldn't catch hold of any of them. A glance at the clock above the mantle told me it was past midnight, and I yawned reflexively.

"Bedtime," I told the creatures. "It'll all be here tomorrow. The world won't end before then."

17

Sunlight streamed through the sheer curtains at seven the next morning, dappling the bedspread with its rays. The creatures were curled up at my feet, breathing heavily. I sat up and stretched, feeling refreshed. It was the soundest I'd slept in a week.

I leaned forward and ruffled two coats of golden fur, earning a purr and a pant in response. "Up and at 'em, kids. Busy day ahead."

Padding down the stairs on bare feet, I made my way into the kitchen. The village shops didn't open until noon on Sundays, but a couple of tasks lay ahead of me before I could greet customers. First, I wanted to research Phillip Sonder. Why did Brie have his photos? What was his significance? Then I needed to bite the bullet and visit Raul at the police station to surrender the illicit envelope. I hoped I wouldn't be subjected to a lengthy lecture.

I started the coffee maker and eyed the creatures. "You know what we should do while I await my caffeine fix? Have a training session. Time to see if we can teach a middle-aged dog and a cat of indeterminate age new tricks."

Woody thumped his tail, ready to oblige, but Carl glared at me. I dropped into a crouch and clasped my hands in front of his face. "Please, Carl. Cooperate. You don't want to embarrass yourselves. Or me."

The cat gave me one last disdainful look and shot toward the stairs. Woody watched him go, looked at me apologetically, and trotted off after the cat. I sighed, wondering how I was going to wrestle the two of them into submission.

Right now, I wasn't up for the fight. I poured myself a cup of coffee and sat at the table, pressing the power button on the laptop. When the browser appeared, I tapped Phillip Sonder's name into Google and scrolled through the list of references, clicking on the first one that seemed promising: a sparsely-written obituary. Cancer had taken the man some five years ago. Survived by a sister and two nieces. Laid to rest in Baltimore. No additional details.

Back to Google. Another link led me to the site of an obscure magazine, *Overseas News*, where I found his name listed as a freelance photographer. I clicked the blue hyperlink and found myself looking at the photos from the envelope. I'd found him. But I still didn't know why. What was Brie doing with photos taken by a deceased freelance photographer?

As I puzzled over the mystery, my phone rang. I picked it up from the table and smiled at the sight of Tonya's name. "Good morning, sweet—"

She interrupted me, her voice tense. "Have you read *Sophie's Scoop* this morning?"

"What?"

"You haven't. Read it now. Call me back when you've finished."

She disconnected, and I quickly pecked at the keyboard, summoning Sophie's website. The words *Sophie's Scoop* danced across the top of the page in a gaudy, attention-getting display. When I read the headline beneath the banner, I blanched. "Murder at Sundance Studio."

By now, my Loyal Readers have undoubtedly heard all about the gruesome crime perpetrated within the confines of our peaceful village. To summarize: The victim, Brie Bohannan, arrived in the village with a group of Big City journalists to attend a business retreat. Our own Callahan Cassidy discovered Ms. Bohannan, a former rival, strangled to death Friday morning in the Sundance Studio darkroom. A key to the gallery was discovered in the unfortunate woman's pocket.

My eyes widened. I knew Raul wanted to keep that clue close to the vest. How had Sophie uncovered it? My answer followed immediately.

You're probably wondering how this information came to me. Alas, I cannot reveal my source. Rest assured, Sophie keeps her sources private. Dear Reader, you may always trust me.

At any rate, Rock Creek Village's well-intentioned detective Raul Sanchez has pared down the suspect pool to four of the victim's cohorts. Due to pesky libel laws, This Reporter is unable provide the suspects' names. But perhaps my Loyal Readers can deduce the identities. One holds a very high position at his newspaper, and another serves as his administrative assistant. An esteemed photographer at the paper is the third suspect. Rounding out the group is a young female reporter who so happens to be the photographer's lover. One of his lovers, anyway.

Here's where the story takes a scandalous turn, complete with marital affairs, lust, jealousy, and love triangles—all rife within this group of supposed professionals.

I devote my next installment of Sophie's Scoop *to the seamy underbelly of* The Sentinel *staff, revealed in my interview with the aforementioned female journalist.*

One last aside. Strangely enough, in light of the circumstances, Ms. Cassidy herself does not appear to be a suspect in the murder. Interesting, given the nature of her rivalry with the victim and the fact that the crime took place in Ms. Cassidy's gallery. Oh, and she found the body (again). We must remember, however, that Ms. Cassidy's father is our own former Chief of Police. Additionally, Ms. Cassidy and Detective Sanchez appear to have a relationship that borders on a partnership.

Loyal Readers, to get the scoop, tune in Tuesday to read the next in my series "Murder at Sundance Studio." In the meantime, leave your own ideas and thoughts in the comments. Together, perhaps we can solve this heinous crime!

I pushed back from the table as a quick fantasy flashed through my imagination, one that involved tracking down Sophie, wrestling her to the ground, and twisting her nose until she begged for mercy. But I restrained myself, instead sucking in a breath, holding it, and exhaling to a count of eight, as my therapist had taught me when I needed to combat anger or anxiety. I sipped my coffee and walked over to the bay window that overlooked my backyard. Two hummingbirds fluttered around the feeder, blurred wings flashing streaks of teal and orange. I spotted a silver Clark's nutcracker fluttering his navy blue feathers on the branch of a pine tree. A chipmunk danced through a patch of sunlight, dark stripes trailing down his flanks.

A shimmering, ghostlike image of myself reflected back to me from the glass, and I saw that she was smiling. A quick self-inventory revealed that my heart rate had slowed, and my respirations came evenly. Surely everyone understood that *Sophie's Scoop* was sensationalistic gossip. Surely her innuendoes and conspiracy theories couldn't do my business any harm.

Reassured, I pressed the icon of Tonya's face on my speed dial, ready to share my optimism. Before I could even say hello, she subjected me to a barrage of four-letter words disparaging Sophie's character, her ability, her lineage, her entire physical being.

"Slow down there, sailor," I said. "You're making me blush."

A harrumph came through the line. "That woman rankles me."

I chuckled. "May I remind you that you're the fine editor who gave Sophie her first journalism gig?"

"An act that will probably have me turned away from St. Peter's heavenly gates." She sighed. "Anyway, girlfriend, you seem awfully calm. I expected the Tasmanian Devil. Instead, I get the Dalai Lama. I'm terribly disappointed."

"I'm sure people will see Sophie's blog for what it is. Anyway, don't they say any publicity is good publicity?

Maybe customers will be lined up at the studio door this afternoon, wanting to get a glimpse of the conniving, murderous wench who owns it."

"Your idealistic view of human nature will inevitably leave you writhing in cosmic pain, I fear. But hopefully you're right and the writhing will take place amidst mounds of filthy lucre."

I laughed and changed the subject, telling her about the engagement photo shoot I had scheduled for the afternoon. It would be my first portrait session in natural surroundings, and I was excited and nervous about pulling it off. She offered best friend reassurances, citing my talent, my eye, my charm. I allowed myself to bask in her praise, and we agreed to meet for drinks at the lodge afterward. She said she'd invite Jessica and Summer to join us.

When we hung up, I found myself humming as I anticipated an afternoon filled with photography and an evening filled with friends.

Then I glanced at my computer screen, where the words "Murder at Sundance Studio" threatened to turn my cheerfulness into anxiety.

18

W hen I pulled into a spot in front of Town Hall, home to the police station as well as the rest of the municipal offices, I wasn't surprised to see Dad's truck parked nearby. As far as I could tell, he showed up for a visit at least once a week. Much as he loved running the resort, this place had served as his second home for over thirty years. He still required regular infusions of his old haunt to maintain his equanimity.

Once inside, I found him leaning on the front counter chatting with Marilyn, the department's administrative assistant. Marilyn pointed toward me, and Dad turned around, smiling. "Sundance, what a happy coincidence. What brings you here?"

I patted my bag and looked at him sheepishly. "You're probably not going to be happy about this…" When I explained my breaking and entering escapade in Brie's suite, he frowned and stretched out his hand. I shuffled through my purse and retrieved the room key, which I placed in his palm. "Don't worry. I'm here to give Raul everything I found."

"Which you should have done yesterday," he responded sternly. Then a gleam flickered in his eyes. "Mind if I sit in?"

A few minutes later, Dad and I were seated at a wooden

conference table across from Raul and Frank. Since it was technically their day off, both were casually dressed. But from the moment I'd offered up the envelope, their attitudes—particularly Raul's—were anything but casual.

He had studied each sheet of paper with intensity, passing them on to Frank one by one. When the men had perused all the pages, Raul straightened the stack and folded his hands on top of it.

"So, you discovered this evidence yesterday and sat on it all night. I imagine you even photographed the contents." It wasn't a question, so I remained silent. The side of Frank's mouth twitched, and Raul shot him a sidelong look of exasperation. "All right," Raul said, after a sigh, "interpret for us, one page at a time."

I started with Melanie's email, filling them in on the outburst I'd witnessed in the Rocky Mountain High coffee shop.

"Ah," Frank said. "We wondered where Sophie had gotten her little exclusive."

I remembered Sophie's comment in her blog about Raul treating me like a partner, and I winced. When I lifted my eyes to his, they didn't seem any angrier than usual, so I moved to the next subject: Preston. After I told them about Preston's secret and Brie's blackmail attempts, I saw Raul and Frank exchange a look. "You already knew?" I asked.

"You don't hold the patent on investigative skills," Raul said. "We are trained detectives, you know."

"How did you find out?"

"Anonymous tip," Frank said. "We're getting a lot of them lately."

Impatient, Raul flipped to the collage of war photos. "Tell us about these. How are they significant?"

I shrugged. "I'm not really sure. I did some research and discovered they were taken by Phillip Sonder, a photographer who died five years ago. He wasn't particularly famous or renowned. No connection to Brie, at least not that I've uncovered."

Raul's forehead creased as he scrutinized the photos. Then he set them aside and tapped a finger on the last page in the stack, the note referencing my Felden photo. "Looks like Callie Cassidy made the pile of shame. Why am I not surprised?"

I scowled. "It's not like I go looking for trouble."

Dad patted my knee. "Of course not, Sundance. It just seems like…well, they say lightning doesn't strike twice in the same place, but you seem to be an exception to the rule."

I threw up my hands. "Can we just stick to the matter at hand? I need to get to work."

Raul rearranged his face into a serious expression. "Far be it for police business to interfere with your work. Let's finish up then. Any idea who sent this note about you to Ms. Bohannan?"

"Not an iota." I shrugged. "But at least it explains where she got the key and how she gained access to my darkroom."

"But not where the anonymous tipster who sent the note got the key," he said.

"Honestly, I'm flummoxed. I have no clue where it came from." I jabbed my finger at the note. "But this is a bald-faced lie. There's no evidence in my file cabinet because I did not stage that photo. I think whoever wrote this knew the thought of catching me in some scandal would get under Brie's skin. He dangled the idea like a carrot to lure her to my darkroom."

"An ambush," Raul said.

The room was quiet for a few seconds. Finally, Frank pointed to an object near Raul's hand. "Why don't you show her the notebook? Maybe she can put some meaning to the contents."

"Maybe we should just deputize her and get it over with," Raul grumbled. But he relented, sliding the object in front of me. "We found this in the desk drawer of Brie's suite. Take a look."

I opened the cardboard cover of the reporter's notebook and began flipping through pages of interview notes, story ideas, phone numbers—typical reporter detritus. "Turn to the page with the paper clip," Raul said.

When I found the page, he reached across the table and pointed. "Any idea what this means?"

I studied the scribbles, a series of letters and numbers that made up Brie's personal shorthand. All reporters developed their own way of transcribing information, but no two methods were exactly the same. Still, this particular code was relatively easy to decipher.

And it made my gut clench.

"*LW. March 10. GSW. JJ Jail*," I muttered, reading the line.

Dad's face filled with concern. "What is it, Sundance? You just went pale."

"A painful blast from the past, that's what." I turned to Dad. "I'm guessing LW is Levi Waltham."

Now it was Dad's turn to react, and I saw him stiffen. "March 10," he said. "The day the young man died."

I nodded. Raul and Frank glanced at each other. "Someone want to fill us in?" Frank asked.

I took a deep breath. "Levi Waltham was my original source for a story I did in *The Sentinel*. The one that sent an innocent man to jail and ultimately caused me to resign."

Raul's eyebrows lifted. "JJ," he said. "Jameson Jarrett."

I nodded. "Levi came to me with a tale of hazing and abuse within the fraternity, spearheaded by Jameson Jarrett. But you already know all this."

Frank leaned his elbows on the table and folded his hands. "I know it's tough, Callie, but in case it might be relevant, take us through it again."

I felt my eyes glaze, but I swallowed hard and told the tale. "After I broke the story, the police charged Jarrett with assault and battery. He was subsequently convicted. A couple of months later, Levi Waltham recanted his accusation. Said he'd fabricated it because he was jealous that Jameson had been named frat president. So I turned the new evidence over to the police and resigned. Brie

Bohannan took over coverage of the fallout." I clutched my hands in front of me. "What you may not know is that Levi later committed suicide. On March 10. It wasn't a huge story. Didn't get a lot of space in the papers."

Everyone wore a somber expression. "So now we understand LW and March 10," Raul said. "And JJ—that's Jameson Jarrett. Do you think GSW stands for gunshot wound?"

"That'd be my guess," I said. "Levi's parents said he'd been experiencing bouts of depression since the trial. On March 11—the morning after Levi's death, apparently—his parents had been unable to get hold of him, so they went to his apartment. Found him dead on the floor. Self-inflicted gunshot wound, the M.E. said. Levi left a note. The contents never made it into the press, but from what I heard, it said he couldn't live with the guilt."

Tears threatened, and I squeezed my eyes shut and willed them away. So much tragedy. So much guilt to go around.

When I opened my eyes, Raul's eyes were soft. Still, he needed answers, and I understood that. I needed them too. "And *Jail?* What did Ms. Bohannan mean by that?"

"I'm not certain, of course, but she was likely considering a follow up piece, a human interest story. You know, examining the ripple effects of the false claim, how many lives it damaged. She was probably making a note that Jarrett was still in jail when the suicide occurred."

"I can't help but focus on this link between Callie and Brie Bohannan—both of them covering the Jameson Jarrett story," Dad said. "I'm wondering if he needs to be on the suspect list."

I shook my head. "Last I heard, he was in Miami, living with his mother. Preston sent me a clip of a TV interview maybe a month ago, in which Jarrett professed his forgiveness for everyone involved in the *fiasco*…" I made air quotes. "Said he was going to spend the next few months using beach therapy to recover from the ordeal before enrolling in law school."

Dad's expression was skeptical. "Well, that was a month ago." He pursed his lips and looked at Raul and Frank. "I have to tell you, I'm concerned about Callie's safety."

Raul jotted a few words on the pad in front of him. "We'll check it out. Make sure he's still in Miami."

Dad nodded, but he was still obviously ill at ease. I could only imagine how he'd react if I told him about the hooded figure outside my house, so I kept that bit of information to myself. But I did offer a little consolation. "Maybe it will make you feel better to know that Ethan had the studio's locks changed yesterday."

"Ethan handled the lock change?" Raul asked. "So he has access to the new keys."

My frustration boiled over, and I slapped my palm against the table. "Stop it with Ethan already. Quit wasting your time. I'm telling you, he's perfectly trustworthy."

Raul crossed his arms, trying to rein in his own frustration. "I guess Ms. Bohannan must have waved a wand and magically manufactured that key we found in her pocket. Perhaps her killer teleported into Sundance Studio." He snapped his fingers. "Maybe that's how your infamous poop depositor gained entrance to the gallery too."

I gritted my teeth. "I don't know how anyone got inside. I just know Ethan McGregor had nothing to do with any of this."

Dad stood. "Listen, we're all a bit tense right now. Probably best to call it a day."

Frank rose as well. "I agree. We'll let you know what we find out on Jameson Jarrett."

He and Dad headed down the hall. Raul and I got to our feet, and when I lifted my eyes to his, I saw concern there. "Listen, Callie, are we good?" he asked.

I graced him with a tiny smile. "Of course. We may not be partners, as Sophie said, but you're like the brother I never had. If we didn't lose patience with each other occasionally, the world would fall totally out of sync."

Raul chuckled. "Can't let that happen, can we?"

19

After my meeting at the station, I sat in my car in the parking lot long enough to call Preston and caution him to be prepared for further questioning. On a whim, I asked if he'd heard anything more about Jameson Jarrett, but he hadn't. I wasn't surprised. Dad might be worried, but I thought the possibility that Jarrett had hotfooted it from Miami to Rock Creek Village to murder Brie Bohannan was a stretch.

I stopped by the townhouse to pick up the creatures, then drove the short distance to the gallery, pulling my red Honda into a reserved space behind the row of village shops. Willie Wright's silver Mercedes was parked in his spot, and I saw him bent into the backseat retrieving his briefcase. By the time I climbed out of my car, he had slammed the door and started scurrying toward the alcove near his office.

"How's it going, Willie?" I called out.

His eyes skittered around, never settling on mine. "Fine. Just fine. In a big hurry. Talk to you soon."

I watched him go before I opened my car's back door. I hadn't bothered with the cat carrier for the quick trip here, so Carl leapt out of the car, and Woody scrambled out after him. "Am I being paranoid, or is Willie acting strangely?" I asked them. Neither creature spared me a glance before dashing toward the studio's back door. I followed, using my brand new key to open my brand new lock.

As I followed Carl and Woody through the hallway and into the gallery, my mind clicked through reasons Willie might be giving me the cold shoulder. Maybe he was, as he'd said, simply busy. Maybe a sudden run on local properties occupied his thoughts. Maybe his mother had guilted him about not visiting her. Maybe he was focused on what he'd eat for lunch.

Or maybe, just maybe, he and the other villagers held me responsible for the precarious status of the Fireweed Festival.

As if I asked for someone to be murdered in my darkroom, I thought.

I'd just worked myself into a full-blown snit when Woody halted abruptly in my path. With a screech, Carl scratched at my calf. My mood shifted from irritated to alarmed. Just as they had the other night when the hooded figure stood outside my home, my guardians were letting me know something was wrong.

I sniffed the air but detected no foul odors. Carl scuttled into the shadows pooling across the gallery floor and leapt atop the sales counter. Woody rushed over as well, standing on his hind legs to rest his front paws there.

Dim light seeped through the slats of the front window blinds. Before I approached whatever had caught the creatures' attention, I needed better illumination. I walked toward the front door and gave the knob a quick twist to make sure it was locked. Then I flipped the light switch and flooded the gallery with incandescence.

Slowly, I turned to look at the sales desk, where Carl was clawing what appeared to be a bolt of cloth. Woody nudged it with his nose. I noted with relief that it was too small to be a body.

Still, my heart pinballed inside my chest. I took my cell phone from my bag and positioned my finger over Raul's speed dial. Given everything I'd seen the past couple of days, I wanted to be prepared.

I crept toward the counter, one step at a time. Carl turned

to me, eyes shining. Woody whimpered.

It took me a few seconds to understand what I was seeing. When I did, I sucked in my breath.

A simple, old-fashioned Raggedy Ann doll stretched limply across the polished wood, her black threaded mouth grinning up at me.

And she had a leather watch band clasped tightly around her neck.

"How do people keep getting in here?" Raul demanded, his dark eyes blazing. I shivered, and Sam's arm tightened around my shoulder.

"I don't know. I told you we had new locks installed yesterday, and I am a hundred percent sure I bolted both doors before I left last night. This morning, I entered through the back—definitely locked. And I checked the front as soon as the creatures alerted me that something was up. Also locked."

The detective folded his arms, his biceps bulging beneath the short sleeves of his polo shirt. He'd arrived within ten minutes of my call.

But he hadn't been faster than Sam, who may have set a land speed record sprinting down the street from his cafe. I felt like a damsel in distress with two manly knights vying for the right to rescue me. As a self-proclaimed strong, independent female, it was not a role I usually felt comfortable in, but today I was glad for the chivalry.

Raul stomped to the window, lifted the blinds, and ran his hand across the window frames. Plate glass, thick, not designed to open. Then he raised his eyes and examined the ceiling. Finally, he paced the perimeter of the room, checking, I deduced, for breaches. After a fruitless search, he shoved his hand into his pockets and strode back to the counter. "What about the rear of the studio? Other than the back door, I don't recall any means of egress."

"No windows at the back of the building," I said. "No openings or vents in the ceiling large enough for a human to squeeze through."

"I'm going to have a look for myself." He disappeared through the arch in the back wall.

I sighed in frustration, and Sam pulled me toward him. "He's just doing his job. We both want you safe."

Now Sam was taking Raul's side. My, how the tides had turned.

I rested my head on Sam's broad shoulder, breathing in the pleasant aromas of sandalwood and fried bacon. "I know. And I'm grateful. I want nothing more than to have this mystery solved—no matter who does the solving."

I wriggled from his grasp and climbed onto a stool, contemplating the little doll with the band around her neck. Was she a threat? A prank? A horrible joke? None of it made sense. "Who hates me this much?"

Raul walked back into the room. "Whoever it is, they hated Brie Bohannan more."

"Are you thinking whoever planted this doll also murdered Brie?"

He gestured toward Raggedy Ann. "I'd say the strap around her neck indicates a corollary."

"Not necessarily," I ventured. "Everyone knows what happened here. Someone might've used that knowledge as a way to scare me." I tapped my finger on the doll's stuffed midriff. "This feels…juvenile. A convenient way to hurt me."

Sam raised his eyebrows. "Juvenile…you're thinking of the twins."

"I am. I believe they've been responsible for each incidence of vandalism. And the fake Instagram site, too, I bet."

"But not the murder?" Raul asked.

"Banner and Braden don't strike me as violent. Sneaky, yes. Vindictive, no doubt. Angry and retaliatory. But murderers? Of a person they don't know, had never met? It doesn't fit."

Raul nodded. "You're probably right. But there's one way

to find out. I'll bring them in."

"About time," Sam said. "Those two need to be held accountable."

I drummed my fingers on the counter. Since last winter when the twins had maliciously informed Elyse that she wasn't Sam's biological daughter, he'd held an understandable grudge against them. But grudge aside, he wasn't wrong. Banner and Braden Ratliff had to be stopped—before they crossed a line that would make them outright felons. But I wasn't sure hauling them to the station was the best path. Just an hour ago, I'd been talking about my huge mistake in the Jameson Jarrett incident. I hoped I'd learned something from that.

No, I wasn't willing to throw the twins to the wolves. Not if there was another way.

"Listen, Raul," I said, "can you hold off for a day or two? Give me a chance to talk to the boys myself? If it doesn't work out, then you can take the scared straight approach."

Sam opened his mouth to object, but I shot him a look and he snapped it shut. Raul stared at me. "Please," I said. "I promise I won't do anything foolish."

Finally, Raul heaved a sigh. "Okay. I have so much on my plate today that I'm going to agree to your plan. I'll give you the rest of today, and that's it." I started to speak, but he cut me off. "No arguments. Unless you manage to reduce those boys to quivering puddles of remorse by morning, they're all mine."

20

A soft breeze wafted across the meadow, swirling the bride-to-be's long, auburn hair gently across her face. In an unscripted moment, her future groom reached out and tucked a curl behind her ear, caressing her cheek with the back of his hand. I pressed the shutter button four times in quick succession. So much love in that simple gesture.

Our two-hour photo shoot had gone even better than I'd hoped. The weather had cooperated nicely, offering up a deep blue sky with a few tissue paper clouds to add depth. I'd captured images of the couple's feet entwined in the flowing water of Rock Creek. Then they'd posed on the wooden bridge spanning the creek. More shots against a dramatic backdrop of craggy mountain rocks and atop a giant boulder. We ended in an open meadow, among the red and pink and purple wildflowers, with an unexpected herd of elk dotting the horizon behind them.

Perfect. We wrapped up where we'd begun—in front of the Knotty Pine resort. I promised proof sheets by Wednesday, and we parted ways. The happy couple walked to their Wrangler, arms wrapped around each other's waists. As they climbed into their vehicle, I noticed Tonya's metallic gray Chevy Tahoe in the parking lot. A few spaces away, I spotted Jessica's black Prius. A glance at my watch told me it was ten after five. With this group, if you were late, you were certain to be the primary topic of conversation. I hurried through the sliding glass doors and into the lobby.

Jamal stood at the buffet table adding fruit to a crystal bowl of Sangria. He pointed toward the corner of the Great Room, where my friends nestled on couches in a cozy nook. His puppy dog eyes lingered on Tonya. Though my best friend was practically old enough to be his mother, he definitely had a crush on her.

Speaking of puppy dog eyes, I saw Woody snuggled up next to Tonya at one end of the leather couch. On the adjoining loveseat, Carl had squeezed between Jessica and Summer, graciously allowing them to stroke his fur. Glasses of Sangria and little plates covered with hors d'oeuvres rested on a pine coffee table. I wanted in on that action, and Jamal apparently read my mind. He raised an empty glass and lifted his eyebrows.

"Yes, please," I said. He ladled wine and fruit slices into a crystal goblet while I grabbed a plate and piled it high with fancy cheese and crackers, stuffed mushrooms, and an unidentified delicacy in a paper baking cup. "What's this?" I asked.

"My newest creation," he said with pride. Jamal attended culinary school on weekdays, and my parents provided him with a weekend stage on which to practice his art. "Pepper jelly goat cheesecake on a toasted pecan crust. Careful, though. I used an Asian Sriracha hot chili sauce, so it has a little kick."

I wasted no time sinking my teeth into his masterpiece. Creamy, spicy, and crunchy, all mixed into one small appetizer. "Delicious," I said, licking my lips. "So unique. You are soon to be a five-star chef, Jamal. Hope you'll remember us little folks when you achieve fame and fortune."

"Thanks, Callie. You and your folks will always have a table at the fancy restaurant I'm going to open. Someday."

"Are the folks off on date night?" My parents had a standing Saturday tradition—getting all dressed up and driving into Boulder or Denver for dinner and often a show.

He nodded. "Should have seen your mom. Beautiful, as always. Your dad cleans up good, too."

Sangria in one hand and plate in the other, I joined my friends, reflecting on the oddity of the four of us becoming such a close circle. We couldn't be more different, as evidenced by our choice of Sunday attire. Summer, a yoga instructor and lifelong hippie, wore flowing cream-colored linen pants and a matching shirt tied above the waist, accentuating her slim figure. Jessica had donned knee-length denim shorts and a T-shirt emblazoned with the name of some grunge band I'd never heard of. True to form, Tonya had chosen a "casual" dress worthy of a runway model's wardrobe—a mid-length, mint green, polka-dotted frock with skinny straps and a scoop neckline.

I glanced down at my own ensemble: capri-length, army green cargo shorts, a short sleeved, button-up blouse, and dirty hiking boots. "Don't judge," I said to the group. "I had an afternoon photo shoot."

Tonya snickered. "I just hope you were the photographer and not the subject, girlfriend."

I ignored the jab and plopped down next to Woody. "So, what are we talking about? Not me, I hope."

"Ah, ego," Tonya said. "As if no one has anything to talk about but little old Callie. Whatever did we do in this sleepy town before you graced us with your presence?"

"Speaking of gracious presence," I said, "I can't believe you've decided to abandon your handsome hunk and join us peons."

Jessica laughed. "Stop it, you two. You bicker like sisters." When she turned to me, I noticed a gleam in her eye. "To be honest, though, we *were* talking about you. More bad news at Sundance Studio, huh? Tell us all about that doll." She sounded very much like the high school journalism teacher she was.

"How did you hear?" I asked.

Summer pointed at Jessica. Jessica pointed at Tonya. Tonya turned her palms up and shrugged. "I'm editor of the newspaper, sugarplum. I hear things."

My lips curled up. "That you do. You're apparently not shy about repeating them, either."

"Speaking of my newspaper—"

I wagged a finger at her. "No comment. Not on the record, anyway."

She folded her arms and pouted. "Callahan Cassidy, I'm your best friend, and this is our hometown. I was okay that *The Sentinel* got first dibs on coverage of Brie Bohannan's murder—I mean, she *was* their employee. But even Sophie Demler beat *The Gazette* to the story. The least you can do is provide me with a little insider information. Just a quote or two…"

Timing hadn't worked in Tonya's journalistic favor. Since her newspaper was issued on Friday mornings, it was already printed by the time I'd discovered Brie's body. As far as the story in *The Sentinel*, I'd read it, and Tonya didn't have much to complain about. They'd published a small piece buried in the back of the first section, a bland statement about Brie dying under "suspicious circumstances." No details, per Raul's request.

"*Sophie's Scoop* hardly counts as journalism," I said. "All she really did was hint at facts everyone already knew and cast aspersions on yours truly."

Jessica waved impatiently. "Never mind all this negotiation. Just tell us about the doll."

I gave Tonya a pointed look. "Off the record?"

She sighed dramatically. "Fine. But you owe me. Like always."

It didn't take long to summarize the series of events. I'd arrived at the studio, walked in, found the doll. Raul showed up, searched the place, bagged the evidence. Ethan and Alexis came to work at noon, and the rest of the day proceeded uneventfully.

Except I still hadn't coerced myself back into the darkroom.

"Any signs of forced entry?" Summer asked.

"Nope. And the intruders couldn't possibly have gotten hold of a key. Ethan had the locks changed yesterday because of the murder. And the poop."

Two of the three sets of eyes widened. Jessica and Summer looked at each other, then at me. "Poop?" Jessica asked.

I looked at Tonya. "You didn't tell them? Color me stunned."

"I'm the soul of discretion," she said.

I shifted to face Jessica and Summer. "You heard about the vandalism at the studio?" They nodded. "There was yet another incident on Thursday, in the form of a large and stinky pile of animal excrement deposited on the gallery floor."

"She stepped right in it," Tonya said.

I shot her a withering look. "Anyway, they still managed to get inside. I can't figure out how."

The group grew silent for a moment. Finally, Jessica spoke. "You said *they*. You must think more than one person vandalized the place." She tapped her index finger against her chin. "Do you believe the same people who planted the poop also killed Brie Bohannan?"

I scrunched up my face. "No, I don't. It's just a feeling, no proof to back it up. But I'd say the vandals and the killers are not one and the same. And I think I know the identity of the vandalizing, breaking-and-entering, fake-Instagram-posting hooligans."

I paused, basking in a moment of drama. But my audience wasn't having it. Tonya made a hurry-up motion, Summer and Jessica stared expectantly, and Carl meowed. Even Woody upped the pressure, nudging my arm with his wet nose.

"The twins," I said with a flourish. "Banner and Braden Ratliff."

My friends nodded. No one seemed surprised. "I've heard they hate you," Summer said. "No offense, but you probably earned it. When their mother was killed, you did kind of blame their father. And then the boys themselves. And then you told everyone their father cheated on their mother and they had a half-sister…"

"Point taken," I said. "But that's no excuse for wreaking all this havoc."

Jessica's eyes narrowed. "They're sneaky little—" She stopped when Summer gave her a disapproving look. "I wouldn't put it past them. But you still haven't explained how they've been getting into the studio."

I shrugged, watching as the wheels spun in Jessica's head. "I have an idea how we can get to the bottom of it." She leaned forward, elbows on her knees, and outlined her plan.

Summer nodded pensively. "That could work. And I know just how to deal with them when they're caught."

21

A few hours later, the four of us—Tonya, Jessica, Summer, and I—were crammed into my tiny office at the studio, sitting on thick cushions borrowed from Yoga Delight. Scented candles emitted gentle light and soft fragrance. We sipped wine from red solo cups and chattered about innocuous subjects. As I was discovering, this was how friendship worked.

Even when the friends had gathered for a little cloak-and-dagger surveillance.

Earlier, the women had accompanied me on my dreaded return into the darkroom. It hadn't been easy to reenter the scene of the murder, but with my support system by my side, I managed. Now I knew I'd actually be able to resume work in my sacred space.

Someone's stomach growled, and I realized it was mine. It was ten o'clock, and we'd long since digested the hors d'oeuvres from the lodge. A knock at the back door signaling the arrival of provisions came at the perfect moment. "Dinner's here," I said.

We all struggled to our feet—except Summer, who seemed to levitate—and moved as a group to open it.

"Who is it?" Tonya trilled.

"Land shark." Everyone giggled. "It's Sir Sam, bearer of nourishment for the damsels of the Round Table."

I unbolted the door and swung it open. Brandishing two steaming containers, Sam led the way back into my office. "Simple fare today, I'm afraid. You ordered too late for me to whip up anything special. Chicken enchiladas, Spanish rice, queso blanco. Flan for dessert."

Jessica put the back of her hand to her forehead. "I'm swooning. If I were straight, I'd forget all about being friends with Callie and steal you away."

He grinned at her and kissed my cheek. "Not a chance. I know a good thing when I've got it."

Summer smiled and put an arm around Jessica. "Don't we all."

"I'm feeling like the odd woman out here," Tonya said with an exaggerated frown.

"Poor baby," I cooed. "Shall we summon David?"

Sam headed back to the office door. "All right, ladies, I'm drowning in estrogen here, so I'll make my exit. My disapproval of this stakeout is on the record, but I'm aware my opinion doesn't carry much weight. Just...keep out of trouble."

I walked him to the door, and he gave me a long, grave look. "All kidding aside, this plan of yours—"

"It's not mine. Jessica and Summer devised it."

"Whatever. Things could go sideways in a hurry."

"Power in numbers."

He gripped my chin between his forefinger and thumb and gazed into my eyes. "You're crazy, you know that?" He kissed me then, and I heard my friends tittering like schoolgirls.

An hour later, our stomachs were full, and our wine supply had dwindled. Summer leaned back against the wall, her long legs stretched in front of her. Jessica lay on her side with her head in Summer's lap. Tonya rested on her back, hands laced across her stomach. Conversation had waned, and my eyelids had just started to droop when a sudden, low thump from the gallery startled us all upright. Summer blew out the candle, and the four of us huddled together in the dark.

The thump was followed by the grating sound of wood sliding across wood. I grabbed the baseball bat propped in the corner and tiptoed out of the office, stopping just inside the arch leading into the gallery. I could feel Summer's warm breath on my neck as she moved in behind me. Tonya's fingers wrapped around my elbow. Jessica's face pressed on my shoulder. We were the Four Musketeers.

Or, depending on how this played out, the Four Stooges.

I'd left the blinds slightly open, allowing light to filter in from the street. As we watched, one of the wheeled wall partitions rolled slowly across the concrete floor—one inch, two, three. We saw fingers clutching the side of the partition. Then a face peered around its edge.

My friends and I eased back a step. I craned my head around the wall, risking another glimpse, just as a husky figure emerged into the gallery. Then another figure appeared, similar enough to the first that they could be…

Twins. Just as we'd suspected.

I faced my friends. "Ready?" I whispered, as I handed the bat to Jessica. Hours ago, we'd choreographed our next moves. Now we'd see if our little dance proceeded as planned.

"Go!" I shouted. I flicked on the light. Jessica dashed into position between the boys and their mode of entry, brandishing the bat like a home run hitter. Summer glided toward the front door to block that escape route. Tonya stood spread eagled in the arch to prevent the boys from exiting through the back.

I walked casually toward the twins, watching as their eyes widened and their jaws dropped open. "Surprise," I said.

In unison, their mouths snapped shut. One twin's eyes darted to the other, who attempted to stammer out an explanation. "We're just…just…"

"Just caught in the act, that's what." I nodded to the bag dangling from the fingers of the twin on the left. "Another little gift, I assume." I sniffed. "At least this one doesn't stink. Anyway, we'll get to the contents of the bag in a moment. For now, take a seat."

I pointed to two folding chairs in the center of the gallery, positioned beneath the beams of the overhead spotlights. One twin jerked his head around, looking back toward the partition. Jessica shifted her grip on the bat. "I wouldn't, if I were you. I was an All-American softball player in college. Hit three-twenty my senior year."

The boy sighed, and his brother groaned. Their shoulders sagged. After a moment's hesitation, they slumped onto the chairs. "Are you calling the cops?" one asked.

"I could." I held up my phone. "Detective Sanchez's number is on my speed dial, and I know for a fact he'd be delighted to provide you two delinquents with overnight accommodations." I settled onto a facing chair and leaned my elbows on my knees. "But it doesn't have to go that way, gentlemen. It all depends on you." I let them squirm for a second. "We have questions. You'll answer them. If you try to deceive us, even once—one minuscule white lie—you'll spend tonight sleeping on thin, lumpy mattresses and peeing into a steel toilet in the corner of a cell."

They looked at each other, resigned. "Okay. We'll talk," one said.

I nodded. "First off, which of you hooligans is which?"

The twin in the blue t-shirt said, "I'm Braden." He tilted his head toward his brother, in a brown t-shirt. "That's Banner."

"All right, then. Braden, what's in the bag?"

The paper bag crinkled as he tightened his grip. "Listen, Ms. Cassidy. All of this is just a...a—"

"Prank," Banner said. "A practical joke. We'd never hurt anyone."

"What's in the bag?" I repeated stiffly.

Braden sighed, fumbled with the bag, and pulled out a carton of eggs. "We weren't going to throw 'em at your pictures or anything. Just break 'em on the floor, smear some gunk on the doorknobs, stuff like that."

I gritted my teeth. "Just a little minor defacement, right? Not to mention a bit of breaking and entering. No big deal."

My friends had formed a semi-circle behind me, and I looked up at Tonya. "Ms. Stephens, do you know what penalty those crimes carry? Legally speaking."

She tapped a long, tapered fingernail against her lips. "I just so happen to have researched those very same crimes earlier this evening. I'd say we're looking at a sentence of six months, with monetary damages in the ballpark of five thousand dollars."

"And don't forget the civil case Ms. Cassidy could file," Jessica chimed in. "Compensation for damages, aggravation. Could tack on a few thousand more."

The color drained from their identical faces. "Of course, if you were responsible for murdering Brie Bohannan on the premises, that's a different story," I said. "That's life without parole."

The bag dropped to the floor. I winced, picturing broken shells and runny yolks. Braden quaked so hard his chair jiggled on its legs. "We didn't do that, I swear, we couldn't. We didn't kill anyone."

Banner cut in. "Please, Ms. Cassidy. You gotta believe us." He glanced at his brother, who gave him a nod. "Listen, we admit to the—what'd you call it?—vandalism. You know, like, as a joke. But we didn't do the murder. I swear it."

I stared at them, unblinking. Then I got up and walked to the wheeled partition, shoving it aside to reveal a pocket door. I peered through the opening and into a nook hidden behind a tall shelf in A Likely Story, David Parisi's bookshop. When I pulled the sliding door closed, it left a thin, nearly indiscernible cleft in the wall, easily mistaken for a spot where builders had joined walls. No knob, no latch. Secreted as it was behind the moving partition, I wasn't surprised no one had noticed it. "How did you know about this?"

Banner cleared his throat. "That was our mom's shop before…you know. V&K's Fine Fashions. We found that secret door a long time ago, back when we were in middle school. After the art lady's store closed up, we came here a lot." He shrugged. "It was a good place to party at night. Then when we moved back from Denver, we saw Mom's old shop keys in the house, and, well…"

"You decided it would be an easy way to terrorize me, right?"

"We didn't really think the key would still work," Braden said. "Guess the new guy didn't change the locks. When it did, and we found the door between the shops was still there, it felt like—fate, you know."

Banner looked at me with glistening eyes. "When our mom died, when she was killed, everybody in town started talking about us. First, they said our dad killed her. Some people said we'd done it. Murdered our own mom." His voice cracked, and he took a moment to compose himself. "Then all the other stuff came out—Dad's cheating, a half-sister. We had to leave town, finish our senior year in Denver. It was humiliating." He drew a breath. "We blamed you. When we came back to the village a couple of weeks ago and saw your place, how good everything was going for you, we kinda…snapped, I guess."

"You wanted to hurt me the way you felt I'd hurt you."

He nodded and dropped his eyes. His brother took up the narrative. "We never would have done anything serious. We just wanted to…I don't really even know."

"Did you create that nasty Instagram site?"

Banner's face colored, but he nodded. "Yeah."

"And you left the doll on the sales counter with a watchband around her neck? Knowing a woman had been murdered here in just that way?"

Braden nodded, but neither boy could make eye contact.

"Which of you stood in front of my house the other night? Wearing the hoodie?"

They both looked confused. "Don't know what you're

talking about," Banner said.

"We never went to your house," Braden added.

I studied their faces. Why would they admit to all the other depraved acts and deny standing in front of my house? I decided I believed them—Hoodie Person hadn't been one of the twins.

"Are you gonna call Detective Sanchez?" Banner asked.

I smacked my hands on my knees and stood. "Not at the moment. We have something else in mind."

I moved aside, and Summer took my seat. Tonya and Jessica and I stood to her side.

In a move I could never hope to replicate, Summer folded her ankles across her thighs, sitting cross-legged atop the narrow chair. Her hands rested on her knees in a full-on guru pose. She closed her eyes and breathed deeply for a full minute. The boys squirmed in their seats.

When she opened her eyes, Summer spoke in a low and lilting tone, the one she used during meditation class. "In some cultures, when a person breaks a rule or otherwise hurts another person, members of the community gather to speak not of the wrongdoer's transgressions, but rather of his goodness. The idea is that all people are essentially good, but sometimes they travel afar of that goodness. Words of affirmation, they believe, wield more power than do shame and punishment. There is even a Bantu word for it: *ubuntu.*"

She closed her eyes and took in a deep breath. "Tonight, we practice *ubuntu.*"

Jessica stepped toward the boys and crouched in front of them, grasping one of Braden's hands and one of Banner's. The twins looked confused, but they didn't resist. "I remember a day, must have been your junior year. It was early, and I had just pulled into the school's parking lot. A bus pulled up and a little girl, kindergartner I'd guess, stepped off, looking lost and scared. The other kids rushed by her, oblivious. You two were the only big kids around. You each took one of her hands, just like this." She tipped her chin to their joined hands. "Then you walked her across the parking lot to the elementary school. You thought no one was watching, but I was. I saw the goodness in you that day. I know it's still there."

She rose and returned to her spot behind Summer. The twins stared straight ahead, eyes shimmering. Tonya moved in front of them, wearing a gentle expression. "I remember the joy on your mother's face the day you were born. I remember her pride when you started school. Victoria and I weren't close, but everyone in the village knew how much she loved you. She saw the goodness in you. So do I."

A tear dribbled from Braden's lower lid. Now it was my turn. "I moved out of the village before you were born, so unlike these ladies, I don't have any examples to illustrate your goodness. But I look forward to collecting some in the future. I've heard enough from my friends to believe in your potential. For that reason, I won't file charges." I gestured to the bag at Banner's feet. "Let your future actions make this a blip on the radar. You are free to go." I gave them a wry smile. "But this time, I'd prefer you to use the front door."

At first, neither boy moved, and I assumed they were judging my sincerity. Were they being tricked? Set up? I got the idea they weren't accustomed to being treated with mercy.

"It's okay, boys. I mean what I say. As of now, we have a fresh start. Make it count."

Banner bent and retrieved the bag of eggs. I looked at the bottom of the paper sack and was relieved to find no evidence of leakage. When Banner straightened, he wore a mixture of shame and gratitude on his face. "I don't know what to say, Ms. Cassidy. Except thanks."

Braden snuffled and reached out to shake my hand. "Yeah. Thanks. Nothing like this…well, it won't happen again. You have our word."

I escorted them to the front door and opened it. Cool night air drifted inside. The boys plodded down the sidewalk, and I felt a sense of relief that we'd resolved the vandalism saga. I thought we could safely eliminate the twins from the list of murder suspects.

Unfortunately, though, we were no closer to unmasking Brie's killer.

22

I stifled a yawn as I walked to Snow Plow Chow the next morning. It was after eight, but I hadn't gotten to sleep until almost two. Still, the sacrifice of a few hours' sleep would be well worth it if the Ratliff twins adjusted their attitudes—and more importantly, their behaviors.

Inside the cafe, I took a moment to revel in my surroundings. Sam had created a warm, inviting space for his customers. Booths lined the periphery, with free standing tables and chairs dotting the center space. A couple of living room style seating areas surrounded a stone fireplace.

Best of all, he'd recently updated the artwork from the tacky Old West paintings of grizzly old men and their covered wagons to a more modern look. I'd provided him with a series of local landscape photos that gave the cafe the mountain vibe it needed.

And each of the canvas photos sported a discreet price tag. Sam had already sold two of them, which I'd quickly replaced. As Ethan told me, you couldn't have too much exposure.

Dan, the cafe's head waiter and seating host, bustled toward me. It was always tough for me to discern whether the man was smiling or sneering, but in my new benefit-of-the-doubt frame of mind, I chose smiling. "Mornin', Mizz Cassidy," he said.

"Now, Dan. How many times do I have to remind you? We're friends. Call me Callie."

He seemed pleased. "Sure thing. Doin' okay, Callie? Heard those Ratliff boys been givin' you trouble. If you need old Dan to kick some—"

"No, no, all is well," I interrupted. "I think the twins have mended their ways." I lifted crossed fingers.

He nodded. "Well, if that don't work out, you know where to find me." He gestured to the restaurant, about half filled with breakfast customers. "Get you a table? Or you just here to see the boss man?"

"The latter," I said.

His face scrunched in confusion. "You need a ladder?"

"No, I mean, I'm just here to see Sam."

As if the mention of his name had made him appear, Sam came out of the kitchen carrying two plates covered with pancakes, bacon, and omelets. "Couple more orders ready in the kitchen." Dan nodded and trudged away. Then Sam gave me a sunny smile. "Morning, beautiful. These are for Elyse and Alexis. Follow me over. Maybe you can offer a little moral support."

My brows rose, and I trailed him to the booth where the two girls sat. I said hello as he deposited the plates in front of them.

"Morning, Callie." Though Alexis's voice was cheerful, her eyes were puffy. She didn't let them linger on me long. "This food looks great, Sam. Thank you."

"Yeah, thanks Dad. And hi, Callie." Elyse cocked her head slightly in a silent hint for us to leave.

I hesitated. "Everything okay?"

"Fine," Elyse said. "Girl talk."

Alexis nodded as she unwrapped her silverware. "It's all good."

"Well, I'm glad the studio is closed today. Go have some fun." I put a hand on her shoulder. "Call me if you need anything. Or if you just want to talk."

"I appreciate that, Callie. Honestly, though, no need to worry about me. Just boy stuff. You know how it is." She reached for the syrup bottle and began drenching her pancakes in amber liquid.

Elyse shot us another look. "You two old folks run along now," she said, injecting levity into her voice. "We youngsters need to figure out how to save the world."

Sam took my elbow and led me away. I glanced over my shoulder and watched the girls lean toward each other, speaking earnestly.

"What's going on with those two?" I asked after we went in the kitchen.

He shrugged. "Who knows? I expect it's just what Alexis said—boy troubles."

"Relationships are hard," I muttered.

He looked at me inquisitively and then turned to the grill, laying strips of bacon on the hot surface. "Elyse and I have our monthly father-daughter date tonight. I'll see if I can pry any information out of her. Though she's been a little hard for me to read lately."

"I'm glad Alexis and Elyse are friends," I said. "Girls that age need someone to talk to. Alexis never tells me much of anything personal. I didn't even know there was a boy in the picture."

"She's barely out of her teens. You're an adult—and her boss. It makes you an unlikely confidante." He wiped his hands on his apron and took me in his arms. "I, on the other hand, will be glad to tell you something personal."

Across the kitchen, Rodger grinned, and I gently disengaged from Sam's embrace. "Must have lost my head," Sam said, chuckling. "I forgot about your super sensitivity to PDA." He went back to the griddle and flipped the sizzling bacon. "I'm making you breakfast. While you eat, you can tell me all about last night's escapade."

He spent a few minutes cooking my favorites—French toast, cheesy scrambled eggs, and two slices of bacon, crispy to the point of almost being burned. Then we headed up the narrow stairs to his office. We sat on the worn leather couch, and I began eating. Between bites, I summarized the evening's events. I grinned at the surprise on his face.

"You didn't think our plan would work, did you?"

"I admit it. I figured those boys would deny everything, cuss you out, and begin plotting their next attack." He took a sip of coffee. "Who'd've thought kindness would penetrate those thick skulls?"

"Careful," I said. "You're talking about your daughter's half-brothers. You're practically their stepdad."

He shot me a feigned glare. "Half-brothers, yes. Stepdad, never." His mouth curved into a smile. "Still, I'm impressed. I should have known, if anyone could pull off such a character resurrection, it would be Callie Cassidy."

"The credit really goes to Summer," I said through a bite of eggs. "She came up with the idea. And Jessica devised the trap to catch the boys in the act. They had no choice but to listen—other than going to jail."

I sopped up a puddle of syrup with the last morsel of French toast and smacked my lips. "My compliments to the chef."

He leaned toward me, his face recklessly close. "I think you have a little something right here on your lip. Here, let me…"

23

I caught myself humming as I left the cafe a few minutes later. My camera bounced against my chest as I headed off to shoot photos. Like all the village retail shops, Sundance Studio was closed on Mondays, but that didn't mean I got the day off. Building a business meant I maintained an unending to-do list.

When I arrived at the lake, I was pleased to find a crowd of tourists—families at the playground, kayakers paddling through the water, couples stretched out on blankets. I spent an hour meandering through the park, taking candid shots as well as asking people if they'd like to pose for portraits. Once I captured the subjects on digital film, I handed them a business card with the gallery's name and website and promised their pictures would be posted and available for purchase by the next day. Ethan had assured me that building an online presence would lead to substantial in-gallery sales. Customers would enjoy the pictures they saw online, maybe even buy a copy or two. The next day, they'd be strolling down Evergreen Way, and—*Hey, look, Sundance Studio. Callahan Cassidy. That's the photographer who took our adorable family pictures. Let's stop in. What's this? What an amazing landscape photo! Wouldn't that look great over the couch, honey?*

I walked to Mt. O'Connell and repeated the process.

Photos of laughing children sliding down the slope in carts. Parents, here's a business card. Two dogs frolicking in the grass. Pet owners, here's a business card. I worked for another hour, exhausting my stack of cards.

My next stop was the Knotty Pine. Due to my late night, the creatures had bunked with Mom and Dad, and I needed to check on them. I waved to Dad and went through the door leading to my parents' private quarters. When I topped the stairs, Woody greeted me with doggie enthusiasm, rising on his hind legs to slurp my cheek. Even Carl seemed pleased to see me, purring and twisting between my ankles.

After a few minutes of snuggles, I went into the kitchen and found Mom bent over another cake. Four tiers this time, and the two bottom layers measured about an inch larger than the two top layers. No tilt. The cake followed the same theme as the last one—a mountain meadow covered with wildflowers. The bottom layers created a visual image of the meadow itself, while the top two layers represented the mountain.

And it was stunning.

Mom gave me a quick hug and gestured toward her creation. "What do you think? Progress?"

"Mom. It's extraordinary. I can't even put into words how incredible it is."

"Now don't go blowing sunshine at me, sweetheart. I need the objective eye of a professional photographer."

"I'm not exaggerating, Mom." I grinned as I put an arm around her and gave her a squeeze. "You're gonna wiiinnnn," I sang.

She jabbed an elbow into my ribs, but her eyes shone. "Don't get carried away. Winning isn't my objective anyway. I simply hope to make a good showing."

"Mother. You once told me false modesty is unbecoming."

"It's so difficult when one's words come back to haunt." She picked up her piping bag and dabbed a tiny green leaf next to a yellow buttercup. "Speaking of contests, how is the training going? The pet pageant is this Sunday, you know."

I sighed. "I don't even know where to begin. They won't cooperate, and it's not like I'm a pet whisperer. They're more likely to train me than vice versa."

"Don't be silly, dear. They're just like every student I ever taught—hungry for leadership. Provide them with loving guidance and approval, and they'll respond. They're highly intelligent, after all."

I looked across the room at the two golden fur balls. Woody lay on his back, tongue lolling and paws in the air. Carl sat next to him, his green eyes studying me with cynicism. Highly intelligent, I wanted to tell my mother, didn't equate to highly obedient. In fact, I would guess it was often the reverse.

Still, I did want us to make a decent showing. I'd Googled pet tricks when I'd entered the creatures in the pageant and settled on a high-five maneuver I thought they could master. If I could get them in sync, the feat would be impressive.

Hopeful, I grabbed the box of treats Mom kept in her pantry. Woody immediately pulled himself into sitting position and lifted his paw, ready to shake.

Carl gave me the evil eye, spewed forth some kitty cuss words, and hightailed it out of the kitchen.

"Come back, Carl," I said, shaking the box. "You're a smart boy. I know you're capable of a simple trick."

Mom grinned. "It's not that he's not capable, darling. It's that he's not interested in selling his dignity for a bite-sized tidbit. He's simply too proud."

I looked at my drooling golden retriever with his paw poised in the air and his brown eyes focused laser-like on the doggie treat. No pride there. I shook his paw and tossed him a treat, which he caught in his mouth mid-air.

Mom pointed her spatula at him. "This one will work for food. Focus your efforts there. Perhaps Carl will see him getting all the attention and feel compelled to show the pup how it's done."

"More likely, he'll whisper insurrection into Woody's ear and lead him into rebellion."

Mom laughed. "A definite possibility."

I worked with Woody for fifteen minutes, finally coaching him to sit on his haunches and hold up a paw, slapping it forward in a high-five gesture. Occasionally, I'd spy Carl peeking around the corner, his green eyes intent. Mom could be right. The cat might come around. Too bad we only had five days—that is, if the Fireweed Festival even occurred.

I rose from my crouch and shook a cramp out of my calf. "Have you heard anything about the status of the festival?" I asked.

She picked up a spatula and smoothed an area of blue frosting. "I'm still not worried. I think the meeting will go smoothly. Are you prepared to say a few words?"

My brow knitted. "Meeting? What meeting?"

She turned to me, surprised. "You haven't heard?"

"Clearly not," I said.

"The Chamber scheduled an emergency meeting this evening to discuss the festival. They sent an email this morning."

I pulled out my phone and checked my mailbox. "Nothing," I said. Was it simply an oversight, or had I been deliberately snubbed?

"Oh, dear. Well, I'll forward it to you when I'm through here. Apparently, they want the members to vote on whether to cancel, given…the circumstances."

"Whose idea was this?" I asked.

"Willie Wright's, or so I'm told. His business doesn't depend as much on tourism, so he can afford to have doubts. You'll be there, right? I don't imagine his motion will gain any traction, but every voice should be heard."

"I'll be there," I muttered. "When and where?"

"Five o'clock in the Town Hall meeting room. As I said, I think you should be prepared to speak. You can reassure the business owners."

I wasn't sure what kind of reassurance I was expected to offer. Was I supposed to pinky swear that there wouldn't be another murder in my darkroom? Or that the crime would be solved by Thursday afternoon? So much pressure.

But as I watched my mother adding the finishing touches to her work of art, and I knew I needed to rise to the challenge.

I left Woody and Carl in my mother's care and tramped down the steps into the lobby. The news about the Town Hall meeting had darkened my mood. Maybe spending some time at the gallery uploading and editing tourist photos would put me in a better frame of mind.

Dad was on the phone, so I didn't bother to stop at the registration desk. As I approached the lobby exit, the glass doors slid open and Preston lumbered inside, head down and hands shoved into his pockets. He was so distracted he nearly bumped into me.

I reached out and touched his arm. "Everything okay, Preston?"

"Oh. Didn't see you. A lot on my mind, I guess. I've just come from the police station. Your detective raked me over the coals."

"Will you please quit calling him *my* detective?" I tugged Preston to a nook near the door. "How did it go?"

He shrugged. "Who knows? They didn't detain me, so I suppose that's a good sign. But I'm also not permitted to leave the village." He ran a hand through his hair. "At least now they know all my dirty secrets. Nothing left to hide."

"You're innocent," I said. "The truth will prevail."

"Not always the case, as you well know." He frowned. "Anyway, I'd prefer not to discuss it further. I'm going up to my room to raid the mini bar." He glanced at me, saw my expression. "Just one drink. Two at the most. And I'll have Pearly's deliver me a thick steak to soak up the alcohol."

I squeezed his arm. "This is going to turn out all right."

He gave me a weak smile and turned toward the elevator.

I snapped my fingers as a thought flitted through my mind. "Wait a second. Can I show you something first? Won't take but a minute."

As he retraced his steps, I pulled out my phone and scrolled through the photos, stopping when I got to the ones attributed to Phillip Sonder. I turned the screen toward Preston.

"This collage was found among Brie's belongings. Do you happen to recognize these photos?"

He took the phone and enlarged the image. "Sure," he said. "These are photos from Dev Joshi's portfolio, the one he submitted as part of his application a year or so ago. Good stuff. They're the main reason I hired him. Why would Brie have them?" He scrolled across the image, his eyes landing on the name scrawled at the bottom of the page. "And who's this Phillip Sonder?"

He handed the phone back and shook his head. "Never mind. I don't want to know. I can't handle one more mystery today. If there's nothing else, the minibar summons."

He walked to the elevator and disappeared through the doors as I tried to process the information. Then my jaw tightened as the answer clicked into place. Dev Joshi had passed off a dead photographer's pictures as his own in order to secure a prestigious job at *The Sentinel*.

My mind reeled. Brie must have discovered Dev's plagiarism. I recalled how defensive he was of her at the happy hour, and Melanie saying Dev was the only one who even liked Brie. Why? Because he had no choice. She was blackmailing him, and he had to play nice.

No doubt about it. Dev's secret upped the ante in terms of motive.

I remembered the Instagram shot of Dev with Brie on his back. He hadn't appeared even slightly burdened beneath her weight. He was certainly strong enough to wrap a camera strap around her neck and choke her to death. As for opportunity, Dev could easily have sent Brie the anonymous note and lurked outside the gallery until she arrived on the scene. When she entered, using the ill-gotten key, he'd followed her inside and committed the deed.

But how had he gotten the key in the first place?

Also, he had an alibi, flimsy as it was. In fact…could Melanie be Dev's accomplice? Raul and I hadn't ruled out a two-person scenario. Guilt would help explain Melanie's distress at the coffee shop.

When I finally yanked myself from my musings, I saw my father watching me, wearing a quizzical expression. He gestured me toward the desk. "What's going on, Sundance? That brain of yours is about to overheat."

"Nothing much," I said, aiming for nonchalance. I wasn't prepared to share my suspicions just yet. I'd been down the road of accusing the wrong person before, and I didn't care to make that journey again. No, Dev deserved a chance to explain himself first.

"Hey, I wanted to check in on Dev, see how he's holding up. Which cabin did you put him in?"

Dad looked at me skeptically. "He's in your old homestead, Creekview number one."

I nodded. I'd spent a few months living rent-free in the tiny cabin just a few yards from the lodge when I'd moved back to Rock Creek Village in December. "Thanks, Dad." I headed toward the door. "I'll see you tonight at the big Town Hall meeting fiasco."

"Hang on, Callie." I turned back. "I doubt you'll find Mr. Joshi in his cabin right now. He borrowed some of our fishing gear about fifteen minutes ago and headed toward the creek. Said he needed some time alone."

I smiled. "Okay. I'll look for him there." I waved over my shoulder and hurried out the door, feeling Dad's eyes on my back.

24

The wooden bridge spanning Rock Creek lay about fifty yards behind the lodge. As I hiked toward it, I checked the sky. Gray clouds had blotted out the blue. Gusts of wind blew strands of hair across my cheeks and forehead. I pulled an elastic band from my pocket and coaxed my unruly mane into a ponytail.

The closer I got to the creek, the more I could detect its familiar fishy scent. If Dev was indeed communing with nature, pole in hand, this is where I'd find him.

I stepped onto the wooden planks of the bridge and scanned the scene. The clouds created a dramatic diffused lighting that caused my hand to brush against the ever-present camera around my neck. Smudged shadows cohabited with bright speckles of sun. Flecks of light glinted off the white spray like flashes from tiny fairy paparazzi. A photographer's fantasy.

But before I could find myself distracted by the call of the wild, I spotted Dev in the distance. Intent on his work, he hadn't noticed me on the bridge, so I watched like a spy as he slung a fishing pole across his legs and explored the content of a tackle box sitting open next to his red Converse shoes. He pulled out a thin nylon line and began tying it around a hook. His fingers moved easily, expertly, as he looped one knot and then another. His hands were strong and muscular, and I could easily picture them yanking a strap tight around a person's neck.

I glanced over my shoulder, acutely aware that I was alone in the woods with the man.

Still, Dad knew where I'd headed. And I wasn't afraid of Dev, not really. Though I did wish I had my pepper spray.

I crossed the bridge and eased down the embankment, making my way toward my quarry. Stealthy as I was, he never heard me coming. That is, until my heel slid on some loose dirt. One of my hands shielded my camera protectively, while the other pawed at the ground for something to stop my descent. No luck. I plummeted down the bank, my feet scrambling for purchase. Just as I was sure I was doomed for a dunk in the bubbling water, a hand reached out and grabbed my armpit, halting my trajectory. I looked up and saw Dev's face hovering above me.

"Need a lift?" he asked.

I breathed a sigh of relief. "You saved me from getting drenched." I touched my camera. "And you saved my Nikon from an untimely demise. Thank you."

"No problem," he said, helping me to my feet. "Are you okay?"

I couldn't help but notice his ripped arms. At about six-four and two-thirty, most of which was muscle, his physique was imposing. I brushed pebbles and dirt from my pants. "No injuries—just wounded pride."

His quick smile never reached his eyes. He flopped back onto the blanket he'd spread out on the bank and started fiddling with the fishing pole. "I'm guessing you didn't end up here by accident. Looking for me?"

I studied his face. His bronze skin glistened with perspiration, and he wore a brooding expression. Since Dev's hiring, he and I had both been on Preston's investigative team, but I didn't know him well. I'd worked as a convergence media journalist, operating mostly on my own, so we'd never had the chance to collaborate. On the few occasions we'd interacted, he'd seemed a nice enough guy—certainly not someone I'd typecast as a murderer.

But now, with his tense jaw and tight lips, I could see the potential.

I lowered myself onto a flat boulder near his blanket. "Dad told me you were down here. I wanted to see how you're doing."

His eyes locked with mine for a moment. Then his shoulders relaxed. He shifted his gaze to the thick pine trees, the clear babbling creek, and the soft patches of light penetrating the canopy.

"Beautiful out here. Peaceful."

I stayed silent, sensing he needed space before he'd open up.

"You've got the life, Callie," he said. "Maybe I'll follow in your footsteps. Find a little town in the mountains. Use my skills to photograph beauty instead of horror."

"It's been a good change for me," I said. "My soul feels lighter than it ever has."

He stared at the rushing water with a faraway gaze. When he looked at me again, I saw pain in his eyes, followed by reluctant acceptance. "You've found out."

I nodded. "I have, yes."

He heaved a sigh. "I knew someday it would all come crashing down. Strangely, though, now that it has, I feel almost relieved. The life I thought I wanted as a hardcore photojournalist, it's been…"

"Stressful? Exhausting? Occasionally even gut wrenching?"

"Exactly. Even so, I would have liked to make the change on my own terms, not be forced into it by that miserable…"

A bolt of anger flashed across his face, igniting a tiny ember of fear within me, but I didn't budge. After a moment, the fire went out of his eyes, and he continued placidly.

"I turned thirty-three in February. Brie presented me with a gift, a package wrapped in shiny white paper and topped with a big blue bow. I was shocked—the woman rarely acknowledged me other than to bark out orders or criticize my work. I remember thinking, maybe she finally respects me. Likes me, even." He paused, reliving the memory. "It was a magazine, an old, dog-eared copy of *Overseas News*. I knew right away that she'd found my secret."

"What did she want in exchange for keeping it quiet?"

He gave a bitter chuckle. "Nothing much. Only everlasting servitude. Unquestioning loyalty. Lobbying on her behalf for whatever she desired—a certain story assignment, a promotion, whatever. She told me I'd do her bidding, or she'd ruin my career."

He passed a hand across his eyes. "Two months I've lived in purgatory."

"It must have been awful," I said softly. "Did Melanie know?"

"She sensed something—an unholy alliance of some sort. But I never told her. It's created a rift in our relationship, probably irreparable at this point. Just another casualty of Brie's destruction."

I took out my phone and scrolled to Brie's Instagram picture—the one that showed her riding Dev's back as he looked up at her with a passionate intensity. When he saw it, his face colored.

"This was shot in April, at a celebration for an award we won," he said. "Before Brie started blackmailing me. I'd indulged in one too many cocktails, and when she jumped onto my back—well, I admit it. I was attracted. But the moment passed, and I came to my senses. Part of the reason Brie posted that picture in the first place was to humiliate Melanie and cause trouble between us. And it worked. The woman was psychologically savvy, I'll give her that."

I bit the inside of my cheek, wondering how far to take this conversation. I decided to push him a little further. I tensed my leg muscles in case his reaction provoked the need for a quick exit.

"I hate to say this, but everything you've told me…the blackmail, the tampering in your relationship…the police might see it as a motive worth investigating."

He paused for a moment, then spoke in a matter-of-fact tone. "I know how it looks. But here's the thing. I'd already decided to confess my sins. That afternoon, before your party, I put Brie on notice that I was going to tell Preston first thing the next morning and hand in my resignation."

"What did Brie say to that?"

"She laughed at me. Said she didn't think I had the spine to follow through, but if I did, good riddance. There were plenty more where I came from." He toed a small rock at his feet, sending it skittering down the embankment and into the creek. "Before I could follow through, she was dead."

The story rang true, but ultimately, Dev couldn't prove a word of it. The only other witness to the conversation was no longer available. "I assume you never ended up telling Preston."

He stared at his feet. "I chickened out."

For his own sake, Dev needed to come clean—preferably before Preston and Raul found out on their own. "It's not too late," I said gently. "It's never too late to do the right thing."

Dev was still for several seconds. Then he nodded. "I'll tell Preston tonight. Right after I contact Detective Sanchez and tell him everything."

"I think that's a perfect plan," I said, relieved that I wouldn't be the one to turn him in.

I glanced at my watch and realized I needed to hurry if I wanted to clean up before the Town Hall meeting. I struggled to my feet and brushed the dirt from my rear. "I've always held you in high esteem, Dev. You'll get through this and come out the other side stronger and happier. I'm living proof."

He smiled wistfully. "You can be my role model. Maybe I'll find a hidden village somewhere and open a gallery of my own."

"Just not too close. I don't need the competition."

I climbed the embankment and stepped onto the bridge. When I looked back toward Dev, he was packing away his fishing gear. He lifted his hand. "See you on the other side."

25

A quick shower and a change of clothes rendered me semi-presentable for the meeting—when I left home, anyway. Parking was in short supply by the time I arrived at Town Hall, so I was forced to park a block away. As I hurried toward the building, blustery winds swirled around me. Thick gray clouds hung low in the sky, like a sodden towel just waiting to be wrung out. A few giant drops of rain tapped at my cheeks.

When I finally made my way into the packed room, Tonya waved me to a seat next to hers in the back row. I slouched onto the red cushioned banquet chair and exhaled a pent-up breath.

She reached over and touched a knot in my hair. "Darling, what happened here?" Then she swiped a thumb across my cheek. "And is that mascara? I know you don't go in for makeup much, but it's supposed to go on the lashes."

I nudged her hand away and swiped the skin beneath my eyes. Then I combed my fingers through the tangles in my hair. "A storm is coming. I barely beat it."

She sat back in her chair and gestured to the crowd in the room. "I'd say the storm has already descended."

She had a point. Nearly all the local business owners had crowded into the compact meeting room, and unless I was paranoid, many were staring daggers at me. Tabitha, Pamela, Fran—even dear Mr. Pearly—sent me stern looks. I found some comfort in the front row, where Mrs. Finney sat next to my mother and father. Jessica and Summer took up chairs nearby.

Then, from the third row, Sophie raised her camera and snapped a picture of me. I took a page from Alexis's book and began to raise my own hand, middle finger at the ready, but Tonya grabbed my arm. "Now now," she said. "Let's not make a scene." She glanced over her shoulder. "Where's Sam? Isn't he with you?"

"He and Elyse went to Denver for their monthly father-daughter date. Dinner and a show. He's squeezing in all the time he can with her before she goes off to college this fall. I'm serving as his proxy tonight."

"He trusts you with his vote. Now that's commitment."

"And where's David? Have you worn the poor man out so that he couldn't even make it to the meeting?"

She smirked. "Quiet, little girl. He's Italian, you know. Perpetually tardy. He'll be here."

Conversation in the room ceased as Willie entered the room and strode authoritatively to the podium. He tapped a finger on the microphone and leaned in so that his lips nearly touched it. "Is this thing on?" he asked. Metallic feedback screeched through the room. From her seat beside the podium, his assistant whispered a few words, and he pulled back an inch.

"Good evening, citizens. Thank you for attending this emergency meeting of the Rock Creek Village Chamber of Commerce." He scanned the audience before turning to his notes. "The first and only order of business entails whether to continue as planned with this year's Fireweed Festival…" He shot a pointed look my direction. "Or cancel it, in light of recent circumstances."

A cacophony of voices immediately rose from the audience. Willie raised an authoritative hand. If he'd had a gavel, he'd have smacked it on the podium.

"Quiet down, please," he said. "Let me provide a summary, then we'll hold an open forum before voting." The voices subsided, and Willie cleared his throat. "As you know, a violent crime occurred in Rock Creek Village over the weekend." Villagers shuffled in their seats, many of them turning toward me. Willie paused to let them have their looks. I straightened my spine and held my head up, meeting their collective gaze. In my peripheral vision, I saw Tonya wink at me.

"The concern," he resumed, "is that the recent murder will impede the Fireweed Festival's attendance, costing us more than we'd make in profit." Another murmur rippled through the audience, and Willie again quashed it with a raised hand. "Further, since the killer has yet to be apprehended, visitors to Rock Creek Village might potentially be in danger. Would we be liable if a visitor were injured…or worse?"

His face creased theatrically. "Additionally, there's the potential of negative press coverage. Holding the festival might spur neighboring towns—even Boulder and Denver—to highlight our misfortune. Last but not least, we must consider the weather. Forecasts suggest a storm brewing to our west may move across the mountains, bringing significant rain and possibly damaging winds."

My hand went to my hair, as if it provided credibility to Willie's argument. He scanned the room and again leaned too close to the mic. "Rock Creek Village has been unwittingly dragged into a confluence of circumstances not within our control. As such, it is my informed opinion that, out of an abundance of caution, we are obliged to cancel this year's Fireweed Festival. And I so move."

His assistant stood on script and craned her head toward the mic. "Seconded."

Willie nodded. "I will now open the meeting for public discussion. If you choose to speak, you may approach the microphone."

A few villagers stirred, but no one rose to address the

assembly. Mom turned in her chair and stared at me. I gave my head a little shake. She raised her left eyebrow microscopically. I knew what that meant.

I sighed and got to my feet. Willie pursed his lips. "The chair recognizes Callahan Cassidy of Sundance Studio. Please approach the podium, Ms. Cassidy."

"I'll stay here. The room isn't so large that everyone can't hear me. Besides, we're among friends. No need for the formality."

My mother's eyes twinkled. I paused and gathered my thoughts. "I will keep this brief. First, I want to address Willie's concern about liability. Quite simply, it holds no merit, as anyone with any sense knows. Is Denver legally responsible for every tourist's well-being? Is New York City? Washington, D.C.? Of course not. That would be absurd. Besides, the risk is negligible. For heaven's sake, people are more likely to get in an accident driving into town than…well…"

From the podium, Willie opened his mouth to speak, but I waved him off. "Let me finish, please. From what I've been told, the Fireweed Festival is an integral part of Rock Creek Village's economy. Losing it would take a big bite out of our profits. And despite the circumstances, as Willie calls them, I feel confident that people will still attend. If I know anything about human nature, I predict they will arrive in even greater droves than usual. Sad commentary, perhaps, but true nevertheless."

A number of the villagers nodded. I clasped my hands in front of my waist. "A woman was murdered in our village, in my gallery. She was someone I knew, and no one here is sorrier than I am about that." I locked eyes with as many of my fellow business owners as I could. "I've known most of you my whole life. Tabitha, I worked one summer in your shop. Pamela, as a kid, I bought your fudge for my parents every Valentine's Day. And when I moved back and opened my studio, you all made me feel welcome and accepted."

I paused. "I didn't ask for this to happen. But I will do

everything in my power to help the police solve this crime before the festival opens. You have never let me down, and I won't let you down either. Thank you."

Tonya draped an arm around me after I fell back into my chair. My mother beamed at me. Sophie scribbled furiously in her notebook. Nearby, Tonya's top reporter, Phil, took notes of his own. Willie opened his mouth and snapped it shut. The room was quiet for a long moment.

Then a crack of thunder broke the silence, and Willie sneered. "Be that as it may, there's still the weather—"

Mrs. Finney jumped to her feet. "Oh, my bloody drunk uncle," she said, eliciting a snicker from the audience. Despite her age, which I guessed to be late sixties, she created an imposing figure. Her height, broad-shouldered stockiness, and impressive fitness level meant few people dared cross her—least of all Willie.

Now he flinched beneath her glare. "Willie Wright, you want to cancel the festival because of a weather forecast? Malarkey. If it rains this weekend, we'll simply gather our things and take them inside until it stops. We're hardy folks." A smattering of applause filled the room. "At any rate, my knees tell me the storm will pass by Thursday morning. My old joints predict the weather as reliably as any meteorologist. When they tell me it'll pass, you can trust them."

Willie cleared his throat and attempted to regain his authority. "Mrs. Finney, with all due respect, it is less than prudent for us to make town decisions based on your knees."

Mrs. Finney lowered her chin like a bull preparing to charge. She shook a finger at him. "Young man, an eagle's eyes view the world much differently than do his talons." She looked around the room, nodding sagely. "You all know I am correct. So I ask you, is there really any need for further discussion? Let the Fireweed Festival commence!"

She returned to her chair and folded her hands primly in her lap. Another crack of thunder sounded, and my father stood. "Ladies and gentlemen, I propose we take a preliminary vote. If it proves necessary, we can continue the debate after that."

Willie threw up his hands in defeat. "The motion on the table is to cancel this year's Fireweed Festival. All in favor, say aye."

The room was silent.

He sighed. "Opposed, please say nay."

The chorus of nays made the room sound like a horse stable.

"Very well, the nays have it," he muttered, gathering his stack of notecards from the podium. "The Fireweed Festival shall open as scheduled Thursday morning, rain or shine." He scowled in my direction. "I can only hope we're not hurtling forth with a murderer in our midst."

26

After Willie marched out the side exit, the rest of the villagers trickled toward the front doors. Many of them paused to offer me words of encouragement. Speaking up at the meeting seemed to have made me the belle of the ball. My mother had been right. Yet again.

As the crowd dispersed, David Parisi approached us and pressed his lips to Tonya's cheek. "Ciao, mi amore," he said. She lit up in a way I hadn't seen in years. Maybe ever.

"Where've you been?" she said, her voice husky.

"Io sono arrivato tardi," he replied. "So I stood near the back wall. Don't worry, I was present for the theater."

He leaned in and kissed me on one cheek, then the other. Very European. Not my style, but to each her own, I supposed. "Ah, piccola!" he said to me. "You handled the crowd with great self-assurance. Consider me at your disposal. Whatever I can do to help you solve this terrible crime. But domani, tomorrow, amica mia. Right now, I must whisk this bella donna away from here. I request her presence for a special surprise."

Tonya smiled up at him and then turned to me. "Are you all right, sweet potato? I can stay if you need me."

I gave her a quick hug. "I'm fine. Just make sure I'm first to hear the juicy details."

She patted my cheek and let herself be swirled away.

By now, the room had nearly emptied. A few villagers stood in a group, chatting. Sophie remained in the third row, writing notes in a little book. Phil had already left. My parents were making their way toward me when my father stopped and pulled out his phone, squinting at the screen. At the same time, I noticed Sophie retrieving her phone from her bag. Then my phone vibrated against my thigh. Once I freed it from my pocket and read the message, my mouth went dry. Then I lifted my eyes to Dad, who took my mother's elbow and led her over.

"You heard?" he asked.

I nodded. Mom looked at me, then Dad. "What is it?"

He leaned in and whispered a few words in her ear. Her lips set in a firm line. "Let's go," she said.

A police car had blocked off the entrance to the Knotty Pine lot, so Dad parked on the street, and I pulled my car in behind his. An hour of daylight remained, but the clouds made it darker than usual. Flashing red lights reflected off the wet pavement. The earlier rain had regressed to a thin blanket of drizzle, which gave the scene a hazy aura.

The bustle of activity centered around a white Toyota Sienna parked in a spot near the lodge. A few feet away, I saw Gary Padgett shifting nervously from one foot to the other. A group of resort guests congregated beneath the lodge's portico, watching and whispering. Jamal had positioned himself like a guard at the lobby door. On the porch of the closest cabin, Melanie and Dev stood apart from each other, and I sensed the distance was more than just physical.

Suddenly, my peripheral vision picked up a blur of motion. It turned into Sophie, who marched up the driveway with a predatory gleam in her eye. Dad and I had gotten word of the police presence from Jamal. I wondered idly who served as Sophie's source.

Lights glowed from the interior of the minivan. The sliding side door was open, and Frank stood next to it, arms crossed. Clad in snug-fitting dress slacks, another man's rear end poked out from inside the vehicle. I couldn't be positive, but I figured it belonged to Raul.

My parents and I huddled together, waiting. At last, the half-person wriggled from the van. The detective, as I'd suspected. He held something in his hand, but I couldn't make it out. Frank moved closer and studied the object. Then Raul gestured, and three people emerged from the shadows and walked toward him.

Flanked by officers Tollison and Hardesty, Preston Garrison suddenly stopped short. Tollison reached out to grip Preston's elbow, and Preston yanked his arm away. In response, Tollison grabbed Preston's shoulder, while Hardesty restrained his other arm. The officers glanced at Frank, who lifted his chin. Then Tollison removed a set of handcuffs from his belt, pulled Preston's arms behind him, and cuffed his wrists.

I hurried toward the van, with Dad on my heels. "What's going on?" I demanded. No one responded.

I took a step toward Preston. Hardesty positioned herself between us. "I'll have to ask you to take a step back, ma'am," she said.

One look at Hardesty's toned arms and her unbudging stance discouraged me from testing her resolve. Instead, I swiveled toward Raul. I might lack the muscle, but I had unbudging down to a science. "Are you arresting Preston? For what?"

It was a silly question, really, and it incited no response. Then my eyes fell to the item in Raul's hand. It was a cell phone, an iPhone, from the looks of it. And I immediately deduced it had belonged to Brie.

Frank took the phone and secured it in a plastic evidence bag. Raul looked at me. "Take it easy, Callie," he said. Despite his gentle tone, his face carried a warning.

I took a step back. For one thing, I didn't really have a dog in this race. Preston had been my boss, and occasionally more, but I wasn't particularly beholden to the man. He'd confessed his motive to me earlier. And judging from the presence of the phone, Raul had uncovered a solid piece of evidence on which to arrest the man.

A few fat drops of rain splattered around us, etching a dark, polka-dotted pattern onto the already damp concrete. Frank glanced up to the sky. "Looks like it could unload any minute. Let's move."

He headed toward the department-issued SUV, and Raul followed him. "Wait," I said, thinking as fast as my brain would go. Raul hesitated and then turned back. "The minivan was rented in Preston's name?"

He nodded. "He's the only registered driver, and the only one with keys. We got an anonymous tip about the phone this afternoon. The judge just issued a search warrant."

"Did you find anything else?"

"Can't say." He turned and trotted off toward the SUV.

I bit my lip as Tollison placed a hand on Preston's head and lowered him into the back seat of the squad car. Preston looked at me, his eyes wide, and I realized I'd never seen him frightened before. Then looked past me at Gary. "Get in touch with Nicole," he called. I knew he was talking about Nicole Harrison-White.

"Will do, boss."

As Gary jogged off to the lodge, my attention was drawn to Sophie. She darted toward the police car with her phone extended, preparing to snap pictures of Preston in the back seat of the police car.

It was probably unintentional on my part—I'm pretty sure it was—but my foot moved slightly into her path. She tripped, and her phone flew from her hand, skittering across the pavement. Sophie slid a few inches after it.

Time seemed to stop for a moment. I took a breath and went to Sophie, taking her arm and pulling her to her feet. She scampered to retrieve her phone, and her face crumpled.

Then her expression morphed into rage. She stomped

back to me, stopping only when her toes touched mine. "You broke my phone. And you did it on purpose!"

I took a step back. "It was an accident, Sophie. You were in a hurry, and you stumbled over my foot. There was no evil intent."

Her lips pulled back in a snarl. "You'll pay for this, Callahan Cassidy. I'm going to write—"

Suddenly, my mother's hand appeared, and her fingers closed around the back of Sophie's collar. Mom pulled her backward, and Sophie's feet clambered across the asphalt. "That'll do, young lady," she said, her voice stern.

I was transported back into the halls of high school, where my English teacher mother held no qualms about meting out discipline. Apparently, Sophie was reliving the same memories. She looked at my mother like a teenager who'd been caught skipping class. "Yes, ma'am," she mumbled. Then she thrust out the hand clutching her phone. "But look what Callie did…"

Mom released Sophie and put her hands on her hips. "I see that, and I'm not pleased with either of you right now." She shot me a sidelong glare. "I'm certain Callie will take care of any repairs to your phone—" I knew better than to object, so I merely nodded.

Before she could scold us further, a siren wailed behind us. We watched as the squad car bearing Preston rolled out of the parking lot and turned onto Evergreen Way, headed toward the station.

Then the intermittent raindrops turned into a sheet of water. Like rats on a sinking ship, we scattered. Sophie splashed across the parking lot to her car, while Frank and Raul took off in the Expedition. As my parents and I hurried to the lobby doors, I glanced toward the cabin. Dev and Melanie were nowhere to be seen.

27

few guests lingered under the portico, pretending to watch the rain but surreptitiously tapping on their phones. I figured they were sharing the whole spectacle on social media. They'd stumbled into an intriguing vacation, complete with a murder, an arrest, and a confrontation in the parking lot. Rock Creek Village would be viral before we knew it.

Jamal met us inside the door and handed over fluffy white towels. He took one look at Mom's face and rushed off to tend the buffet. Mom ruffled the towel across her hair and wrapped it around her shoulders. Then she went upstairs without so much as a backward glance. Dad stepped behind the registration desk. I wiped myself down as best I could and trudged after him. "She's mad," I said.

"Smart as a whip, aren't you?" Dad said. "I'm not going up there for a while. I'd suggest you avoid it, too. Give her a few minutes to cool down."

"Absolutely," I said. "But it really was Sophie's fault…"

Dad narrowed his eyes at me and took a seat at the desk. "So, they've taken your old boss into custody. Think they made the right move?"

I considered his question. "That phone is incriminating, for sure. But when you think about it, the parking lot is easily accessible. Anyone with a slim jim could have planted the phone in the rental car." My mind flashed on Dev, watching the scene of Preston's arrest play out from the cabin porch.

Dad stretched out his legs and crossed his ankles. "The most logical solution is usually the right one. We know Garrison had a motive."

I shrugged. "Could be. But it just doesn't feel right. Besides, Brie had gathered dirt on a lot of people. Preston wasn't the only one with a motive."

He locked his hands behind his head and frowned. "Listen, Sundance. I know what you said at the Chamber meeting. And you've always had the desire to protect the people close to you. But it's time to take a step back. The police have a suspect in custody. Let them do their job."

I gazed off into the distance. It was sound advice, but I knew he wouldn't have followed it either. "Dad, we're justice seekers, you and I. You wouldn't let Preston be falsely accused any more than I would. If he killed her, fine, he deserves whatever he gets. But I have to know for sure."

He sighed. "I was afraid of that."

I kissed his cheek, sandpapery with a day's worth of stubble. "If it makes you feel any better, you can go ahead and forbid me."

An hour later, the creatures and I returned home. I filled their food bowls and offered treats. Then I ate a peanut butter and jelly sandwich and half a bag of barbecue chips. Who said I couldn't make a decent meal?

Next, I nestled into the corner of my couch with a legal pad on my lap and tried to make sense of this murder. I just couldn't unravel it.

My phone trilled with an actual call. I was so used to text messages that it took me a second to figure out what was happening. The screen flashed the words, No Caller ID. Probably a sales call, but considering the current state of affairs, I decided to answer.

"Callahan Cassidy?" A smooth, professional-sounding

female voice flowed across the connection.

"Who's calling?" My voice was frosty, but to my credit, I refrained from adding, *Whatever you're pitching, I don't want any.*

"Nicole Harrison-White here. Editor in chief of *The Washington Sentinel.*"

My heart may have skipped a beat or two. Very few people elicited a sense of hero worship in me, but Nicole Harrison-White topped the list. As one of the first women to break into the journalistic boys' club, she had blazed a path many female reporters subsequently followed. I'd only met her in person a handful of times—once at my Felden Award celebration, I recalled with pride. Now this warrior of feminism was calling *me?*

"Ms. Cassidy? Did I lose you?"

I forced myself to mimic her professional tone. "No, I'm here. It's a pleasure to talk to you, Ms. Harrison-White." I slapped my palm against my forehead. *A pleasure?* I realized I sounded star struck. If we'd been face to face, I'd probably have stammered and asked for an autograph.

"Yes, well, I'm afraid my call isn't a social one." I pictured her seated on the white leather couch in her expansive office. Through the picture window behind her, the lights of Washington, D.C., glittered. In my vision, she wore a tailored suit, and her designer heels lay in a heap near her desk. Honestly, though, it was just as easy to visualize the woman in fatigues with her hair tucked under a ball cap.

Or, unfortunately, in a skimpy bikini with Preston's hand on her hip. Ugh.

"What can I do for you, Ms. Harrison-White?" I asked

"First of all, you can call me Nicole."

"All right, Nicole. And of course you'll call me Callie."

"Yes, of course. Now, let me get down to business. I've just been in touch with Mr. Padgett, who informed me that the police in your little town—Rock Creek Village, right?—have detained my managing editor."

"Yes, I was present at the time. I can assure you—"

"No time for assurances. What are you doing about it?"

"What am I doing?"

Through the line, I heard her exhale. "Ms. Cassidy—Callie—need I remind you that Preston Garrison and I launched your career? That it was your work at our newspaper that earned you that Felden Award? That we defended you in your recent time of trouble? Must I remind you of the handsome severance package we provided when you chose to leave us?"

Her pitch had risen with each consecutive question, to the point that I feared the window behind her might shatter. Gone was the calm, self-assured professional. Now, she sounded manic. It seemed excessive, but I thought I understood her distress. If Preston was arrested and went to trial, her name would be drawn through the mud. Everything she'd accomplished would be overshadowed by that one scandal.

"I remember," I said. "I am indebted to you, and to Preston. And I'm doing what I can, but—"

"I'm told you're friendly with the detective on the case," she cut in. "And if my sources are correct, your father once served as chief of police. You have pull in that little town, Callie. Use it."

"Are you suggesting that I attempt to influence the legal system?"

"That's precisely what I'm suggesting. I've arranged for *The Sentinel's* attorney to fly out there tomorrow. He should arrive in Denver midday and make his way to Rock Creek Village by early afternoon. Do whatever you must to schedule an immediate bail hearing. I don't want Preston spending a single minute more than necessary in jail."

"I-I'll…do what I can…" I said.

"Callahan, you've navigated combat zones. I'm sure you can deal with a local-yokel police detective and small-town judge."

Now my dander was up. Local yokel? I pictured Raul, Frank…my father. How dare she? "Listen, Nicole, you can't just—"

But she had no intention of hearing my response. "Better yet, you should just uncover the identity of the real killer yourself. I hear you have experience with that. Let's set a deadline. Journalists work best under time constraints. We'll say two days. I believe in you, Callie. Now make it happen."

I heard a click, followed by soft static. Just like the old days, I'd received my assignment.

28

My body pulsed with the adrenaline that accompanied the beginning of an investigation. As Ms. Harrison-White—*Nicole, I corrected myself*—had suggested, I'd always been deadline-oriented. And though she'd been hamhanded with her demand, and condescending to boot, she was right. The faster this murder got solved, the better. Then the Fireweed Festival could proceed without a shroud hanging over it. Preston could walk free and resume his life, unencumbered by suspicion.

And a murderer would no longer be lurking around in our village.

After a brief call to reassure Sam I was fine, I spent the next few hours refining my list of suspects, motives, and alibis. Carl never strayed far from my shoulder, meowing every time I added a new thought.

Despite the cat's counsel, the list didn't evolve much. Preston remained at the top, for obvious reasons, with Dev a close second. I wedged Melanie into the third spot. All three had a solid reason to want Brie dead, and all three had weak alibis.

I thought about Gary Padgett and drew a line through his name. It was obvious he couldn't have carried out the physical act of Brie's murder. He could be a co-conspirator,

I supposed, but it seemed unlikely.

I called Dev's cabin to ask if he'd followed through on talking to the police, but he didn't answer. I tried Raul twice, but my calls went straight to voicemail. No one wanted to talk to me. It was just like my good old days as a pesky journalist.

Finally, my brain blurred and my eyes refused to stay open, so I went to bed. I'd have to face my assignment tomorrow with fresh eyes.

After a dreamless, six-hour sleep, I was wide awake at daybreak. My phone log affirmed that no one had called me back or texted, but it was still too early to resume my campaign of harassment.

But it wasn't too early for obedience training.

I went downstairs and opened the back door. Carl refused to leave the kitchen, but Woody bounded outside joyfully. I followed him onto the patio. Muted light filtered through the sheet of clouds., and gusty winds rattled the leaves on the shrubs. I thought of Willie's dire forecast, which led me to wonder again why he was so angry with me.

Finished with his doggie business, Woody pranced toward me wearing a huge grin, as if he'd just invented the cure for bad breath. The two of us went back inside. I found a not-too-stale donut in the pantry and bit into it. Then I pulled out the treat box and sat cross-legged on the floor. Woody drew close and sat expectantly.

I grinned. "Good dog. But we're doing something different, remember?" I held out a hand, palm up, and lifted it.

He cocked his head quizzically. Then the light bulb flashed. He pulled himself up on his haunches and lifted a furry paw, waiting for a high-five.

I squealed with delight and tossed Woody the treat. After he wolfed it down, he joined me in a happy dance.

From the corner of my eye, I saw Carl watching us. Rather than his usual expression of disdain, he appeared semi-interested. "You want in on this?" I asked.

He paused for a moment, before screeching *ack, ack, ack* and vaulting across the back of the couch. It was his usual response to most of my requests, but this time, perhaps his refusal was a little less sincere…The pet pageant was still four days away. Did we have a shot?

An hour later, I stopped to pick up a box of Mrs. Finney's pastries for my employees—and one for myself. I rationalized that the donut I'd eaten earlier didn't count since it had been stale. I spent a few minutes filling my friend in about Preston's arrest. I'd worried about her reaction, given their past association, but she took it in stride. "The wheels of fate sometimes spin askew," she told me. "But they eventually stop exactly where they should." I nodded wistfully.

To my surprise, the lights were on when I arrived at Sundance Studio. I hurried inside and found Ethan on a ladder, a gray-speckled paintbrush in his hand.

"Morning, boss," he said, swiping paint across the now non-existent crease.

I walked over and examined his work. "Ethan, this is above and beyond the call of duty. When I told you about the hidden door, I didn't expect you to take care of it. I planned to hire someone."

He grinned. "I'm much cheaper labor than you could hire." He gestured to the bag in my hand. "I work for food. Plus, I enjoy stuff like this. It was actually pretty easy. You can learn anything on YouTube. I used cement to seal the opening, and now I'm touching up the paint. Should be done before the gallery opens."

"You're a godsend. What am I going to do when you go back to your teaching job this fall?"

"I'll still be around. Who knows, if business skyrockets, maybe I'll quit teaching and work here full-time."

"I'd love nothing better." Right now, I could only afford to pay Ethan minimum wage, plus a commission on online sales—certainly not enough to replace his teaching income.

The thought of online sales propelled me to the task at hand. I left Ethan to his painting and headed to the computer behind the sales counter. I uploaded the photos I'd taken at the lake yesterday and used the software we'd purchased to catalog them with order numbers and prices. Before I'd even completed the task, two orders came in, and I called across the gallery to tell Ethan.

"Told you so," he said. "And it's just the beginning. I predict you'll be able to hire me full time by next summer."

"If we do that well, I might have to make you a partner," I murmured.

"I heard that," he said. "Put it in writing, please."

I'd resumed work on the computer when I was interrupted by tapping on the front window. The gallery wouldn't open for an hour yet, and the blinds were still drawn, so I ignored it. Then the sound escalated from light tapping to insistent rapping. I climbed off the stool and opened the blinds to find Tonya peering at me.

"Let me in," she mouthed through the glass.

Once I unlocked the door, Tonya swept across the threshold. She ran a hand over her wind-blown hair, which settled obediently into place. Today's fashion statement involved a yellow floral tunic over clingy white pedal pushers. The red of her lips coordinated perfectly with the flowers on her patterned blouse. So summery and bright, she made me smile.

Only her worried expression on dampened the effect.

"What's wrong?" I asked.

"I need to talk."

I bolted the door behind her. She greeted Ethan, and when he noticed her expression, he diplomatically pulled headphones from his pockets and tucked the buds into his ears. "Don't mind me," he said. "Just listening to some oldies." By oldies, I knew he meant nineties music, and I was glad the songs were playing in his ears instead of over the gallery's speakers.

Tonya followed me to the sales counter and took a stool across from mine. Her eyes shimmered. Tonya rarely displayed sadness, yet here she was, close to tears. I put my hand over hers. "What is it? Tell me."

She turned her gaze to the window, not meeting my eyes. "It's David…"

Immediately, I bristled. "He dumped you? I knew there was something wrong with that man. You're better off without—"

She shook her head. "No, it's nothing like that. It's…wait, you think there's something wrong with him? What are you—?" She waved. "Never mind. We'll deal with that another time." She took a deep breath. "Last night's date was a dream—a gourmet meal at a secluded mountain venue. Candlelight, soft music. And then…"

"Yes?"

"He proposed."

My hand flew to my throat. "*Proposed?* As in, marriage?"

Her head bobbed. "One knee. Huge diamond. The whole bit."

Tonya and I were in our mid-forties, and neither of us had ever married. But suddenly I found myself in a serious relationship with Sam—he'd even uttered the L word, for heaven's sake. And now Tonya was possibly—engaged? It felt surreal.

"What was your answer?"

She wrung her hands. "I said maybe."

"*Maybe?* How'd he take that?"

"He said a few words in Italian that I didn't understand. But I didn't get the impression he was pleased."

"Oh my." My mind reeled. "How'd you leave things?"

"I told him I needed time to think. He drove me home, and I drank myself into oblivion. Today's hangover isn't helping the decision-making process. So I came to you."

We stared at each other. After a few seconds, she said, "Well? What should I do?"

My knee-jerk reaction was that she should tell him heck

no. They'd only met a few months ago and had been dating maybe six weeks. It was too soon for a commitment. Besides, I couldn't get a good read on the man. He seemed nice enough, though perhaps a little over the top with the charm. But before I gave her my instinctive response, I paused. Who was I to counsel against rashness? For that matter, who was I to counsel on matters of the heart?

I squeezed her hand. "Do you love him?"

She smiled softly. "I do. At least, I think I do. But I'm not sure I can tell the difference between love, lust, and infatuation. Am I feeling this way because I'm a woman of a certain age? Is this love, or fear of being alone for the rest of my life?"

I understood the sentiment perfectly. The same thoughts had flitted through my own mind just the other day. "Too bad there's no manual with instructions about falling in love," I said finally. "Sometimes I think it's just a leap of faith. Is David someone you can see yourself growing old with? Sharing rolls of toilet paper and tubes of toothpaste? Values and interests?"

She laughed. "All this philosophizing. When did you become such a deep thinker?"

I grinned, relieved at the sound of her laughter. "You want to know what I think? There's no hurry. If he's the one, he'll wait until you're sure. If he's not willing to wait, he's not the one."

She closed her eyes for a moment, and when she opened them, the pooled tears had evaporated. "I knew you'd have the answer. You're—"

But then the sight of a certain someone walking past the window had me leaping to my feet. "Hold that thought," I said. "Back in a flash."

"Where are you—"

I didn't take the time to respond. I'd seen Willie, head down and shoulders slumped, and I was after some answers.

29

By the time I got through the door, Willie was climbing the steps to his office. "Willie, wait," I called. "I need to talk to you."

Without even glancing at me, he waved over his shoulder, as if shooing away a housefly. "I'm really busy, Callie. Email me and we can set up an appointment."

His haughtiness rankled me. Then I realized maybe it wasn't haughtiness I was hearing. Maybe it was fear. His days-long attitude toward me suddenly made sense. Willie didn't want to talk to me because he was afraid. Of what?

He paused on the landing, digging his keys from his pocket and unlocking his door. I hurried up the stairs, catching up to him before he was able to shut me out. I donned my best investigative reporter voice. "Willie, I need a few minutes. That's all. Just talk to me."

He froze with his hand on the knob. Then he sighed, surrendering. "Fine. But not out here. Come in."

I scuttled into the large office, waiting while he flipped on the light and removed his jacket, hanging it on a coat tree near the door. He gestured to a leather chair and moved around his desk, settling himself into a broad leather executive chair. As I perched on the edge of my seat, he leaned over his desk, sorting through a stack of mail, feigning indifference. "What can I do for you, Callie? Are you interested in purchasing another property?"

"Willie, you've been acting strangely toward me for days. Since the murder, actually. And then you tried to cancel the Fireweed Festival and get people to blame me. What's going on?"

His focus never left the papers on his desk, but I knew he wasn't really seeing them. "I'm not treating you any way in particular, Callie. As Chamber president, I'm under quite a bit of stress organizing the Fireweed Festival, especially with the dreadful weather forecast. And yes, the crime in your gallery only served to amplify my anxieties. Perhaps that's what you're sensing."

I stared at him. He squirmed, and his eyes darted to the wall beside his desk. Just as quickly, they returned to his hands. I shifted in my seat and followed the direction of his fleeting gaze. A grouping of framed documents decorated the wall—a college diploma, a certificate declaring him Chamber of Commerce president, a newspaper article announcing the opening of his realty office.

And mounted next to the arrangement was a metal key case.

I felt an electric current pulse through the wires of my brain. The pieces started to fit together. Willie's curious behavior. A metal case I was certain was filled with keys to the multiple properties he represented. The gallery key found in Brie Bohannan's pocket.

"She got it from you," I said.

Willie's face turned crimson. "I don't know what you're talking about. As I told you before, I'm quite busy today. So if there's nothing else…"

He stood and gestured toward the door, but I stayed put and pointed at the key case. "You probably keep a spare key to every property you lease, in case of emergency or a delinquent tenant or such." I tilted my head. "What motivated you to hand mine over to Brie?"

He gave a mirthless snort. "That's nonsense. You've gotten carried away with your own sense of importance, I'm afraid."

I ignored the comment and stared at him silently. When it was clear he wasn't going to continue, I rose. "Have it your way. I'll let Detective Sanchez handle this." I tapped a finger on the desk. "But before I make my way to the police station, perhaps I'll have a quick chat with Sophie Demler. She loves anonymous sources, and her *Sophie's Scoop* blog has quite the following. I'm told our fellow villagers consume it voraciously."

In a split second, his face went from crimson to ash gray. "You can't…"

"I don't want to. But I will." I put my hands on my hips. "Why did you give Brie that key?"

When he exhaled, he deflated like a balloon. He dropped back into his chair and put his head in his hands, raking his fingers through his gelled hair. I sat down and waited, sensing he was on the cusp of a confession. At last he spoke, never looking up. "I didn't give her the key. It was stolen."

My eyebrows lifted. "Stolen? When? How?"

"I don't know exactly." He finally lifted his eyes to mine. "I didn't even realize it was missing until I read in Sophie's blog that they'd found a key in the dead woman's pocket. I had a terrible hunch and checked my key case immediately. Sure enough, the backup key to Sundance Studio was gone."

I let the scene play out in my mind as I sat down. "Willie, that's an important piece of evidence. Why didn't you go to the police right away?"

He fumbled with the envelopes on his desk again. "The thing is, I'm not always reliable about locking the door to the office. Or the key cabinet. I mean, Rock Creek Village has always been a safe place, until…"

I knew how that sentence concluded in his mind. *Until you came back.* But now wasn't the time to chase that thought. "You're saying someone could have waltzed in here anytime and taken any key they wanted?"

Willie didn't respond, so I continued. "All right. But that doesn't answer my original question. Why didn't you tell Detective Sanchez?"

He rubbed his eyes. "I've worked hard to build a life here, a reputation. Things haven't always been easy for me. But now I have standing in the community, a position of importance. If I'm seen as derelict in my duties, as jeopardizing the safety of people's homes and businesses, I'm ruined. My practice, my Chamber presidency, gone." He snapped his fingers. "Poof."

A woman murdered, my gallery compromised, the Fireweed Festival at risk of cancellation, our local economy endangered, and Willie was worried about his reputation?

Still, though he might be a shallow man, I didn't think anything he'd done had ultimately sparked the chaos. Key or no key, a murderer intent on harm would find a way to follow through.

Across from me, Willie emitted a small groan. "If Sophie finds out, the whole town will know. My life will be destroyed."

I fought the urge to roll my eyes at his self-pity. I'd indulged in it myself a time or two, so who was I to judge? "Listen," I said. "I can't promise you Sophie won't find out. But I can assure you it won't be from me." He looked up at me hopefully. "Detective Sanchez, on the other hand, must absolutely be told about the stolen key. Unless there's more to the story than you've told me, I doubt the information will be made public."

He reached across the desk and grabbed my hand. For a moment, I was afraid he might actually kiss it. "I swear there's nothing more. I've told you everything I know. Please ask Detective Sanchez to keep my confidence."

I withdrew my hand. "He'll do what he can, I'm sure. He's not out to harm anyone. But the thing is, this isn't all about you, Willie."

His face filled with chagrin. "Of course. Just…if you'd put in a good word for me, I'll be forever grateful."

Behind me, the door opened and a young couple entered the office. Willie stiffened, his eyes pleading with me. I rose and reached across the desk. "Thank you for your time, Mr.

Wright. You have given me a lot to think about. I'll be in touch."

He shook my hand and got to his feet. "I'll look forward to it," he said, the image of professionalism. "If you have any further questions, please don't hesitate."

As he walked over to greet his clients, I gave them a friendly smile and exited, pausing on the landing outside to look around. The office space was fairly isolated. It wouldn't be hard to sneak up here in the dark of night and steal a key. But whoever had done it must have known about the spares, as well as Willie's lax security. It seemed unlikely that one of the visiting journalists would have been privy to such information.

My skin crawled. For the first time, I entertained the idea that the killer might be a resident of Rock Creek Village.

30

As I descended the stairs, I spotted my mother walking along Evergreen Way. I remembered her displeasure last night and considered hiding in the alcove, but it was too late. She'd seen me.

"Well, look who we have here," she said, shifting her umbrella to pull me into a one-armed hug. In her tan Burberry raincoat and matching boots, she looked almost as elegant as Tonya.

I gave her a wary look. "You're not mad at me anymore?" I asked.

"Of course not, darling. You know I'm not one to stew over misdeeds. What's done is done, that's what I always say."

Was it? I didn't seem to recall the woman who'd raised me letting go of her grudges quite so easily. Perhaps her inversion table worked miracles after all.

"I'm on my way to meditation class," she said. "Why don't you join me? I haven't seen you there in days. No wonder your behavior last night was so…maladjusted."

Ah, there she was—the mom I knew and loved. I smiled in recognition.

"Can't today, I'm afraid. Too much to do, especially now that the Fireweed Festival is a go." I knew better than to bring up the murder investigation.

"All right," she said, only a hint of disapproval in her tone. "Well, anyway, running into you here has saved me a phone call. Will you come for dinner tonight? Your father is grilling steaks, and I'm making homemade rolls. For dessert, we'll taste test a prototype of the cake I'm entering in the festival baking contest."

The image of all that food made my stomach rumble. "That sounds amazing, Mom. I'll be there."

She beamed. "Lovely, dear. I've invited Sam and Elyse as well. And Mrs. Finney will be joining us too."

"A regular dinner party," I said. "Do you mind if I bring Tonya? She's…going through something right now, and I think it would do her good to be among friends."

"Absolutely." She leaned in and lowered her voice. "Please don't tell me that David Parisi has broken her heart. He seemed like such a lovely fellow."

"No, nothing like that. But I'm not comfortable saying anything more. Maybe she'll fill you in tonight."

She pursed her lips as she tried to decipher the secret. Giving her a peck on the cheek, I hurried into the gallery, mentally preparing my apology for abandoning Tonya in her hour of need. But I needn't have worried. She was gone, and Ethan looked up at me from his spot at the computer.

"Tonya had to get to work," Ethan said. "She said to tell you she'd think about what you said."

I glanced at my watch and saw it was after ten. I'd spent more time with Willie than I'd realized. "Yikes. The morning has already gotten away from me. I meant to have three or four photos printed by now. I'd like to have a healthy inventory prepared for the festival."

"Take a look at this." He pointed to the computer screen. I moved around the counter and looked over his shoulder. "Four more orders from your shoot at the lake. Two of those buyers also purchased additional photos from the available stock."

I studied the orders. One person had chosen the sunset over the Rockies landscape I was so proud of. Another had settled on a wildlife photo featuring a lone elk grazing against a backdrop of wildflowers.

"I'll package them up and ship them today," he said. He grinned and rubbed his hands together. "This is just the beginning, Callie. You're going to be more in demand than you ever imagined."

"From your lips to God's ears. But it also means more work. Maybe it's time to train Alexis in the darkroom."

Ethan picked up a mug and took a sip of coffee. "Guess you could, if she were here."

I scanned the room. I'd been so frazzled I hadn't even registered her absence. "Did she call in sick?"

He nodded. "Something about a migraine, but I couldn't make out all the details. She was kind of slurring her words."

That was worrisome, especially in light of her emotional state at the cafe yesterday. I dug my phone from my pocket and pressed her number. After eight rings, I disconnected.

Just then, the bell over the door tinkled, and two twenty-something guys entered the gallery. I recognized them from the park and smiled as I approached.

"Good morning, gentlemen. I shot photos of you two yesterday. Welcome to Sundance Studio. I'm Callie Cassidy, and this is my associate, Ethan McGregor." The men introduced themselves as Bradley and Tim, and we all shook hands.

Tim gestured toward the photos displayed in the gallery. "I must tell you, Ms. Cassidy, Bradley and I are enraptured with your work. We browsed your website last night and just had to come take a peek in person."

My smile broadened. "What kind words. Is there anything in particular you're looking for? Color scheme? Content?"

"Anything and everything," Bradley said. "We've just purchased a cabin on the outskirts of town. Summer place, you know. We're in the market for some quality artwork. Your photos seem ideal. Do you mind if we browse a bit?"

I tried to quell the dollar signs flashing behind my eyes.

A new cabin. Loved my work. Maybe they'd buy one of my high-end pieces. "Be my guest. If you have any questions, I'll be happy to assist."

The men strolled toward the side wall, whispering and pointing as they moved from one display to the next. A steady trickle of customers kept me from obsessing too much over their progress. While Ethan went to the back to retrieve a customer's online order, I sold a few landscape postcards and a matted five-by-seven. During a lull, I tried to contact Raul about Willie, but he still wouldn't answer his phone. My irritation at him grew. He'd given me no information about Preston's arrest, and in the meantime, I'd uncovered clues that might aid his investigation. He simply couldn't keep ignoring me like this.

I checked on Bradley and Tim, who were still making their way around the gallery. I was starting to think they might browse all day and walk out without buying anything. Next, I texted Tonya, apologized for rushing out, and invited her to dinner at my parents' house. She forgave me—largely, I think, because of the offer of Mom's cooking. Then I tried Alexis again. Still no answer.

As Ethan joined me at the counter, the two men ambled back toward us. "We've come to a decision," Bradley said.

"It was quite difficult," Tim added. "If we had adequate space, we'd take everything you have."

Bradley smiled and draped an arm around Tim. "For now, though, we'll settle for five of them."

My heart rate accelerated. Was he talking about five of the large photos? The good stuff, as Ethan called it? We followed the men around the gallery as they pointed out the works they'd chosen. Sure enough, the pieces were among the most expensive I offered.

Ten minutes later, we'd rung up the hefty sale. Ethan said he'd package the photos, and Bradley and Tim told us they'd return for them after lunch. I gushed a heartfelt thank you as they left. They said they'd be telling all their friends about Sundance Studio.

The store was empty for the moment, and quiet. Ethan stared at me. I stared back. Then we both started laughing. "Best sale we've had," I said.

"So far." He grinned. "You need to get in the darkroom. When a sale like that comes along, you'll soon have trouble keeping up with demand."

I knew he was teasing me—at least a little. Most of the photos I printed in the darkroom were smaller in scale—the matted prints, the postcard-sized photos. The larger display photos and the ones printed on canvas we contracted out. I realized with a surge of joy that I'd need to place a new order this week to replenish what we'd sold.

And I'd need to shoot more pictures. One of the studio's guarantees was that each of the larger prints was unique, meaning I couldn't simply have copies made of what I'd just sold.

So much to do. And, of course, rumbling beneath it all was an unsolved murder.

But right now, my mind was on Alexis. I'd suffered from an occasional migraine myself, and they could be nasty. And the poor kid lived alone, with no one to look after her.

"Do you think you could hold down the fort for an hour?" I asked Ethan. "I'm worried about Alexis, and I'd like to grab some soup from the Snow Plow Chow and take it over to her."

Ethan shooed me toward the door. "Definitely. Even I'm a little concerned. I'll take care of the gallery—and start packaging that big sale."

It was past noon, and a lull in the rain meant Snow Plow Chow was filled with hungry diners. In the kitchen, Sam bagged a container of French onion soup, along with some crusty garlic bread and a Caesar salad. If this didn't knock the migraine right out of Alexis's head, nothing would.

As I thanked him and grasped the handles of the paper take-out bag, Elyse sidled up beside me. "Want some company? I'd like to check on her too."

I glanced at Sam. "Can your dad spare you?"

She raised an eyebrow. "He doesn't pay me a dime, you know, so I can come and go as I please."

"Someday I'll give you a spreadsheet detailing every dollar I've spent on you over the past eighteen years, and then we can discuss how I don't pay you a dime," he said, grinning affectionately at her. "You owe me free labor for the next twenty years or so. But it's fine. Go on and leave the dirty work to the rest of us."

Since the break in the rain seemed to be holding, Elyse and I decided to walk the half mile to Alexis's apartment complex. As we made our way through throngs of tourists, she filled me in on her mom and stepdad's second honeymoon. A few months ago, Kimberly and Parker Lyon had been through a rough patch, to put it mildly. Now, they were trying to see if they could resuscitate their troubled marriage. From what Elyse said, the attempt was going well, and the couple was currently indulging in croissants and fancy wine in Paris. Next stop, the French Riviera.

Then our conversation turned to Alexis. "I don't know much about her personal life," I admitted. "Just that her family is in Virginia."

"There is no family," she said. "Both her parents are dead, no brothers or sisters. And she's from Florida."

I stopped in my tracks, and Elyse had to double back. "What's wrong?"

"She never told me her parents had passed. The poor girl is all alone in the world."

"Not anymore," Elyse said. "Now she has us."

We started walking again. "Well, I'm pretty useless," I said. "I don't know even the smallest details about my own employee."

"Jeez, Callie. Quit beating yourself up. It takes time to get to know people. Alexis is a really private person. You have to be patient."

I glanced at her. Elyse was a lovely girl, with her father's lustrous blond hair and sparkling blue eyes and her mother's full lips and high cheekbones. "Elyse, you are wise beyond your years. Okay, then, let's talk about you. Have you gotten everything you need for your dorm room?"

A cloud drifted into her eyes. "About college…"

I lifted my eyebrows. "I thought you'd been accepted. Did something happen?"

"Yeah, that's all fine. It's just…" She sighed. "I don't really want to go."

"What? I thought you were pumped. Couldn't wait to take classes, isn't that what you said?"

She shook her head. "It's not the classes. I'm still excited about that part. I just don't want to live there." She gestured around us. "I love Rock Creek Village. Moving to Boulder doesn't feel right."

Now I understood. Homesickness was setting in at the mere thought of leaving. "It's only an hour's drive. You can come back on weekends."

"Exactly. Only an hour away. At least half my classes will be online. I should just live here and commute when I need to be on campus. Think of the money it would save on room and board."

"Hmm," I said. "I think this is way above my pay grade. It's a conversation to have with your parents."

"Okay, but maybe you can tell my dad—"

"Hey, Callie." A deep voice boomed from nearby. "Find any dead bodies today?"

Looking around, I saw that the words came from one of two boys I didn't recognize, who were lounging on a bench just past the row of shops. One of the boys mimed wrapping something around his friend's neck, and the friend stuck out his tongue and bulged his eyes. A regular Dumb and Dumber act. They grasped their sides and writhed in laughter.

My face reddened. "Just ignore them," Elyse whispered. "I know them from school. A couple of losers, that's all."

"Hey, Elyse," one of them shouted. "Figure out who your dad is yet?"

That was the last straw. I marched toward the boys. But before I could get there, two figures charged past me like bulls and pulled the boys off the bench by their collars.

My mouth gaped. Banner and Braden Ratliff.

"Hey, boys, stop!" I called, worried what they were about to do. But then Banner gently sat his conquest on the bench, and Braden did the same with his. The twins gestured toward me. "This is a nice lady," Banner said. "What's gotten into you, bothering a woman you don't even know?"

Braden pointed at Elyse. "And this is our sister. Show some respect."

Elyse's eyes went wide. Banner stared at the boys. "Listen, Tommy. Doug," he said. "You're not so bad. Your moms raised you better than this. Make it right. Apologize to Ms. Cassidy, and to Elyse."

Tommy and Doug looked at each other, stunned. Perhaps they'd expected Banner and Braden to join in the hilarity. Or maybe they'd prepared themselves for a swift punch in the nose. What they hadn't expected was a soft-spoken scolding. But wide-eyed, they responded.

"Sorry, Ms. Cassidy," Tommy mumbled. "That was uncalled for."

"Yeah," Doug said. "Sorry, Elyse."

Banner clapped Tommy on the shoulder, and Braden patted Doug on the back. "Feels good, right? Come on, guys. Let's go to the Fudge Factory. We'll tell you all about *ubuntu*."

Tommy and Doug looked dazed, but they headed down the street with Banner and Braden. When they were a few feet away, the twins glanced over their shoulders at us. Banner winked, and Braden gave us a thumbs up.

My heart swelled with an almost motherly sense of pride. No way of knowing yet if it would stick, but the twins seemed to have embraced their lesson.

I couldn't wait to tell my friends.

31

For the remainder of our short journey, Elyse and I talked about Banner and Braden's about-face in attitude. I told her about the intervention at the gallery, and her eyes filled with hope.

"Maybe the boys and I can actually have a relationship," she said. "Especially if I don't go off to Boulder."

We turned past the lake and walked a short way down a side street to the charming apartment complex where Alexis lived. After climbing the pebbled staircase to her second-floor unit, I knocked gently, hoping the soft sound wouldn't intensify her painful headache.

Elyse leaned her ear to the door. "I hear rustling."

After a few seconds, Alexis's muffled voice came through the door. "Who is it?"

She sounded weak, and I felt a flare of worry. "Alexis, it's Callie and Elyse."

"We came to check on you," Elyse said.

"And bring you food."

The bolt clicked as Alexis turned it, and the door cracked open. In the small gap, her face appeared, pale and drawn. Behind her, all the lights were off, obscuring the interior of the apartment.

Elyse's forehead rumpled in concern. "Are you okay? You look terrible."

"Gee, thanks," Alexis mumbled.

I nudged Elyse in the ribs with my elbow. "You look like a woman with a migraine," I said. "Have you taken anything?"

She brushed a hand across her eyes and squinted into the light. "It's all right. I get them sometimes. I have a prescription. Took it a while ago and slept a little. A couple more hours ought to do the trick. Sorry for missing work. I might be able to get there later today."

"Don't you dare," I said. "Ethan and I will be fine. We just came to see how you're doing." I held the bag forward. "And to bring you lunch. You need to keep your energy up."

She reached an arm through the door and took the bag. Her eyes met mine, and I saw gratitude. "Thank you, Callie. You didn't have to do this for me."

"Do you want me to keep you company?" Elyse asked. "I can get your lunch ready and sit with you while you eat."

Alexis shook her head and grimaced with the pain of the movement. "That's sweet of you, but I think I'll just try to eat and then climb back in bed. Sleep is usually what does the trick."

"We'll leave you to it, then," I said. "But we're only a phone call away if you need anything."

As she closed the door, Alexis gave us a weak smile, and Elyse blew her a kiss.

At the bottom of the stairs, Elyse pulled out her phone and silently read a text. "Hey, would you mind if we split up? A friend wants to meet for coffee at Rocky Mountain High. If it's okay with you, I'll run on ahead."

Before I could decide if that statement was a slam against the slow pace of middle age, my own phone vibrated. When I saw the screen, I waved her on her way. "Go. Have fun. I need to take this call anyway."

She scurried off toward the village as I answered, not sure what I was going to say to Nicole Harrison-White.

"Good morning," was the best I could come up with.

"Callahan, Nicole Harrison-White here. Our attorney,

Saul Sanderson, has arrived in Rock Creek Village. He tells me he has checked into the Knotty Pine resort. I'd like you to meet him there and accompany him to your sheriff's office."

Her condescending words released the temper I'd barely lassoed in last time we talked. "Nicole. Just to let you know, this is not Mayberry. Small though it is, Rock Creek Village is actually graced with a full-fledged police department and top-tier officers and detectives."

A long pause ensued. I expected a reprimand, but instead, Nicole responded with what sounded like amusement, which infuriated me even more. "You're sounding a tad touchy today, Callie."

"Perhaps that's because I'm not used to being treated as an errand girl. Your expectation that I am here to serve you is a misguided one. I no longer work for your newspaper. Therefore, you are not the boss of me."

I cringed at the juvenile phrase. Not particularly the professional, competent image I was trying to create. But I plowed ahead. "However, since the murder occurred in my gallery, and the victim was a former co-worker, I am invested in a successful outcome to the investigation." I paused. "Besides, I like Preston. I'll do whatever I can to help him."

"Ah, yes. I've heard you like him."

"As do you, from the evidence I've collected. Regardless, I don't believe he killed Brie Bohannan, so I am happy to assist in clearing him however I can. Including escorting his attorney to the police station."

A long pause. "I appreciate that, Callie," she said finally. "I apologize for my tone. I realize that I can come across as haughty on occasion, usually when I am especially worried. It was not my intent to treat you badly."

I smiled. Despite everything, I liked this woman. Climbing to the heights she'd reached had taken stamina and grit. And her willingness to apologize only increased my respect for her.

"No worries," I said. "Now, if I'm to get your Mr. Sanderson to his meeting with Preston, I need to run. I'll contact you as soon as I can." We said our goodbyes and disconnected.

I didn't actually run, but I upped my usual pace to power walk speed, which garnered a few amused glances from locals who weren't accustomed to seeing me hightail it anywhere. When I made it to the gallery—sweating and chuffing, but in record time—I paused to catch my breath. Thanks to a not-so-regular exercise program and semi-regular visits to Yoga Delight, I wasn't in the same flabby, couch-potato condition as I'd been when I returned to Rock Creek Village six months ago, but I wasn't ready for a marathon, either.

"Ethan," I said, "I know I'm asking a lot of you today, but I'm going to need to be away for a couple more hours."

"Making a clean getaway?" he asked, noting my breathless state. "Did you rob a bank?"

"Hardy har har. No time to explain right now, but I'll fill you in when I return."

"Sure," he said. "We haven't been that busy since the big sale. But before you go—this emergency isn't about Alexis, is it?"

I reassured him that his co-worker was going to recover, then trotted out the back door to my Civic.

Minutes later, I'd rounded up the attorney, who sat stiffly in my passenger seat, clutching his briefcase in his lap as if it contained the nuclear codes. At a stoplight, I glanced across at him. Mr. Sanderson was a small, mousy man, probably late fifties, with a bushy mustache that looked like a chipmunk sleeping on his lip. In the five minutes we'd been together, he'd barely spoken two words.

"It's good of you to come," I said, attempting to claw through his reticence.

"It's my job," he replied curtly.

I waited for him to elaborate, but nothing was forthcoming. "I've been involved in the investigation from the start," I said. "In fact, I'm the person who found her. Brie, that is. She was, um, in my darkroom. As you probably know, I used to be with *The Sentinel*. Convergence media specialist. You might have heard of me…" I realized I was rambling. "Anyway, I just thought you might have some questions for me."

He stared out the windshield. "I prefer to collect information from my client and the authorities."

All right, then. We drove the rest of the way in silence, and as soon as I pulled into a parking space, Mr. Congeniality exited the car and strode toward the door, without a word of thanks to his chauffeur.

But I wasn't about to sit in the car and await his return. I hurried in after the lawyer and saw him standing at the receiving desk, watching while Marilyn called to summon Raul. As the attorney waited, he glanced at me. "Thank you for providing transportation, Ms. Cassidy. No need to wait. I'll make other arrangements when I've completed my duties here."

He turned away, clearly finished with me. Luckily, I had a thick skin. And I wasn't going anywhere—not until I got my own audience with the detective.

Just then, Raul emerged from the hallway leading to the department's offices and interview rooms. He scanned the waiting room, and when his eyes landed on me, he frowned. When I mouthed, "I need to talk to you," he inhaled, and I figured he was gathering his patience. I tried not to take it personally.

"Take a seat," he said. "I'll be with you as soon as I can." Then he ushered Mr. Sanderson down the hall and out of sight.

32

S hortly" turned out to be twenty minutes, during which time I texted Sam, then Tonya. Both of them were still on for dinner and probably confused about why I was asking. Then I texted Ethan. A few customers, he said, but he could handle it.

I spent a few more minutes worrying, first about Alexis, then about the fact that Sundance Studio wasn't getting much foot traffic this afternoon. The memory of the two men who'd dropped a significant wad of cash this morning helped to ease that concern. Even if no one else made a purchase all day, Bradley and Tim had given us our best day in the gallery's short history.

My phone dinged with a text from Ethan, this one containing a hyperlink. *Check this out*, he said, adding a wide-eyed emoji. When I clicked on it, the breath whooshed out of me. I read the article twice, more slowly the second time. I couldn't believe what I was seeing.

Raul appeared at the end of the hallway then, and gestured for me to join him. When I got out of the chair, I had to look down at my feet to make sure they were firmly planted on the ground and not dancing on a cloud.

"What's with the secret Mona Lisa smile?" he asked.

I shook my head, slightly dazed. "It's too much to go into right now. I'll tell you later, after I've had a chance to digest the news myself."

He narrowed his eyes, and I knew he was debating whether to push me. When you're a detective—or anyone whose career revolves around investigation—it's difficult to be left in the dark.

But he let it go and stepped back so I could precede him into his closet-sized office. Inside, Frank lounged in a metal folding chair, long legs stretched almost across the width of the room. I plopped down into another metal chair, and Raul walked around the desk and sat in yet another metal chair, this one padded. It was good to be the king.

Frank popped a toothpick into the corner of his mouth. "So what's up, Callie? Got some intelligence for us? Other than the breaking news we read in *Sophie's Scoop*?"

"She hasn't posted anything new today, has she?"

"Not that I've seen. I've got Marilyn checking the blog regularly. With you and Sophie solving all the crime in town, Raul and I are becoming irrelevant."

I scowled at him. He was teasing, I realized, but being lumped with Sophie gave me a pit in my stomach. "Listen, Chief Laramie. Do you want to know what I found out or not?"

Frank chuckled. "So it's Chief Laramie now, is it? Of course we want to hear your information. I have a three o'clock tee time. We need you to wrap up the case before then."

"Enough, you two," Raul interrupted. He folded his hands on the desk like a high-school principal. "Callie, we're very busy. As soon as Preston and his lawyer are finished conferring, we'll need to head back in there. What do you need to talk to us about?"

Humph. As if I wanted to spend my day in a tiny room with these two anyway. Still, I had business to attend to myself, so I jumped right in. "First thing: Have you heard from Dev Joshi?"

Raul looked at Frank, who shook his head. Then he flipped through a stack of pink message slips and pulled one out. "Looks like he called about an hour ago. What's it about?"

"I should let him tell you."

"Callie, if you know something, spill it."

I hesitated, but then thought of Preston down the hall planning his defense on murder charges. The police needed all the details. "Okay, but I want it on the record that Dev reached out to you of his own free will."

Raul sighed. "So noted."

"Well, as it turns out, Preston wasn't the only person Brie had been blackmailing." I filled them in on Dev's plagiarized photos, his fear over his career, and his decision to tell Preston the truth and resign. "He confronted Brie hours before she was killed and made it clear her extortion days were over."

As he pondered this, Raul tapped his pen on the desk. He looked at Frank with a silent question. "Yep," Frank said. "Bring him in."

Raul picked up the phone and contacted Officer Tollison, instructing him to collect Dev and bring him to the station. "He's not under arrest," Raul said. "Just tell him we want to ask a few questions."

When he hung up, he looked across the desk at me. "There's more?"

"Yes." I felt the Mona Lisa smile on my face again. "I figured out where the key in Brie's pocket came from."

Frank's eyebrows lifted as Raul's knitted together. "Where?"

"Willie Wright's office." I repeated our conversation, ending with Willie's confession about the key's theft from his unattended, unlocked office. "He said he was going to call you."

Raul checked his messages again and shook his head. Then he shuffled through a stack of pink message slips on his desk. "Nope."

I bit my lip. "Maybe he was putting it off until the end of business today. I know he's very concerned about the information getting leaked. He thinks it'll ruin his reputation and cost him his Chamber presidency."

Raul tossed the stack of messages onto his desk. "You know, it would've been nice to know all this before Preston's lawyer got here."

"If you're blaming me, you can stop right there." I folded my arms. "I've called you any number of times and left several voicemails. It's not my fault you couldn't be bothered—"

"I've been a little busy, as you can see." He swept a hand across the piles of paper on his desk. "Sorry I didn't have time to listen to you trolling for details on the investigation."

Frank raised his hands. "That'll do, both of you." He rubbed his chin, thinking. "Seems like our deductions were right, Sanchez."

"What deductions?" I asked. Neither man answered. "Hey. Remember that the victim was a woman I used to work with. She was killed in my darkroom. The suspects are people I know. I'm deeply involved here. Besides, I've done a lot of your legwork. You owe me."

As Frank stifled a grin, Raul bristled. But finally, he leaned back in his chair. "We've decided it's unlikely Preston is the murderer. We'll let the lawyer do his dance, but we're not going to argue against his request for bail."

"What changed your minds?"

Raul shot Frank a glance but neither man would my eyes. "Gut feeling," Raul said. "Mostly, anyway. Garrison seems too polished. Not the type to get his hands dirty."

I studied one man then the other, and I knew I wasn't getting the whole story. "There's more to it, isn't there? Tell me."

Frank's face had colored slightly. He cleared his throat. "Turns out Garrison has an alibi. An…online site…he visited. Video chats that would be difficult to fake. And that's all we're prepared to say."

My mind raced. Internet records? Video chats? Something that made Frank blush? I chased my thoughts down a distasteful path. Ugh. This just kept getting seedier.

Happily, a knock at the door saved us from further embarrassment. "Detectives?" Marilyn popped her head through the opening. "Mr. Sanderson says he's concluded his consultation with his client."

She backed out of the office, and the three of us stood. "Callie, thank you for the information," Frank said. "Rest assured, we will pursue your leads. Even if it means canceling my tee time."

He sauntered off down the hall, but Raul paused beside me. "One more thing. We tracked down Jameson Jarrett. Credit card records confirm what you told us—he's in Miami, apparently celebrating his release in high style. Bar and restaurant tabs in the hundreds of dollars this week alone. Hardesty called Jarrett's mother, and she confirms he's staying with her."

I nodded. I'd figured as much, but it was still a relief to hear it.

"Will you let Chief Cassidy know?"

I gave a little snort. "Does Frank know? If so, I'd guess my father does, too."

"You're probably right." He gave me a serious look. "I'm sure it's too much to ask that you stay out of this. So I'll just tell you to get in touch if you hear anything."

"I'll try," I said. "But it's up to you to pick up the phone."

I waved at Marilyn on my way out of the station. Mr. Sanderson had assured me he no longer needed my services, so I felt no sense of obligation to him, or to Nicole, to stick around. I slid inside my car and shut the door, closing my eyes. It had been a long day—a long week—and stress threatened to consume me. I took a moment to implement a meditation strategy my therapist had taught me, breathing in for a count of four and out for a count of eight. I let my mind empty of all thought. The method worked so well that I nearly dozed off. After giving myself a full body shake, I turned the key in the ignition, rolled down the windows to get some fresh air, and pulled out of the parking lot.

As I drove, I let my mind roam, free from thoughts of murder or suspects or lawyers. The radio played an old John Mayer tune, and I sang along. A stoplight at the entrance to the park turned yellow, and rather than blow through it as I would have when I was a city girl, I rolled to a stop.

Across the park, a family picnicked on a blanket. Nearby, a boy threw a Frisbee to a yapping border collie. Then my gaze landed on a bench near the water. Two figures sat next to each other, and when I squinted, I could see that the one on the left was Sophie Demler. The other woman's face was partially hidden, but I recognized her. It was Melanie Lewis. And she didn't look happy.

33

Reverting to my big city ways, I jerked the steering wheel and made an abrupt right onto the little road leading into the park. The move earned me an angry honk from the car I cut off, but no harm, no foul.

I parked and jumped out of the car, trotting the short distance to the park bench. Sophie looked up as I approached, and I wasn't surprised at her lack of enthusiasm when she saw me coming. She clutched the phone in her hand a little more tightly.

Crouching in front of Melanie, I put a hand on her knee. "Everything okay?"

She snuffled and wiped the back of her hand under her nose, then put that hand on mine. I resisted the urge to run back to the car for my hand sanitizer. "No," she said, a sob catching in her throat. "Nothing's all right. I just…I just…" Her voice hitched, and she covered her face with her hands.

Sophie's lips were tight, but her eyes gleamed. She wanted to be mad at me, but even more, she wanted to spill some gossip. "Dev broke up with her," she said, her voice verging on gleeful.

The words caused Melanie to sob harder. Sophie tightened her grip around the young woman's shoulder. "There, there," she said, in an almost passable imitation of compassion. "Keep talking. You'll feel better."

After a few more snuffles, Melanie regained some composure. "He said it's over. That he's starting a new life, and there's no room for me." Her face contorted, and I feared she was going to plummet back into sobbing incoherence.

But she rallied and looked at me with pleading eyes. "He said he talked to you, Callie. I know he likes you, respects you even. Maybe you can convince him to give me another chance."

I shook my head, but kept my tone sympathetic. "It's not my place, Melanie."

Her demeanor changed in an instant. She leapt up from the bench, nearly knocking me over in the process. Her face was a mask of rage. "Just leave me alone, then. Both of you. I'll take care of Dev myself." She stormed across the grass in the direction of the lodge.

Sophie and I stared at each other in shock. I rose from my crouch and sat beside her on the bench. "What was all that about?" I asked.

She flipped up her palms. "I only just got here. She didn't tell me anything more than what you heard: the photographer broke up with her. If you talked to Dev, you probably know more than I do. Give me the scoop, Callie. After breaking my phone last night, you owe me."

She leaned toward me, close enough that I could smell her breath. Nothing particularly unpleasant about it, but still. I scooted over until my back pressed against the armrest.

"Sophie, even if I did know something significant, what makes you think I'd share it with you? You said some nasty things about me in your last blog. Then you tried to take pictures of my former boss—my friend—in the back of a police car."

She harrumphed. "Whatever. My blog will post in the morning regardless. I'll simply find other sources." She rose and wiggled her fingers. "Toodle-ooo, Callie. You know how to reach me if you change your mind."

By the time I got back to Sundance Studio, I'd shaken off the strange conversation. The rest of the afternoon flew by as Ethan and I tended to customers. I spent an hour in my office ordering canvases from my vendor to fill the empty spaces on the walls. We barely even had time to talk about the link Ethan had sent me, or to revel in its importance.

When we finally flipped the sign to Closed and locked the door at six o'clock, I had to rush home. Sam and Elyse were swinging by my house in fifteen minutes so we could all go to Mom and Dad's together—and we knew better than to be late for any event hosted by Maggie Cassidy. For Mom, on time means five minutes early.

As we parked at the lodge, Tonya pulled in beside us. She smooched Woody and stuck a finger through the mesh of the carrier on my back to stroke Carl's back. We walked through the lobby and upstairs. Mom emerged from the kitchen carrying serving bowls steaming with mashed potatoes and green beans, and Mrs. Finney followed behind with a bottle of wine in each hand.

"Perfect timing," Mom said, as Dad came in from the balcony with a platter of sizzling steaks. We settled around the dining table. Wine flowed and silverware clattered as everyone passed plates and served themselves food. We laughed and talked over each other the way families do, and I felt as content as I could ever remember.

As long as I kept the knowledge of an at-large murderer at bay.

I watched Mom eyeing Tonya with burgeoning curiosity. Finally, she couldn't take it another second. "So, Tonya," she said, "anything new with you?"

Tonya gave me a sidelong look. I raised my fingers to my lips and made a locking motion. "I've said nothing to anyone. I swear it on my Felden."

She gave me a skeptical look and quickly took a bite of steak, chewing as she pointed at her mouth. "Can't talk right now. Rude."

"Don't worry, I'll wait. I have the patience of a saint."

We all laughed, and Mom pursed her lips. "Hey! I'm the most patient person you all know."

Mrs. Finney pointed her fork at my mother. "The image we see in the mirror is not the one we project into the universe."

My mother waved a hand in front of her face, as if fanning a flame. "Oh dear. Are you implying I occasionally come across as…short-tempered?"

Sam lifted a glass. "I think you're perfect just as you are, Maggie."

I elbowed him in the ribs. "Suck-up."

Mom turned to Tonya and wagged a finger. "Don't think for a second this little sidebar is getting you out of spilling the beans. You have a secret, and I want to know what it is." She swept a hand around the table. "You're among family here. Now talk."

A sly smile crossed Tonya's face. "Fine. But if I talk, you each owe me a secret in return. Not today, necessarily, but at a time of my choosing."

"You drive a hard bargain," Dad said. "But I'm in. I have no secrets anyway."

"Maybe not now," Tonya said. "But someday you'll have one, and when you do, it's mine."

"Enough chatter," Mom said. "Tell us."

Tonya foraged in her pocket and pulled out a small jewelry box. She opened it and swept it around so each of us could get a peek. Inside, a platinum plated ring twinkled in the light, cradling a diamond roughly the size of my kneecap.

Six sets of eyes widened in shock, including my own. Elyse squealed. Sam gasped. Only Mrs. Finney seemed unsurprised, her lips curling up in her famous Cheshire cat grin.

Everyone began talking at once.

"Are you engaged?"

"Wait, is this from David Parisi?"

"Did you say yes?"

"How did he propose?"

Tonya's laugh tinkled like wind chimes, and her eyes gleamed. She looked genuinely happy. I reached across the table and put my hand over hers. "Did you say yes?"

"Not yet."

"Not *yet*," I repeated. "Does that mean…?"

"Listen, you guys. As close as I feel to all of you at this moment, it doesn't seem fair for you to have my answer before he does. So let's drop the subject for now, okay? You'll all be the second to know."

Mom put a hand to her chest. "Oh my goodness. She's going to say yes. I'm going to be a surrogate mother-in-law." She paused. "Tonya, have you told your mother?"

I cringed. Tonya's relationship with her mother, who currently resided in Las Vegas, could at best be labeled tumultuous. Mom knew this, and I wondered why she'd broach the subject right now.

"Not yet," Tonya said quietly. "I'm waiting until I make a final decision."

"Well, let's you and I chat about it over coffee, maybe tomorrow." Tonya nodded, and Mom lightened the mood by clapping her hands cheerfully. "This is big news, people. It calls for cake, don't you agree?"

Dad and Sam helped clear the table as Mom prepared the pièce de résistance. When everyone was ready, she called out from the kitchen. "Close your eyes."

Everyone complied—at least, I assume they did, since I followed orders. Rustling ensued, and we heard the sound of the cake being placed upon the table. "Open them."

The cake was gorgeous, and we collectively oohed and aahed over it, much to Mom's delight. "It's my last practice effort," she said. "The next one I make will be for the competition. Do you think it's good enough?"

"It's gorgeous," Elyse said. "The meadow, the flowers— I can almost smell them. It's so…Rock Creek Village. It's perfect."

Mom's cheeks flushed with pleasure. "Thank you, one and all. If I keep at it, who knows?" She turned to Tonya. "Maybe I'll be ready to tackle a wedding cake."

34

After the cake—as delectable as it was attractive—Mrs. Finney took her leave, saying, "Coffee shop owners must rise before the sun." Tonya departed soon after, but not before Mom issued her a stern warning. "I'll expect to hear from you in the morning."

The rest of us engaged in dish duty, making quick work of it. Then Sam and Elyse and I thanked my parents for the delicious meal and trekked down the stairs.

When we exited through the lobby's sliding doors, cool night air carried the scent of oncoming rain. I worried that Willie's meteorological predictions would come to pass after all. But in the spirit of mindfulness, I accepted my lack of control over the weather. What would be, would be.

I had just finished securing Woody and Carl into the backseat of Sam's car when a white BMW whipped into the parking lot, pulling into an adjacent spot. Mr. Sanderson, Preston's attorney, stepped out of the driver's seat. He hadn't been messing around when he told me he'd make his own transportation arrangements. His rental made my Honda look like a jalopy.

The passenger door opened, and Preston emerged, staggering slightly. I'd never seen him look so haggard and defeated. Without thinking, I walked over to him and gave him a quick hug. "Preston, I'm so happy you've been released. What wonderful news."

Behind me, Sam cleared his throat. "Callie, we really ought to be going."

I shot him a look. "Give me a second." Then I turned to Preston. "How are you? You look tired."

He rubbed his face. "The accommodations weren't especially conducive to rest." He sighed. "I've been released, yes, but your detective strongly urged me to stick around."

Mr. Sanderson circled the front of the car. "Mr. Garrison, I'd advise you not to discuss your case with…" He gave me a sidelong look. "Anyone."

I put my hands on my hips. "Mr. Sanderson, I'm not just anyone. I'm his friend. All I've been doing is trying to help."

Preston smiled weakly. "It's okay, Callie. I'm exhausted, and all I want right now is a hot shower and a soft mattress. How about if I call you tomorrow?"

Mr. Sanderson coughed. "Mr. Garrison, I strongly advise—"

Preston raised a hand, and I was pleased to see a spark of the old Garrison defiance. "We'll discuss your strong advice tomorrow." He bowed his head to Sam, and then to me. "Goodnight, all." As he trudged off to the lodge. Sanderson turned to follow, but not before shooting me a warning scowl.

Sam leaned against the passenger door of the car with his arms folded. Perhaps sensing an oncoming storm that had nothing to do with the sky, Elyse had already climbed into the backseat beside the dog and cat. She pretended to read from her phone screen, but I noticed a few worried glances in our direction.

I stared at my boyfriend. "Don't get huffy, Sam. Preston is a friend."

"He's been accused of murder, Callie."

"So were you once. And I stood by you."

His frown wavered. "Touché." He shook his head in resignation. "Things would be much simpler if you weren't right so much of the time."

I kissed him lightly on the lips and got in the car. Twisting in the seat, I smiled at Elyse. "Storm averted," I said. "Your dad is a reasonable man."

She answered without looking up from her phone. "You've obviously never asked him for money."

Sam fastened his seat belt, started the car, and pulled out of the parking lot. When we passed the street leading to Alexis's apartment complex, I turned back to Elyse. "Have you heard anything from Alexis?"

"I talked to her before we picked you up. She said she's feeling a lot better and expects to be back to work in the morning."

"That's good. What about her boy troubles? Any news on that front?"

Elyse was quiet for a moment, and I saw Sam glance at her in the rearview mirror. "I know you mean well, Callie," she said. "I'm just don't feel right talking about things Alexis told me privately. It feels…icky."

I faced forward in my seat in a rush of shame. "Of course," I said. "I never meant to put you in an awkward position. Sometimes…I revert into reporter mode. Some things are none of my business. I'm sorry."

"No big deal," she said nonchalantly. I sneaked a look at her over my shoulder and saw she was already engrossed in her phone again.

Sam pulled the car to the curb in front of my townhome. When I opened the back door of his car to gather Woody and Carl, Elyse smiled at me warmly. "No hard feelings?"

"Not a one. I'm grateful you were up front with me. I hope you'll always let me know if I'm crossing the line."

Woody trotted to the front door, and I slung Carl's carrier over my shoulder. Ever the gentleman, Sam walked me to my door. "Elyse is spending the night at a friend's tonight. Want me to come back over after I drop her off? I can bring dessert."

"After the cake we just ate? Do you want me to turn into a blimp?"

He ran his hands down my arms. "First of all, I wasn't talking about that kind of dessert. Secondly, I'd love you even if you weighed four hundred pounds."

I felt a flush crawl up my neck. That word again. "Sam, you keep saying…"

His mouth was smiling, but his eyes were serious. "I know perfectly well what I keep saying, Callie. I've felt this way for a long time. I'm just waiting for you to catch up. But I'm a patient man, twenty-five years' worth. Though I must admit, I didn't expect Tonya to get engaged before us."

My heart pounded. I fought the urge to run like an escaped convict. At my feet, Woody whined, and on my back, Carl clawed at the mesh carrier and meowed. I shifted uncomfortably from one foot to the other.

Then I made myself look into Sam's eyes, and an unexpected sense of peace filled me. Suddenly, it all felt so right. I reached up and cupped his face in my hands, felt his fingers tighten on my waist. "I love you too," I whispered, and kissed him.

After the kiss…and subsequent hug…then one more kiss…I convinced him a long day awaited me tomorrow and I needed to get some sleep. When he reluctantly released me, I went inside and put my eye to the peephole, watching as he walked to his car. Halfway down the sidewalk, he turned back and smiled at the closed door. I touched my lips. Love? Like Tonya, I asked myself, was this the real thing?

I made my way to the kitchen, released Carl from his carrier, and poured myself a glass of wine. My head was spinning, adrenaline pumping, blood racing through my veins. The clock on the oven read nine-thirty. Despite my busy day tomorrow, I realized sleep was a long way off.

The only way to calm my chirping nerves was to chase the niggles in my brain.

Settling on the couch, I pulled a legal pad onto my lap and began making a list of facts and persons of interest.

Melanie: Brie had info about her family's mental health. Jealous of Brie and Dev. Best story assignments go to Brie. Prone to rage, mood swings.

Dev: Brie had evidence of his plagiarism. Could ruin his career. Left happy hour to find her. Access to rental van? Weak alibi.

Preston: Blackmail—affair with Nicole. Career on the line. Brie's phone in rental van. Caught sneaking out of Brie's room.

Then I added a list of all the clues I knew.

1. Key in Brie's pocket—sent to her anonymously.
2. Contents of envelope hidden in Brie's suite.
3. Broken fingernail.

I tapped my pen against my chin. I was missing something. Finally, it popped into my mind.

4. Plastic tubing found in darkroom.

I examined the list. All these people had motive, yes, and perhaps each was capable of killing in a moment of rage. But premeditated murder? Something felt off. I needed more.

With a groan, I slammed the laptop shut and gulped down the rest of my wine. Whatever I was missing, I wouldn't figure it out tonight. A busy day of Fireweed Festival preparation loomed tomorrow, and I couldn't afford to face it exhausted.

I let Woody outside for one last bathroom visit, then shut off the lights, checked the locks on both doors, and climbed the stairs, hearing the wind howl in the eaves. Woody stayed close behind me, with his wet nose nudging my calf at every step. When we entered the bedroom, I flipped on the light to find Carl posted beside the French doors with his back arched. He stared through the sheer curtains and issued a mournful wail.

My exhaustion evaporated, replaced with a racing pulse. I tiptoed toward the door and pulled the curtains back a smidge, already anticipating what I'd see.

The figure stood on the sidewalk beneath my window, just outside the pool of light from a nearby streetlamp. In addition to the hood, the person wore a scarf wrapped around the bottom of their face. I couldn't make out their features, but I didn't doubt for a second it was the same person I'd seen there before.

Unlike the last appearance, this time I knew the person wasn't merely a passerby. The presence in front of my house was no coincidence.

35

J ust before dawn the next morning, I went downstairs, treading as lightly as possible toward the living room. Though the sun had yet to rise, ambient light filtered in through the window. I smiled as I gazed down at Sam, asleep on the couch with one long leg flung out from beneath the blanket. Woody roused on the floor behind him, wagging quietly. Carl kept watch from the hearth, his green eyes glowing through the shadows.

Sam snorted softly and rolled to his side, his breathing deep and regular. My heart swelled. Love was so easy when the object of your affection was sound asleep.

I dropped to my knees beside the couch and smoothed back his tousled hair before planting a soft kiss on his forehead. He stirred, maybe even smiled, but didn't wake. As I watched him, the events of the night before replayed in my mind. When I'd spotted the stranger outside, I'd eased open the French door and duckwalked onto the balcony, intending to snap the intruder's picture with my phone. But the masked, hooded figure must have sensed my presence because he, or she, hurried away before I could get a shot.

Despite my earlier bravado, the visit had shaken me. Throughout my often dangerous career, I'd never had someone stalk me at my home. So, feeling chagrined at the hit to my image, I'd called Sam.

To his credit, he'd given no rebuke or lecture. He'd just showed up. Once he'd taken me in his arms and determined for himself that I was unharmed, he handed me a piece of paper he'd found affixed to the door when he arrived.

A blurry picture of a body bag on a stretcher.

Some back and forth ensued: Sam wanted to call the police right away, while I argued that was an overreaction. He pointed out that, when he'd used the same word, I'd thrown a fit. I said that was different…and on we went. Someone was trying to scare me—and admittedly, doing a decent job—but I refused to offer them the satisfaction of summoning the police in the middle of the night.

We compromised, sealing the offending paper in a plastic sandwich bag and agreeing I'd call Raul in the morning. But Sam was unbudging when I told him I'd recovered from my scare and he could go home. Without engaging in any discussion, he'd taken a blanket from the closet and stretched out on the couch. I laid next to him for an hour or so, talking—mostly. After that, I'd calmed down enough to sleep, and I headed up to bed.

Now, I ran my fingers through Sam's silky hair. It was a little longer than he normally wore it, and his usually clean-shaven face carried a three-day scruff. Both were casualties of too many hours at the cafe and not enough time for personal grooming. But in my opinion, it only made him that much more handsome.

"Wake up, sleepyhead," I murmured. "You said you needed to be up by five-thirty to get to the cafe."

Without opening his eyes, he pulled me toward him. "No time for shenanigans," I whispered into his ear. "You're already running late, and you still have to go home to shower and change before you go to the Chow. We'll have tongues wagging if you show up in yesterday's clothes."

"Let them wag," he mumbled against my cheek. "Rodger can handle the breakfast crowd."

He kissed my neck. For a moment, I closed my eyes and let him continue, but then I scrambled up and tugged his arm. "Enough. Get moving. You'll thank me later when you realize I've protected your fragile reputation."

Reluctantly, Sam finally slipped on his shoes and left, but not before reminding me of my promise to call Raul.

After Sam departed, Woody slammed into the closed pet door, shaking his head in confusion. "Sorry, pooch," I said, as I unlocked the cover and removed it. In an abundance of caution, Sam and I had secured the door last night, as if a small intruder might crawl inside through a doggie door. Tentatively, Woody tried again and then disappeared outside. As usual, Carl displayed no interest in the great outdoors. He primly strolled to his litter box in the laundry area.

I yawned. The hour was too early for me, but there was no sense going back to bed. Besides, with the Fireweed Festival slated to open tomorrow, a lot of work awaited me. After shooting a quick text to Raul, I went upstairs and readied myself for the day. With any luck, I could get some quality time in the darkroom before Ethan and, hopefully, Alexis showed up.

Two hours in the darkroom flew by like minutes. The alarm I'd set on my phone warbled at nine-thirty. Time to get the gallery ready for the ten a.m. opening. Today's goal involved printing sixty postcards and forty five-by-seven prints, which would then need to be matted. I'd managed to make a dent, but there was much more to be done.

I turned on the white lights and washed my hands in the darkroom sink, drying them on a towel as I made my way down the hall. A quick peek into the office assured me the creatures were sleeping peacefully on their beds in their home-away-from-home. I headed into the gallery, flipping on lights and opening the front blinds. When I turned the bolt on the door, it flew open immediately, nearly knocking me over in the process. Raul marched inside.

"Let me see that note," he grumbled.

"Wow. Like, 'Good morning, Callie. How are you today?

Do you have a minute to talk?'"

He jiggled his fingers. "No time for pleasantries. Hand it over."

Apparently, no time for complete sentences, either. I walked over to the sales counter to retrieve the baggie and gave it to him.

"Why didn't you call me last night?"

"Even if I had, who knew if you'd answer?" I retorted. "You didn't even respond to my text this morning—just showed up when the whim hit you."

He ignored my sarcasm and studied the note briefly through the plastic before tucking it in his pocket. "Doubt we'll get any fingerprints, but I'll have the techs take a look. Ratliff boys, you think? Another prank?"

I shook my head. "Their vandalism days are over. I'd be willing to bet on that."

He cocked an eyebrow. "Any idea who it might be, then? Did your mystery man exhibit any particular characteristics? Mannerisms?"

"First of all, I'm not even sure *he* is a he. I thought so at first, but the more I think about it, the more I realize I'm just projecting. The person wore a bulky, zip-up sweatshirt and a hood. The bottom of the face was covered with a scarf. I can't even narrow down an age range, though instinct tells me the figure moved more like a young person. I tried to get a photo—"

"You *what*?" His brow furrowed. "Are you saying you went outside?"

"Just on the balcony. But the person ran off."

A beat of silence. Then another. It appeared Raul was quietly counting to ten. Finally, he said, "I would advise you to exercise some caution, but it's never any use with you."

I waved off his irritation. "We've had this conversation numerous times, Raul. I'm not reckless. I take necessary precautions. Let's not waste time with your lecture and my rebuttal. We're both too busy for that."

His jaw tensed, but he relented. "You have a point. I'm

already late for a meeting. Garrison's lawyer is raising a stink, wants us to let him leave the jurisdiction. In the meantime…" He paused. "Never mind. Just—take care of yourself."

As he exited, Ethan and Alexis entered. "Whew," Alexis said, smoothing her frizzy hair. "I have a feeling we're going to get a gully washer."

Ethan snorted. "What twenty-year-old says *gully washer*? You sound like an old woman in a rocker on her front porch shelling peas."

She pointed at me with a mischievous grin. "I heard it from her."

I laughed and looked my young employee up and down. Aside from her wind-blown hair, she appeared ready for the day. She wore khaki slacks, a turquoise polo shirt, and light gray sneakers. Her cheeks were rosy from the wind.

"You seem fully recovered," I observed.

She walked behind the sales counter and tucked her purse into a drawer. "Migraine meds are the bomb. I'm back to a hundred percent and ready for duty."

"What's in those meds?" Ethan quipped. "I could use some myself. I'm not nearly as perky as you."

"What kind of twenty-eight-year-old says *perky*?" she quipped.

I smiled at their banter. "Well, I'm happy to hear you're all better, Alexis. Because if Ethan agrees to handle customers this morning, I want to recruit you for some darkroom work. I have more prints to develop than I have time, and you said before you'd like to learn. Interested?"

She bounced on the balls of her feet with an enthusiasm she'd never displayed before. "Yes, yes, and more yes. I've been ready for weeks."

Ethan said he'd take care of the gallery, and Alexis and I headed to the darkroom, stopping briefly at the office so she could give Woody a hug. As always, she and Carl ignored each other. "I'm not what you'd call a cat person," she told me. "But I'd take this dog home with me in a heartbeat."

"Not so fast." I reached down to rub Woody's belly. "I've grown pretty attached to him myself." Then I stretched out a finger and stroked Carl's spine. "I didn't think I was a cat person either, once upon a time. But when Woody persuaded me to adopt this guy, all that changed. I admit it, I'm smitten with the kitten. If I could only get him to perform a high-five by Sunday…"

We left the creatures to their rough day of napping and continued into the darkroom. Inside, we slipped on goggles and gloves. I'd already filled the chemical trays in the deep sink, and I spent a few minutes training my helper on the relatively simple developing process. The enlargement process—turning negatives into prints—was a more challenging lesson. It also had to be conducted in complete darkness, so we choreographed a method by which one of us could be at the enlarger while the other used the developing trays, and then we'd switch.

It took some time, but we eventually established a rhythm. Alexis turned out to be a quick study.

"You're a natural," I told her. We'd stopped for a moment to turn on the overhead fluorescent lights so I could assess her first independent print. "The colors are nearly perfect. I'd add a little more magenta to enrich the fireweed—" I pointed at the cluster of wildflowers in the photo, "—but the other tones are just right."

She beamed at the praise. We turned out the lights and continued creating. I'd expose a photo, then while I was processing it, she'd do an exposure of her own. After about an hour, we were comfortable enough with the procedure to allow for conversation as we worked.

"This is fun," Alexis said. "But I don't really understand why you do it this way. Seems like it would be faster, and probably even cheaper, to print in bulk through a company with dedicated machinery."

"It would, for sure. But I prefer to do it here. For one thing, like you said, it's just plain fun. I've always enjoyed darkroom work. Seeing an image come to life right in front of my eyes is the ultimate creative experience."

"Almost like giving birth," she said. "Except without the grunting and the pain."

I chuckled. "Exactly. Also, you may not realize this about me, but I'm a bit of a control freak." She snorted. "If I sent these off to be printed, I wouldn't be able to get the blues exactly as I wanted, or the precise cropping. And last, printing photos here makes each work unique, in a sense. Even if I display a dozen photos of the same scene, I can honestly say each of them has been hand-crafted. It makes a nice selling point."

She nodded. "I've heard customers refer to the postcards as Callahan Cassidy originals."

We worked in silence for a few minutes as I considered whether to move on to more personal subject matter. I wanted to get to know this girl, but I didn't want to invade her privacy. I decided to go for it, starting with what I thought would be a benign topic.

"So, you said you'd been enrolled at the university until this semester. What made you decide to quit?"

Through the darkness, I heard a chuff. "Why do boomers all believe if you don't go to college, you're a failure?"

So much for benign. "First of all, I'm too young to be a boomer. Secondly, I didn't say that at all, and I don't believe it. A lot of happy, successful people don't have a college diploma hanging on their walls. Sam, for instance. I wasn't judging you, just making small talk."

After a brief hesitation, she said, "Sorry. Guess I'm a little defensive on that subject." She paused, and I heard her remove photo paper from its container. "I dropped out because continuing seemed like a waste of money. I didn't have any real direction or sense of purpose. I enrolled in a bunch of classes I didn't care about and felt, I don't know, like I was drifting." The enlarger easel snapped shut, and I saw a brief flare of light as Alexis exposed the photo paper, then felt a tiny breeze as she moved past me in the dark. "Honestly, this is the first thing I've enjoyed in a long time."

I smiled at her, though I knew she couldn't see it. "I'm glad to hear it. Because now I can push you as hard as I want while I sit in my office and drink margaritas."

She giggled. "Works for me."

"But for now," I said, "let this one be your last print. We've already exceeded my goal for the morning. Let's clean up and get some lunch."

When we entered the gallery, currently devoid of customers, Ethan looked up from his seat at the computer. "Been this slow all morning?" I asked.

"Steady trickle," he said, pointing to the window. "Inside and out."

I went to the front and gazed outside. Raindrops speckled the window and ran down the glass in tiny rivulets. A gusty breeze whipped the awning. I chewed my thumbnail in concern. "They're supposed to shut down Evergreen Way tonight and start setting up the canopies. But unless this weather calms down—"

The door crashed open before I could finish the thought, flinging a spray of water across the floor. Startled, I took a step back, as a soaked, bedraggled Melanie Lewis sloshed across the threshold.

36

Melanie stood shivering in the doorway, tendrils of wet hair pasted across her mouth like tentacles. Rain dripped from the tip of her nose, from her chin, and from the fists clenched at her sides. A puddle quickly formed beneath her feet.

"Is he here? Is he with you?" she demanded.

Like a freeze frame in a movie, no one moved. Then the film reel jerked forward. Ethan saw the rabid look in her eyes and moved in front of me protectively. Alexis rushed into the hall, and I heard the storage room door creak open.

As Alexis hurried back with an oversized towel, I came to life and moved past Ethan. "Is who here? Do you mean Dev?"

Alexis started patting Melanie's soaking hair, her shoulders, her legs. Then she wrapped the towel around the woman's shoulders and steered her toward a guest chair.

But Melanie had no desire for consolation or comfort. She tossed the towel to the floor. "He was supposed to meet me for breakfast this morning. We were going to talk things over. Reconcile, I thought. When he didn't show up in the lobby as we'd planned, I figured he'd changed his mind. I called him over and over, but he didn't pick up."

"Have you checked his cabin?" I asked.

She finally collapsed onto the chair and reached for the

towel, rubbing it across her face. "I knocked on his door, but he didn't answer. I thought he was just being a jerk, so I went up to my room and had a good cry. Then I got mad. But now…thinking of what happened to Brie…" Her eyes widened. "Oh no! The darkroom. Could he be—?"

I crouched in front of her, my hands on her knees. "Calm down, Melanie. Take a breath. Alexis and I have spent all morning in the darkroom. Dev's not there. I'm sure he's safe and sound, off somewhere thinking. When's the last time you actually spoke to him?"

She looked at me with weepy eyes. "Midnight maybe. He was upbeat, excited even. He said he'd talked to you by the creek and after that he'd gone out shooting pictures. People, he said. Landscapes. Fun stuff. He said he was sitting on his bed going through the photos and thought they were good, that he might even be able to make a living like you do. I thought…" She turned away, tears dribbling down her cheeks. "I thought he was going to invite me to join him on his new adventure. Then, when he didn't show…"

Her breath began to hitch, and I feared she was about to hyperventilate. "Put your head between your knees," I instructed, gently pushing her forward. Once her respirations began to come more regularly, she sat up. "I'm sure Dev's fine," I said. "He probably got so excited over thoughts of the future that he went out on another shoot. You'll find him." But I could feel my own apprehension growing. Shooting photos in this storm? *Was* Dev fine?

In a small voice, Melanie said, "Will you help me look for him?"

I glanced at Alexis and Ethan. "Go," Alexis said. "We'll handle things here."

Ethan nodded. "No worries. Just keep us posted."

I gestured toward the office. "The creatures have food and water, and Carl has a litter box. But Woody will probably need to go out soon…"

"Callie, we've got this," Alexis said, as I rose to my feet. "You two go find Dev."

I looked out the front window. The rain came down even more heavily now, in sideways squalls. "We'll have to take my car." I grabbed my raincoat and led Melanie out the back door.

I drove down Evergreen Way, working the windshield wipers full speed. We parked at the Knotty Pine and splashed across the lot toward Dev's cabin. Melanie had tried to call him again in the car, but he still didn't answer. We hurried onto the covered porch, and I pounded on the door. Nothing. Melanie tried the knob, but the door was still locked. I went to the window, cupped my hands around my face, and peered into the dimly lit interior.

When my eyes adjusted, I sucked in a breath. "Did you see this?"

She rushed over to the window. "Oh no!" she cried.

The room in disarray, as if it had been ransacked. Drawers pulled from the dresser, clothes strewn across the floor, overturned chairs. Someone had definitely been looking for something in this cabin.

Melanie's hands flew to her temples. "I didn't even think to look through the window. What if he's inside, injured?"

"I don't see any signs of him, or that he's been hurt, but we need to get inside. I'm going to run over to the lodge and get the master key. Stay here."

She turned back to the window and rubbed the glass with her sleeve, pressing her forehead against it. I hesitated, worried she might try to break the glass. But there was no more time to waste. I pulled up the hood of my raincoat and sprinted across the wet path.

When Dad saw me, he jumped to his feet. "Callie, what is it?"

I explained the situation, and he snatched up the master key. He ran through the lobby door and through the downpour, his speed that of a man twenty years younger. When he sprang onto the cabin's porch, where Melanie waited, he thrust the keycard into the electronic lock, turned the knob, and shoved the door inward, flicking on the light switch. He swiveled to face us and held up a hand. "Stay here, both of you."

I didn't even bother to respond. I simply rushed in behind him, with Melanie on my heels.

The tiny cabin didn't require much in the way of an all-out search. Dad checked the bathroom, pulling aside the shower curtain to reveal an empty tub. Every other inch of the space was visible from the doorway, and there was no sign of Dev. I dropped to my knees and peeked under the bed. Nothing there but an empty suitcase.

Dad put a hand on Melanie's back and guided her gently toward the door. "Let's get out of here before we contaminate the scene any further."

We stood on the porch. Melanie shivered. Dad pulled his cell phone from his pocket. "I'll call it in," he said.

"T-to the police?" Melanie stammered. "Then you think—"

She crumpled, and Dad put an arm around her to steady her. He looked her in the eye, projecting the soothing demeanor I'd seen since I was a child. "I don't think anything in particular. The police simply have more resources available for a search than the three of us can muster. They'll be better equipped to find Dev."

His manner had the desired soothing effect. Melanie nodded and steadied herself on her feet as Dad made the call. My brain, on the other hand, went into overdrive. Despite Dad's calming words, I knew something bad had gone down in that cabin. I didn't believe for a second that Dev had disappeared for more alone time.

As I gazed into the distance, trying to sort things out, an empty plastic bag skittered across the sidewalk, blown by a puff of wind. I followed it with my eyes. The bag bounced across the grass and then over a bright red object lying a few yards away. I narrowed my eyes. It was a shoe. I flashed to a memory of Dev by the creek, wearing a pair of red Converse shoes. Without uttering a word, I jumped off the porch and charged toward the bridge behind the resort.

"Callahan Cassidy!" Dad yelled. "Where do you think you're going?"

I didn't stop. The rain lashed against my cheeks as I raced onto the bridge. When I reached the middle, I swiveled my head, scanning the creek bed. Nothing. Then I crossed to the other side of the bridge. My eyes searched through the mud and ground cover. Ten yards away, I saw a lump that could be...

Leaning across the rail, I squinted. Yes. I spotted a patch of red and followed it up a leg, across a torso, to a face.

It was Dev, sprawled motionless on the ground with his face turned toward the torrential sky.

37

D ad!" I waved my arms above my head as if I were guiding an airplane to its gate. He leapt off the porch and ran toward me. As soon as I saw that he was on the move, I scrambled around the end of the bridge and stumbled across the muddy creek banks.

A bolt of lightning flashed across the sky, followed by a crack of thunder. The creek rushed angrily across the rocks. A chubby marmot emerged from behind a boulder and darted toward the trees.

Remembering my earlier slide down the bank, I slowed my pace. One false move and I could end up breaking a bone, rendering me useless to Dev. I heard Dad behind me, but I didn't pause to look back. My foot sank ankle-deep into the mud, and I yanked it free with a squelch, nearly losing my shoe.

After what felt like a slow-motion film reel, I reached Dev's unmoving form. When I drew close enough to see the grayish shade of his skin, alarm raced through me. I fell to my knees and pressed my fingers against his neck, searching for his jugular vein. When I found it, I breathed a sigh of relief at his faint but steady pulse.

I felt Dad's presence above me. "He's unconscious, but he's alive," I yelled above the din of the rain and the gurgle from the creek. "Call for an ambulance."

Dad tapped at his phone and lifted it to his ear. I leaned over Dev, slapping his face lightly. "Wake up. Help is on the way."

His head rocked back and forth beneath my touch, but he showed no signs of coming to I conducted a cursory search for injuries. Mud splattered his legs and torso, but they appeared unmarred. Pine needles covered his body and stuck to his face like leeches, making it clear he'd been here a while. My fingers moved across the back of his head, and I felt a wetness thicker than water.

"Head wound," I shouted to Dad, who passed along the message.

I continued to chatter at Dev, keeping my voice calm and reassuring. After a few minutes, I felt Dad take hold of my arm and try to pull me up. "Go back to the cabin with Melanie," he said. "Wait for the paramedics so you can direct them to Dev."

I wrenched loose. "You go. I'm not leaving him."

"I'll stay with him. He won't be alone."

"No." I put on my defiant face, one I knew Dad had seen hundreds of times.

He studied the expression and sighed. "Fine. But I'm not leaving you. Whoever attacked Dev might still be nearby, hiding in the woods."

I stiffened. I hadn't considered that someone might be lurking out there, watching us and waiting for an opportunity. I grew quiet, listening for the movements of the attacker, but all I could hear was the wind whipping through the trees. My eyes darted around the forest, trying to pierce the shadows beneath the trees. Dad crouched next to me and rested a hand on my shoulder. "I doubt anyone would dare mess with the two of us. Butch and Sundance, you know." He gave me a reassuring smile.

My calf began to cramp, so I plopped onto my rear end and massaged it, my eyes never leaving Dev. "He's very weak."

Dad lifted his chin. "I hear sirens. Should be any second."

"You'd better go back up to the bridge so they can find us."

"I told you, I'm not leaving—"

"Just up to the bridge, Dad. We'll be within sight. Plus, with your supersonic hearing and my supersonic vocal cords, you'll know if I need you."

Reluctantly, he got to his feet and tramped through the underbrush, shooting a look over his shoulder every few steps. The wail of the siren grew louder. Though I couldn't see the cabin from my position, I made out the flash of red strobe lights through the trees.

Getting Dev up the bank of the creek through the thick mud proved a cumbersome task. But after fifteen minutes of grunting and tugging, paramedics finally managed to maneuver the rescue basket onto the bridge. They'd done a quick preliminary examination at the creek bed, but the real medical theater began on the bridge. They moved Dev onto a gurney and checked his pupils. Then they took his blood pressure and affixed an IV into the back of his hand. While they worked, Dad and I trudged back to the cabin, where Melanie huddled on the porch, her back against the cabin and her arms wrapped around her knees. Frank stood next to her, his cowboy hat dripping. Covered in a black slicker, Raul hovered near the open door, glancing inside occasionally to observe the progress of the crime scene techs.

As Dad and I stepped onto the porch, Melanie revived from her stupor and sprang to her feet. "Is he—?"

I wrapped my arms around her. "He's alive," I whispered. "He took a blow to the head, and he's unconscious, but his pulse is steady. The paramedics haven't told us much, but they seem hopeful."

Her body collapsed into mine, and she sobbed against my shoulder. "I should have searched for him sooner. I should have looked through the window. If he doesn't make it, it's my fault."

"That's enough," I said in a firm voice. I took her by the shoulders and stared into her eyes. "This is not the time for self-pity or what ifs. Dev needs you to be strong right now."

Melanie hesitated and gave one last sob. Then she scrubbed at her cheeks with the backs of her hands.

The paramedics appeared then, rolling the gurney across the bumpy path. Melanie yelped, and before I could grab her, she sprinted toward them, throwing her body across Dev's torso. Raul ran after her and pulled her off.

One of the paramedics turned to her, calm and professional. I assumed he'd dealt with such hysteria more than once. "Ma'am. You need to stay back. I'm sure you don't want to cause this man any further harm."

Melanie shook Raul off and folded her hands, as if in prayer. "Please, please tell me he's going to be all right."

"What I can tell you is that right now he is stable. But we need to get him to the hospital for further evaluation."

"I'm coming too," she said.

"Are you family?" the paramedic asked.

She thrust her chin up. "Girlfriend."

"I'm afraid we can't allow you in the ambulance if you're not legally related. You can meet us at the hospital."

She shook her head, frantic. I rushed forward and grabbed her shoulder again. "You're doing Dev more harm than good right now, Melanie. Think of what he needs, not what you want."

The medics took off toward the parking lot, and Melanie resumed sobbing.

"How about if I drive you to the hospital?" Dad said. "We'll be right behind the ambulance." He turned to Frank and Raul, raising his eyebrows. "I that's okay with you."

"We need to question her," Raul said. "She shouldn't leave the scene until we get her statement."

Frank crossed his arms. "I don't think questioning her in this state will do us much good. Why don't we let Butch take her to the hospital? I'll ride with them and take her statement along the way."

I could see it wasn't Raul's first choice, but he nodded. Dad glanced toward the lodge, then at his watch. Melanie continued to cry softly, and he put an arm around her. "Raul, I know you need to get Callie's statement, too, but could you do it in the lodge? Jamal isn't on duty for another hour. Maggie's on her way back from a cake seminar in Boulder, but with this weather, I don't know how long it'll take her to get here. I don't have anyone watching the desk."

We all turned toward the lobby entrance, where a group of guests stood beneath the portico, watching the activity. Second time in two days they'd gathered for a bit of unscripted excitement. I noticed that one of those guests was Preston.

One of the crime scene techs appeared at the cabin door and summoned Raul. "That's fine," Raul said. "Go on to the lodge, Callie. I'll be there in a few minutes."

As Raul strode through the cabin door, Dad caught my eye. "Sorry to dump this on you, Sundance."

"It's fine, Dad. I'd need to stay to talk to Raul anyway. Might as well be useful. I'll just call the studio and tell Ethan and Alexis what's going on."

Emergency workers had secured Dev inside the ambulance while we made our arrangements, and now they squealed out of the parking lot, lights blazing and sirens howling. Melanie had grown still enough that I started to worry she might be in shock. "Why don't you get going, Dad?" I said, cocking my head toward her.

"Ready, Melanie?" he asked her. A tremor traveled down her body, but she moved down the stairs. Dad pulled his keys from his pocket and steered her toward his truck.

Frank eyed me with concern. "You've been through an ordeal, too, I'd say. You okay? Want me to walk you to the lodge?"

His words warmed me. I'd known this man most of my life, and I adored him as if he were my uncle. "Thanks, Frank, but I'm good. You know me. All in a day's work."

He smiled kindly and trotted off toward the truck. I

walked gingerly across the sodden path toward the sidewalk, not sure why I was being cautious. Not much more damage to be done—my shoes were ruined from the mud. Looking down, I realized most of me was covered with mud. The raincoat had done little to keep me clean and dry.

More lightning pulsed across the western sky, followed by a rumble of thunder. I pulled my hood tight around my face and hurried toward the lodge. The storm hadn't finished with us yet.

38

J ust a few stragglers remained by the time I made it to the lobby door. They didn't pepper me with questions as I'd feared, but I was aware of the whispers that followed in my wake.

A lone figure stood near the reception desk, but it wasn't a guest waiting to check in. It was Preston Garrison, and his face was etched with worry. "What happened?" he demanded. "Is Dev all right?"

"For all my various talents, I'm not a doctor," I snapped. I took a breath. "Sorry, Preston. Just give me a minute to get cleaned up. Can you wait here at the desk? If anyone needs help, tell them I'll be right back."

In answer, he leaned a hip against the counter and crossed his arms. I went into the closet-sized bathroom behind the office area and shrugged off my raincoat. Then I grabbed a paper towel and swiped at the muddy patches on my pants. Useless. I slipped off my soggy shoes and returned to the desk in my socks.

After I laid the wet garments on the rug by the door, I went back behind the desk and settled onto a stool. Preston raised an eyebrow. "Hate to tell you, but you're still a mess."

"It's been a long day. I'm entitled."

"What can you tell me?" He spoke in a familiarly professional tone as he rested his elbows on the counter, interrogating me with his eyes.

"I can't say much," I said, shooting a glance at the door. If Raul came in and caught me talking to Preston, I'd never hear the end of it.

"Dev is my employee. I brought him here, and I feel responsible. Please, Callie, just tell me what happened."

I hesitated. It wouldn't hurt to give him a broad overview. After all, the way news spread in this village, the story would be common knowledge in an hour. I told him about Melanie showing up at the gallery, seeing the mess through the window of Dev's cabin, and finding the man unconscious beside the creek. "That's really all I know," I finished.

He gave me his signature look, the one intended to wilt the resolve of any source who withheld information. I shrugged. "You can stare me down all day long. I've told you everything I know."

The lobby door opened before he could respond, and Raul strode inside, pausing to read something off his phone. Preston leaned toward me, speaking in a hushed voice. "I'm heading to the hospital. If you learn any other details, please keep me posted."

"Do you think going to the hospital is a good idea?" I asked. "You know, given your…circumstances. I doubt your lawyer would approve."

"I don't need his permission. Dev is a member of my team, and I intend to be there for him."

I smiled. This was the Preston Garrison I'd always known. Steadfast and loyal. Aggressive but compassionate.

He shot a look toward the elevator and whispered. "But if Sanderson comes downstairs, it's not necessary to volunteer my whereabouts." He headed to the door, nodding at Raul as he passed. I braced myself for a lecture from the detective, but he was too preoccupied to scold me for consorting.

"Gotta run, Callie. I'll get your statement later."

My breath caught. "What happened? Is it Dev?"

He nodded. "He's regaining consciousness. I need to get

over there to hear what he has to say."

The pent-up breath whooshed from my lungs. "Thank God," I said. "But he may not be able to tell you anything. A blow to the head, loss of consciousness—that kind of injury often interferes with short-term memory."

"I know," he said. "But I want to be there just in case. I'll call you as soon as I'm done. We can meet at the station."

Then he was gone. I shifted on the stool, suddenly at loose ends. A wave of exhaustion threatened to overwhelm me, but I pushed it away. There was still a lot to do, and first I needed to check in with Ethan and Alexis.

As I pulled out my phone to make the call, an elderly woman marched toward me—a resort guest, from the looks of her. And determined. She was a tiny thing, in her mid-eighties, I guessed. White hair sprouted from her skull like an exploding cotton ball. She looked at me with steely eyes. "Are you planning to put out the Sangria, young lady? That's one of the daily amenities we were promised, as listed on the website when we booked."

Oh, dear. I hadn't thought about the evening happy hour. I lifted my eyes to the antique clock above the huge stone fireplace. "Well, it's only four-thirty," I said. "Happy hour doesn't start until five—"

She puffed out her birdlike chest. "At this rate, you'll never make it on time. Happy hour won't be so happy after all."

I braced myself. Surely I could go toe to toe with this octogenarian. "My father usually sets up the evening festivities, ma'am. As you have likely noticed, we've had an emergency, and he's been called away. Until his replacement arrives, I'm here to watch the desk, but I don't have the first idea how to set up the buffet. If you'll just be patient—"

She tapped a bony finger on the counter. "How hard can it be to throw together a pitcher of Sangria? It's not rocket science."

"Ma'am, if you'll just—"

Then her demeanor altered. Her thin, heavily lipsticked

mouth curved into a sweet smile. She turned and winked at a group of white-haired ladies gathered nearby. "On the other hand, if you could spare an old lady a few details about the goings-on out there, it might improve the evening even better than a glass of wine."

I suppressed a grin. I was being conned. The old gal just wanted insider information so she could be a hero to her friends. "Well, I can't tell you much——" I teased.

She leaned in and lifted a pair of nearly nonexistent eyebrows.

"In fact, I can't tell you anything you didn't see for yourself. We found an injured man by the creek, and he's been transported to the hospital. Perhaps my father can supply more details when he returns. He's the former police chief, in case you hadn't heard. Try grilling him instead."

With a humph, she threw her shoulders back, and stomped over to her friends. When she joined them, she pointed at me and said something along the lines of, "Insolent girl."

I snickered as I settled in at the desk. I picked up my phone and dialed the gallery.

"Sundance Studio." Alexis's voice sounded tense.

"Alexis, it's Callie."

"Oh thank goodness," she said. "Ethan and I have been on pins and needles."

"We found Dev——"

"Is he dead?"

I hurried to reassure her. "He's hurt, but he's alive. They've taken him to the hospital, and I'm told he's regaining consciousness. Detective Sanchez is on his way to talk to him. I'll let you know as soon as I hear something."

"Great news," she said, and I heard her relaying it to Ethan.

I told her I needed to stay on-site until Mom or Jamal arrived. Thunder roared as I spoke, and I heard its echo through the phone line. Outside, a sheet of water filled the space between the sky and the ground. "I'm guessing we don't have any customers this afternoon," I said.

"No, it's been dead since you left." I heard her gulp. "I mean—"

"Listen," I interrupted, "why don't you two close early? Go on home."

She hesitated. "Are you sure? We still have an hour and a half."

"I'm sure. What's the use of having my own business if I can't make executive decisions once in a while? Thanks to your help in the darkroom, we're caught up on Fireweed Festival prep. And I doubt anyone will be doing much shopping the rest of the day, anyway."

"What about Woody and Carl? Do you want me to drop them off at the lodge? Or maybe your house?"

I glanced at my watch. "Mom should be here shortly. I'll swing by the studio after that and pick them up. They'll be fine."

I heard her conferring with Ethan. "All right," she said. "If you're sure."

I walked to the glass doors and peered outside as my mother's Jeep pulled into the parking lot. Accompanying her arrival? A break in the rain. Only my mother could elicit such treatment from the weather gods. "Yep. Mom just pulled in. Looks like the rain is slowing down at the moment. You two skedaddle."

"Okay," she said. "But call me when you hear something."

I assured her I would and mentally added her to the list of people I'd need to contact. It would probably be faster to have Sophie publish the information in a special blog post.

I slipped my phone in my pocket as Mom breezed through the door. She lifted her poncho over her head, hung it on the coatrack, and poofed her silver hair with her fingers. "I must look a fright," she said

As if. In her wide-legged slacks and baby blue silk blouse, the woman was so classy that even a storm couldn't muss her style. "Oh my, yes," I said. "Like something Carl dragged in from the yard. Frightening, in fact."

"Hush, you." She came over and wrapped me in her arms, unconcerned about my damp, mud-caked state. "Oh, Angelface. My poor dear. Always getting into one scrape or another. Your father called and told me what's been going on."

I allowed myself a self-indulgent sniffle before pulling out of her embrace. "Raul said Dev is waking up, Mom. I think he's going to be okay."

"Yes, dear, I do hope that's the case. He seems like a nice young man."

Jamal entered then, and she called him over. "You're early, and I couldn't be happier about it. As you've no doubt heard, we've had a bit of a crisis. I'm afraid we've fallen behind in our evening preparations. Could you get the buffet and Sangria started? I'll be along shortly to help."

"Sure thing," he said. He walked across the room to the happy hour nook and began setting up, much to the delight of the ladies in the lobby.

"And darling," Mom said, still plucking at her hair. "Would you mind giving me just a few minutes to run upstairs and clean up?"

"Go ahead," I responded.

As she bustled upstairs, I returned to my post behind the counter. Jamal had already filled the large urn with wine and commenced slicing oranges and strawberries. The gaggle of gray-haired women clustered around him, giggling like schoolgirls.

No one needed my help at the moment, so my thoughts drifted to Dev's assault. Who was responsible? And what reason would anyone have for attacking him? There were any number of motives for Brie's murder, what with all her blackmail schemes, but from everything I knew, Dev was a victim of evil, not a perpetrator. Yet the disarray at his cabin indicated that someone was looking for something.

I had no doubt his attack was linked to Brie's murder.

Anything other than that would be stretching coincidence beyond belief. But what was the link?

I drummed my fingers on the registration counter and replayed Melanie's comments about her last contact with Dev. They'd agreed to meet…she'd felt encouraged…he'd seemed happy…he was scrolling through the series of photos he'd shot…

Then it hit me, and I jumped up so abruptly I toppled the stool. Dev's camera. In our search of the cabin, I hadn't seen it. I might have overlooked it, I supposed, but as attuned as I was to all things photographic, it seemed unlikely.

I wondered—was Dev's attacker searching for that camera? Could Dev have unwittingly captured an image that made him the target of a killer?

39

Mom came through the door, took one look at my face, and rushed to my side. "What is it, darling? You look pale."

"I'm fine. Just trying to make sense of everything. I assume Dad told you someone trashed Dev's cabin?" She nodded. "I don't remember seeing his camera among his things. And it wasn't on him when I found him by the creek. It just seems odd. I mean, it's his most prized possession."

She snapped her fingers and smiled. "I can help you solve that one, darling." She brushed past me to the storage closet and swiveled the lock on the safe inisde. When it clicked open, she reached inside and retrieved a black bag, holding it up like a prize. "Voila!"

"How did you get Dev's camera bag?" I asked.

"He brought it by first thing this morning and asked me to lock it up for safekeeping. Pardon the pun, darling. I hadn't given it another thought until you brought it up. Do you think it's important? A clue, perhaps?"

"Might be," I said. My phone buzzed before I could share my suspicions. A text from Raul. He was leaving the hospital and headed to the station. Could I meet him there?

Yes, I texted. *Just need to pick up the creatures and drop them off at home. Half hour?*

He responded with a thumbs-up emoji, and I filled Mom in. "Can I have Dev's camera? I'll pass it along to Raul."

She raised an eyebrow. "Can I trust you not to snoop?"

"Mother," I said, drawing out the word as I rolled my eyes. "You know me better than that."

"Callie, darling, I know you precisely that well."

I shoved my feet back into the sticky shoes and slipped into my raincoat, certain the storm had no intention of settling the same favor on me as it had on my mother. She handed me the camera bag, and I ran a hand across it. Mom wagged a finger at me. "Remember, straight to Raul. No peeking."

"Of course not. I'm only trying to figure out how to keep it dry."

She gave me a skeptical look, but walked behind the desk and came back with a waterproof carryall bag. I tucked the camera bag inside and headed out the lobby door.

I paused beneath the portico, scanning the sky. Dark clouds stretched from beyond Mt. O'Connell as far east as I could see, blotting out the sun. Rain fell steadily. I'd have to make a run for it.

Dodging puddles, I climbed into my Honda, pulled off my dripping hood, and placed the carryall gingerly on the passenger seat. A wave of curiosity surged through me. Need, really. I tried to ignore it. Really. I buckled my seatbelt and inserted the key into the ignition. Started to turn it. Stopped. Rested my hand on the bag. Decided to remove the camera bag from inside, just to make it accessible for Raul. Nothing more.

I sighed. Who was I kidding? I was going to snoop.

I sneaked a guilty look at the lodge door, certain I'd find my mother standing there, hands on hips. But I was mistaken. I took that as a sign the fates approved.

I lifted Dev's camera out of the bag and turned it on, my fingers maneuvering familiar buttons. A photo loaded onto the LED screen—the emerald green of pine trees lining the creek. Pressing the arrow, I moved through the images, mostly landscapes. I nodded appreciatively at Dev's eye for composition.

The images changed to people-watching shots, similar to the ones I'd taken in the park and at the base of Mt. O'Connell. His were strictly candid, and I sensed he'd been experimenting with depth perception. The focus shifted from blurred background to sharp background.

There were dozens of shots, and I scrolled through them quickly. When nothing in particular stood out, I began to believe I'd tainted my ethics—and cemented my mother's opinion of them—for nothing. People in the park. Forward. A group at the lake. Forward. A shot of guests on the swing in front of the lodge. Forward. Tourists strolling down Evergreen Way. Forward. A family at the playground near the gallery. Forward.

Suddenly, my subconscious caught sight of something my conscious mind had missed. I scrolled back one shot, then a second, stopping when I came to a group of people reclining on a blanket.

A tingling sensation in my brain told me there was something here I needed to see. I enlarged the image and touched the arrows to navigate around the frame. I didn't recognize anyone on the blanket—but in the background, closer to the lake... A man stood in profile, apart from the rest of the tourists. He looked familiar. I enlarged the image yet again.

Then I gasped, and my heart pounded.

I was looking at Jameson Jarrett. And he wasn't in Miami.

Operating on instinct, the first thing I did was to switch off the camera and remove the memory card from its tiny compartment, carefully tucking it into my front pants pocket. I'd had too many bad experiences with inadvertent photo erasures to risk leaving the card in the camera.

Next, I picked up my phone, fumbling it in shaking hands, and pressed Raul's number. The call went straight to voicemail. "Are you kidding?" I muttered.

Frustrated, I disconnected without leaving a message and tossed the phone onto the passenger seat beside. *No big deal,* I told myself. I was headed to the station anyway, and he couldn't ignore me then. Just a quick stop to retrieve Woody and Carl and drop them off at home.

Luckily, the storm had driven the tourists inside, and Evergreen Way was empty of cars. A sparse few pedestrians made their way down the sidewalk, but they stayed beneath the awnings, not venturing into the street. I made a quick turn into the alley and braked hard at the sight of a scurrying chipmunk, sending my phone tumbling into the wheel well.

I pulled into my spot behind the gallery. Grabbing the keys, I hurried to the back door and unlocked it. I trotted down the hallway and into my office, expecting to find Woody and Carl on their beds. But the office was vacant.

I was perplexed. Alexis and Ethan wouldn't have left the creatures run of the studio. Maybe we'd misunderstood one another, and Alexis was on her way to drop them off at my house.

Standing still for a moment, I listened to the silence. Something felt off. Then I heard Woody's whine coming from the gallery, and I dashed toward the sound.

The studio was shrouded in darkness, except for a single lamp left burning atop the sales desk. It provided just enough light for me to see Woody standing there, trembling. Suddenly, he lunged forward, trying to reach me, but he'd been tethered to the foot bar at the bottom of the counter.

Then I saw the leash wrapped in loops around his snout and knotted in place, keeping his mouth shut tight.

I sprinted across the room and fell to my knees in front of him. "Woody! Who did this to you? Where's Carl?"

As I fumbled with the knot, the hair on Woody's neck rose. His eyes stared over my shoulder, and he growled. I began to turn.

I heard the loud crack even before I registered the blow to the back of my head. My body crumpled to the floor. I made out one last doggie whine. Then the world went black.

40

Before I even opened my eyes, I knew I was in the darkroom. The acrid smell of chemicals—familiar and pleasant, to me, anyway—gave it away. It took an act of will to force my eyelids open, and when I did, my vision was fuzzy around the edges, like I was looking through a warped peephole. So I closed my eyes again and allowed myself to drift off.

The next time I opened them, pain spiked through my skull. Migraine? Like Alexis? It was all too complicated for my compromised brain to puzzle out, so I tried to float back into dreamland.

But it was no use. Consciousness persisted, as did agony.

I went to massage my aching temple, but my hands wouldn't budge. I slitted one eye open and tried to make sense of things. I saw that I was seated in a rolling chair, the one from my gallery. What was it doing in the darkroom? And more importantly, why were my wrists tethered to the armrests with camera straps?

None of it made sense—not to my foggy mind, anyway. I turned my head slowly, trying to get a look behind me. Even that gentle movement hurt my head. I closed my eyes and let my chin rest on my chest as I tried to think. My last memory was of Woody, tied to the sales counter. I'd run over to free him. I'd felt confused, afraid, and then…a thunk across the back of my skull.

Someone had knocked me out.

I drew a breath, willing the lurking panic to subside. Trying to figure out how I got here was a waste of time. What mattered, my gut screamed at me, was getting out. Now.

After another deep breath—four counts in, eight counts out—I felt calm enough to open my eyes again. I slid my eyes down my body. As far as I could see, all my parts appeared intact. Other than the straps digging into my wrists and the throbbing in my head, I was in fine form.

I needed to summon help. Yelling would do no good. No one would hear. I thought of my cell phone and remembered watching it fall to the passenger floorboard when I braked to save the chipmunk. Thinking I'd just be a minute, I hadn't bothered to retrieve it.

Then it hit me: though my hands were bound, my legs weren't. And the chair was on rollers.

If I could wheel my way across the darkroom to the revolving door, I'd be almost home free. There was the issue of the door's raised slider, but I figured I could maneuver the chair over it. Then I'd rotate the door with my feet, exit into the hall, and roll to the phone in my office.

It could work.

My brain transmitted the plan to my legs, but they didn't receive the message. Apparently, being conked on the head left a person limp as a wilted flower. When I finally convinced my feet to move my body an inch, I was hit with a bout of nausea and had to will myself not to throw up.

I wasn't giving up, but I needed a minute recover before trying again.

Then I heard the familiar squeak of the revolving door. My eyes flew open, and adrenaline quelled the nausea. Someone was about to enter the darkroom. Had help arrived? Or was it the killer, returning to finish the job?

My eyes darted across the floor, looking for anything I could use as a weapon. Nothing. For one of the few times in my life, I felt utterly helpless. The door swiveled. The dark gap opened, then grew. I held my breath. But when I saw who was inside, I exhaled in relief.

"Alexis," I said. "Thank God. Quick, untie me. We have to get out of here."

She made her way toward me—too slowly. No urgency at all. "Did you hear me?" I demanded. "Whoever did this to me will be coming back. We have to hurry…"

Then I heard what I'd just said. *Whoever did this to me will be coming back.* I looked more closely at Alexis. She wore a gray sweatshirt with a hood hanging down her back. My mind flashed to the hooded figure outside my home. Then I looked at her feet. Running shoes, and her feet were big.

As the truth dawned, panic threatened to overwhelm me. "Oh, Alexis. Please. Don't tell me it was you."

"Shh." She reached a hand to the back of my head and probed my scalp. I blanched at the pain and thought I might pass out. At this point, that might not be such a bad thing.

Alexis examined her hand. "Bleeding's stopped. You have a nasty lump, but you'll survive." She smiled. "For what that's worth."

It all began to make sense. As she watched me start to understand, Alexis cocked her head. "Well, well. The great Callie Cassidy finally solves the mystery. Guess you're as smart as everyone believes. Almost, anyway."

The door squeaked again. This time, I had no doubt who was coming.

Jameson Jarrett entered the darkroom, holding Dev's camera. He smirked at me and slid an arm around Alexis's waist. "Look who finally woke up."

She took the camera, and Jameson leaned over and tugged the straps on my wrists. "Think these are tight enough? I want them to leave marks."

"They're plenty tight," Alexis said. "Anyway, we don't need marks on her body. Her soul will have plenty of permanent scars by the time this ends."

"Soul scars?" he grumbled. "I'd like something more…physical."

Hearing the menace in his voice, Alexis lowered the camera and touched his bicep. "You took care of that when you cracked that bat across the back of her head. Lot of power in that swing, baby. It'll leave a scar for sure. Your mark will always be on her."

Marks? Scars? What difference would any of that make when I was dead?

Then it occurred to me—maybe they weren't planning to kill me.

Jameson seemed mollified at her praise. He nodded at the camera. "Did you find what you were looking for?"

She fiddled with buttons and flipped levers. "No. I think everything has been erased." Then she flipped open the tiny door on the side. "I see. The memory card is missing—the place where digital photos are actually stored."

Jameson's face twisted in rage. He snatched the camera and launched it across the room. It smashed against the wall, sending shards of plastic and glass through the air as it tumbled to the floor in a broken heap.

Then he was on me, shaking me by the shoulders and whipping my head back and forth. Pain roared through me. "Where is it?" he screamed. "I want those pictures!" I felt the sting of a slap, and then I must have blacked out.

The next thing I knew, Alexis had her arms around the raging man. "The photos don't matter, Jamie," she said in a soothing tone. "By the time anyone recognizes your picture, we'll be long gone. Just a couple more tasks, and before you know it, we'll be on a tropical beach sipping mai tais."

Jameson's shoulders relaxed. Alexis kissed him. "It's okay, baby," she said. "Let me talk to Callie so we can get on with it. We don't want to miss our flight."

"I don't get why you need to do this," he said. "I say we take her out and be done with it. We shouldn't leave any witnesses."

She gave him a pout. "I want the world to know our story. I want us to be famous. We deserve it. Besides, baby, you promised. Just give us a minute."

"All right, all right. Make it quick." He glowered at me before walking to the far side of the darkroom, where he leaned against the counter and started swiping through his phone.

Alexis positioned a folding chair so it faced me and sat, resting her elbows on her knees. "Callie, you are one lucky woman. This was supposed to be a death scene, you know. But then you brought me that silly lunch yesterday, all worried about my fake migraine, and I began to feel a tickle of affection for you. Funny to think a bowl of soup might have saved your life." She sat back and brushed a strand of hair off her forehead. "I like the alternate plan better, anyway. It kills two birds with one stone—so to speak. You'll tell our story and still be left with the aftermath. You'll be haunted by us for the rest of your life. A fitting punishment for your part in what happened to Jamie."

Hearing his name, Jameson glanced up from his phone. "Quit dragging this out."

My head throbbed. With each pulse, blackness flashed across my vision. I shifted, trying to find some comfort. Suddenly, a picture popped into my mind, the last image I'd had before being bonked on the head: Woody, tied up in the gallery.

Outrage thrust out the fear and pain. "Alexis, where's Woody? I swear, if you hurt my dog, I'll—"

She smiled. "I don't think you're in any position to be making threats." Then she gave me a look of pity. "But just to set your mind at ease, Woody is fine. He played his part in our little drama splendidly and was rewarded with a nice treat, laced with a doggie sedative. He'll sleep for a while and wake up bright eyed and bushy tailed. I have a soft spot for that pup. I'd never hurt him."

She held out her arm and traced a finger along a trio of angry welts. "The cat, on the other hand…"

I gasped. "You didn't…"

"No. The thought crossed my mind, believe me, but I had other matters to attend to. I tossed him out the door into the rain—cat torture, I'm told. He ran off down the alley, yowling like the feral thing he is. Maybe he'll find his way home, but if not, no great loss. He's just a cat."

I heaved a sigh of relief, but inside me, the anger boiled.

"Now pay attention," she said. "You're all tied up and can't take any notes, so you'll have to commit all this to memory. You should consider it an honor that we've chosen you to tell the world our story. It's an epic tale—a regular Bonnie and Clyde saga. I'm thinking you might even win your second Felden Award."

I puffed my cheeks and blew out a breath. If I refused to play along, I didn't doubt she'd let Jameson kill me. I'd seen the expression on his face—he was looking for an excuse.

I thought of the meeting I'd scheduled with Raul. Was he missing me yet? If I could find a way to stretch this out long enough, he'd show up and rescue me. A girl could hope.

"All right," I said, mentally donning my reporter cap. "But first, I need some context, some background information. So let's start at the beginning. How did you two meet?"

Her face lit up. "Such a beautiful love story," she said. "Your readers will just die. We met in high school—"

"Wait," I interrupted. "Jameson is twenty-five. You're twenty. How were you in high school together?"

She giggled. "You're so gullible, Callie. I haven't been twenty in, like, seven years now. I was two years ahead of Jamie." She flipped her hair over her shoulder. "I admit, I look quite youthful. It's the product of my pure lifestyle."

From across the room, Jameson called out. "Move it along, Alexis. We don't have all day."

A pained expression clouded her face at the reprimand. I was getting the sense that Alexis was much more enamored of Jameson than he was of her. I wondered how long their little tropical love nest would actually last before he flew the coop.

She shifted in her chair and blinked back tears as she resumed the tale. "I'd been in love with him since he was a freshman. But I was shy, and he was always surrounded by friends. I was too nervous to approach him."

Jameson grunted impatiently. Alexis wrung her hands and quickly summarized the next few years—her graduation and subsequent associate's degree as a dental hygienist. Jameson's departure for the greener pastures of college in Washington, D.C.

"I followed his life through social media," she said. "When he got in trouble—when he was *falsely* convicted—I knew he needed me. I started writing to him in prison. We became pen pals." She shot him a timid look. "And we fell in love, didn't we, baby?"

Her voice carried a pleading quality that Jameson must have recognized. He turned his attention from the phone to her. "That we did," he said. "Nobody believed in me. Not the great Callahan Cassidy. Certainly not Brie Bohannan. Only Alexis stood by me the whole time, through it all."

Cynic that I was, I had an inkling there was more to it than true love. Maybe their pen pal correspondence included a little cash for Jameson's commissary account.

"I drove up to visit him a few times," she continued, "and we both just knew. We were destined to be together. When his innocence was finally revealed, he moved back to our little suburb near Miami. We were finally a real couple."

The mention of Miami reminded me of Jameson's alibi. I faced him. "One thing has me a little confused," I said. "Detective Sanchez tracked your credit card charges and even called your mother. Everything showed you still in Florida. How'd you two pull that off?"

Jameson looked at me like I was a moron. "Lent my credit card to a buddy down there. Told him to go crazy. Not like I'm going to be paying the charges, anyway. As for Mom, the last thing the old lady wants is for her baby boy to end up in jail again. She'll say whatever I tell her to say."

Reverence filled Alexis's eyes, and I could see that, like his mother, she'd drunk Jameson's Kool-Aid. That young woman was officially a lost cause.

41

Back to the story," Alexis said. "Returning to the real world wasn't easy for Jamie. My poor man was angry and depressed, drinking too much. Who could blame him? How does someone fit in again when society has stolen everything? Everyone else got to go on with their lives, but he couldn't."

Inwardly, I rolled my eyes. Any guilt I had over my part in Jameson's conviction was fast evaporating. Yes, I'd printed information that turned out to be false, but I clearly hadn't misjudged the man's character. Jameson Jarrett was a self-serving narcissist, and he'd dragged this lonely, troubled woman down with him.

Still, I hung my head and pretended to sympathize. "I feel responsible. If I hadn't believed Levi's accusations…"

Jameson crossed the room in three strides and loomed over me. "You *should* feel responsible. Because you are."

Alexis put a hand on his chest, and he took a step back. "Partly, anyway," he went on. "Mostly, though, this was Levi's fault. Nothing infuriated me more than knowing he didn't pay a price, even after he admitted lying. Oh, he got kicked out of the frat. Big deal. He still got his degree, landed a job, stayed out of a cage…"

"It wasn't fair," Alexis agreed, riding the wave of Jameson's outrage. "Everyone else moved on, but Jamie couldn't. So we came up with a plan."

For the first time, I saw him look at her with true

affection. "Alexis thought it up," he said. "She saved me. Gave me a new purpose in life."

Alexis allowed herself a moment to bask in his approval, then continued her story. "The first step involved getting even with Levi. He had to pay, so one night, I tracked him to a bar, we had a few drinks, and we...hooked up." She glanced tentatively at Jameson, who rewarded her with a smile. "I followed him back to his place. As we were...getting together...I told him I had a special way I liked to party. I went to my car and got a canister of nitrous oxide I'd smuggled out of the dentist's office where I worked."

"Nitrous oxide?" I asked. "As in, laughing gas?"

"It was perfect," she said. "It doesn't live long in the bloodstream, and it makes people compliant. The only downside is that they all die happy."

I thought of the crease on Brie's upper lip. A ridge left by a plastic mask? That led me to the rubber tubing the police found in the darkroom. It was all starting to come together. "You used nitrous oxide on Brie, too. That's how you were able to control her long enough to get her tied to the chair."

Alexis waggled a finger at me. "Now, now, Callie. A good reporter never interrupts her source. I put the mask over my own nose and pretended to inhale. Then I handed it to Levi and opened the nozzle wide. He was woozy within a minute, practically unable to move within five. That's when I took the gun from my purse, wrapped his hand around it, and put it in his mouth. He didn't even resist."

I visualized the scene, Alexis's cold-blooded actions, and felt my body tremble. "So it wasn't a suicide. But what about the note his parents found on his computer?"

"Easy peasy," she said. "He'd left his laptop on. I just typed a few lines and that was that. Everyone bought it."

Jameson scowled. "Except one person. After Levi was dead, that Bohannan woman started poking around. We knew she didn't believe Levi had killed himself. We figured she'd keep digging, and we couldn't have that."

Alexis wrapped her arms around Jameson's waist. "That's where my man's skills really came into play." She stroked his arm along with his ego. "Jamie is brilliant on the computer, a master hacker. My genius here managed to breach the contents of Brie's computer."

"At first," he said, "I just hoped to find something I could use to expose her for what we knew she was—"

"A ruthless skank," Alexis said. "An oozing sore on the face of humanity."

"But I couldn't believe the dirt I found," Jameson continued. "Nasty stuff. Erotic, some of it." He smirked. "Even a couple of photos of you, come to think of it, all cozied up to that boss of yours. Nothing too graphic, unfortunately, but still. Want to see?" He began tapping on his phone screen.

"No time for that, baby," Alexis said. "We still have another job after this."

"Yeah, okay." Reluctantly, he slid the phone into his pocket. "Anyway, this one email I found mentioned an annual work retreat. When I realized your boss was taking everyone to your hometown, I couldn't believe my luck."

I nodded. "The perfect place to take revenge on Brie and hurt me in the process."

"It didn't take long to create our plan," Alexis said. "Our masterpiece. Within a week, I moved to Rock Creek Village."

"You came here with the sole purpose of killing Brie? In my darkroom?"

She tittered. "That part came later. At first, I had no idea I'd end up working at the studio. That was a lucky twist of fate. I'd researched the village, of course, and figured I'd end up as a barista at Rocky Mountain High or a server at Snow Plow Chow—something along those lines. I only popped into Sundance Studio to get a look at you. But when I saw the Help Wanted sign in your window, it all fell into place."

"And I walked right into your trap."

She shrugged. "You have this thing about helping people.

Some people find it charming, but all I know is, it makes you an easy mark."

Tears pricked my eyes at her betrayal. "I cared about you, Alexis. Ethan cared about you. And Elyse. This village took you in, treated you like family."

Her face clouded over. "Jameson is my family. He's the only one who cares about me."

He draped an arm around her shoulder and gave me a smug look. "This woman is the true hero of the story. Make sure you write that in your article."

She stared at him as if she were gazing upon a god. Any hopes I had of rescuing her from his emotional clutches were dashed. All I could do was keep them talking, and hope for Raul.

"I just can't comprehend the scope of it," I said. "Such an intricate scheme, so complex. If I weren't on the losing side of it, I'd have to say how impressive it was."

Alexis leaned against Jameson and smiled radiantly. Then she rearranged her expression into one that almost resembled sympathy. "I know this must be difficult for you, Callie. All things considered, I think you're a good person at heart. But that doesn't release you from your obligation to pay the piper. You deserve to be punished for starting this chain of events." She locked eyes with me. "That's why we ultimately chose your darkroom as Brie Bohannan's final resting place."

"We figured it'd cause a hit to your business," Jameson said. "That your reputation would be trashed. It hasn't happened yet, but with everything that's about to go down, it will."

I sensed this train was hurtling to the end of the line, and it was too soon. I needed to keep the two of them here a little longer. I furrowed my brow in mock concentration. "It'll make a decent story. But to be an award winner, it needs more details. Some flesh to make it come to life. For instance, how did you lure Brie into the darkroom?"

Alexis's eyes glowed. "You already know some of it. The

note, the key—"

"You stole the key from Willie Wright's office."

"Yep. He helped me rent my apartment. Silly man—he rarely locked his office door, or his key cabinet. So there was really nothing to it. I even made myself a copy so I could get in after the party. And a key to your house. But you'll hear about that later. As for the bait, I knew Brie would jump at the opportunity to smear your name. When she came into the studio, that night I turned on the nitrous oxide tank in the darkroom and let it flow. I slipped on a gas mask and hid. You know the rest."

Her eyes took on a faraway look and she relived the moment of glory. "Brie flipped through your file cabinet for a few minutes before she became disoriented. Then I grabbed her. She scratched me, even broke a fingernail, but she was too weak to put up much of a fight. I shoved her into the chair, put a mask over her face, and attached the hose to it. She squirmed for a minute, maybe two. Then she was out. I wrapped the camera strap around her neck and pulled it tight until she was dead." She shrugged as if taking a life was just another check mark on her to-do list.

I glanced at Jameson, so smug, and decided it was time to stir things up. "For purposes of accurate reporting, let me get this straight. You've done all the dirty work here, right Alexis? All the killing? Jameson is merely the beneficiary of your actions?"

Jameson's fists clenched at his sides, and I braced myself for a blow. But it was Alexis whose hand darted out and struck me across the cheek. "He's not some kind of bystander, Callie," she said. "In addition to all the necessary computer work, he also took care of Dev."

I lifted my eyebrows, and Jameson smirked. "I figured he hadn't recognized me," he said. "Probably didn't even notice me in the background when he took those photos at the lake. But I knew he'd gotten me on camera. It was a loose end, and I had to take care of it. No big deal."

"But it *was* a big deal, baby," Alexis said. "He could have ruined everything, but you didn't let that happen. Tell Callie exactly what you did. For our story."

"I went to his cabin. He wasn't there, but the door was unlocked. I didn't even have to break in. I searched for his camera but couldn't find it anywhere. Then he walked in on me. As soon as he saw me, I could tell he knew who I was. He took off running toward the bridge. Lucky for me, it was raining hard enough that the place was deserted. I caught up to him at the creek, picked up a rock, and..." He lifted his arm and mimed the blow, his fist coming so close to my face that I flinched.

"But like I told Alexis on the phone, he didn't die," I said.

"That was unfortunate," he said. "But in the long run, it's not important."

"What do you mean, not important? By now, he's surely told the cops everything. They'll be out looking for you."

He shrugged. "They won't find us. We just have one more piece of unfinished business. Then we're in the wind."

"What one more thing is that?" I asked.

Alexis smiled. "Show her, baby."

He took out his phone and scrolled. When he found what he was looking for, he turned the screen to face me. It took me a few seconds to make sense of what I was seeing. When I did, I swallowed hard.

Preston had been bound and laid out flat on the floor of my kitchen. His eyes were closed. His mouth and nose were covered with a plastic mask, attached with plastic tubing to a canister. Nitrous oxide, I assumed.

My mind reeled. When I'd last seen Preston, he'd been headed to the hospital. "How did you—?"

Alexis held an imaginary phone to her ear. "Preston, Preston!" she squealed. "There's a hooded figure outside my house. He's coming to the door. Oh, help me. Please." Her voice was a more than passable imitation of mine.

"Of course he came running to the rescue," she said, back to her normal voice. "That's what people do for you. We tied him up and dosed him, then drove his van back into town. When we're finished here, we'll go back to your place to set up the grand finale." She flung her arms outward. "Just picture it. Your former boss—your lover once—strangled in your house, with your own camera strap."

She giggled again, and it was the sound of someone who had broken with reality. "You'll never be able to walk into this gallery without the memory of Brie dead in your darkroom. And the image of Preston dead in your kitchen will forever contaminate your home. You'll never be free of what you did to Jameson. Never."

I froze under the coldness of her gaze. The girl I'd wanted to protect, to mentor, had disappeared. In her place, I saw a psychopath.

She wiped her hands on the legs of her pants. "Now it's time for you to get a taste of the silly juice. Preston's currently using the only mask I have, so your dose won't be quite as intense. And this tank is only about half full. It'll run dry before it kills you—at least, I think it will—but by the time one of your perpetual rescuers finds you, you won't be feeling too well."

While Alexis brought out a canister from beneath the work table, Jameson walked to the wall and yanked down the clothesline I used to hang wet photos. He looped it around my waist and knotted it around the heavy work table, ensuring I wasn't going anywhere after they left.

Alexis positioned the canister about a foot from my chair and adjusted the plastic hose toward me. She crouched beside me and looked into my eyes. "I'm actually a little sad about this, Callie. Under different circumstances, you know, we might have been friends. You could have been the big sister I never had."

She stood up, twisted the nozzle, and joined Jameson inside the revolving door.

42

The revolving door swiveled, and Alexis and Jameson disappeared. Soon after, the back door slammed shut. After that, the only noise I heard was the hissing of the nitrous oxide canister.

I spent two minutes yelling at the top of my lungs, recognizing the futility of my efforts even as I was doing it. The building was well insulated, and the darkroom sidled up against the alley. With the storm raging over the village, there was little chance of anyone hearing me.

Wrenching my wrists against the straps, I felt a tiny bit of give. If I had another hour, I might be able to free my hands and get loose from the chair.

But Preston didn't have an hour.

And with the nitrous oxide filling the room, neither did I. A wave of dizziness fluttered through my head. Not unpleasant, not at all. Relaxing, even. Like the first glass of wine at the end of a stressful day. I found myself craving another glass. I could just let myself doze off…

I fought the urge and yelled some more, mostly to keep myself awake. I figured my best hope lay in getting the gas turned off. If I did that, I could focus on freeing myself.

I stretched my leg as far as I could, trying to touch the canister. A slight roll of the chair. One more thrust. Finally, my toe brushed against it. The canister tumbled over and rolled a few inches away. I breathed deeply. Too deeply. My head felt wobbly, and my eyelids suddenly weighed a hundred pounds each. I closed them and realized my head no longer hurt. I'd give myself a minute to rest, I decided. Then I'd come up with another plan.

When I came to again, it was in flashes, snapshots separated by blackness. I'd break through the blanket of semi-consciousness to feel hands working at the straps around my wrists. Then blackness again. Then I'd hear giggling, realize it was me, and out I'd go. At one point, I opened my eyes to see the ceiling moving above me and understood I was being dragged across the floor. Then drowsiness overcame me again.

The weight of a furry body settled across my chest, and a rough tongue grazed my cheek. I opened my eyes and blinked, feeling a little more alert. Woody's nose appeared, free of constraints, an inch above my face. "Hey, Chief," I said. "I love you too, but you need to give me a little air."

My head pounded and my stomach roiled, but I was starting to get my wits about me. I closed my eyes again, and the memory of Alexis and Jameson flitted through my mind. I recalled the straps, the clothesline, the nitrous oxide.

And then the photo of Preston on my kitchen floor.

I pushed the dog off and lifted up onto my elbows. "They're going to kill him. I need to go."

A face appeared next to me. Then the same face again. I blinked. The gas had me seeing a double exposure. But then I realized it was the twins, Banner and Braden Ratliff.

I rubbed my eyes. "Boys, how did you—?"

They wore guilty expressions. One of them—I still couldn't tell which—pointed toward the front door. I turned my head—too fast, as it turned out. A wave of vertigo nearly caused me to pass out. When I was able to focus again, I saw the broken pane of glass above the knob.

"We heard your dog going crazy." The speaker pointed to himself. "I'm Banner, by the way. Anyway, the blinds were open a little, and we got a look inside. Saw this poor guy leashed up, barking his head off. We knew something was wrong. Tried to get in through…well, you know, the old way. But I guess you sealed that up." His cheeks colored. "We thought we should check it out—fast. Sorry about your door."

"Don't you dare apologize. You saved me. And if I can get home in time, you will have saved someone else, too." I reached out my hand, and Braden helped me to my feet, keeping his fingers wrapped firmly around my arm. The contusion on my scalp pounded, and my equilibrium wavered. But after a couple of seconds, I felt steady enough to stand on my own.

"What was that stuff in the tank?" Braden asked. "We kept getting dizzy from it, even after we turned off the fumes. Had to take turns cutting you loose."

"Yeah," Banner said. "It was like getting high. Kinda cool. In a different situation, I mean. And you kept laughing…"

The door flew open, and the three of us jumped. Sam appeared, his wet hair flattened against his forehead. His eyes were wild as he rushed toward me. "Callie, I've been trying to call. I saw your car out back, then I ran around front and saw the broken window." He stood in front of me and gave the boys a hard look. "Did they hurt you?"

"No, Sam. Banner and Braden saved me. But there's no time to explain right now." As my awareness grew, so did my sense of urgency. I glanced at the clock, unsure how long I'd been out. I only hoped I could get to Preston before it was too late. "I need to go home. Now."

I made a move to the back door, wobbled on my feet, and realized it wasn't safe for me to drive. I looked at Sam. "Will you take me? I'll explain on the way."

He didn't hesitate. "Where are your keys?"

I pulled them out of my pocket and handed them over. Then I turned to the twins. "I need your help. Call 9-1-1. Tell them to send the police to my house, that it's a matter of life and death. Tell them we need Detective Sanchez, too. Will you do that?"

"Consider it done," Braden said.

I glanced at Woody, standing protectively at my side, and thought of his brother. "And maybe one of you can look for Carl. I think they threw him outside."

"Sure thing," Banner said. "And don't worry about the studio. We'll stay here and guard it as long as we need to."

I took a moment to give each of them a quick hug. "We were right about you," I whispered. "At the *ubuntu*. We were right."

Identical blushes colored their faces. Then I shook a finger at them. "But don't be going back in that darkroom for another whiff."

Sam put an arm around me to keep me steady, and we hurried to the back door. Woody darted ahead of us. "No, Woody. Stay." He gave a single, decisive bark and stood with his nose pressed to the door jamb, not about to be left behind. I relented, and the three of us headed through the pelting rain to my car.

Sam drove like a maniac, his knuckles white around the steering wheel. As he maneuvered down the wet streets, I gave him the abbreviated version of what had happened. When I finished, he exhaled. "Hope we make it in time."

After a few minutes that felt like hours, we screeched to a stop in front of my house. I didn't see any cars on the street. Anxiety crackled inside me. Had Alexis and Jameson already killed Preston? And if they hadn't, how were we going to stop them?

Woody scratched at the back window. I looked outside and spotted Carl in the grass near the curb, his fur wet and matted. When I opened my door, Woody leapt over the seat, across my lap, and onto the curb. He touched Carl with his nose, and the cat arched his back.

Sam scrambled out and raced around the car to get to me. Pain thudded across the back of my head. He took my hand, but I shook him off and raced up the wet walkway. As I reached for the doorknob, he grabbed my arm. "We have no idea what's going on in there," he whispered. "If you open the door, they might hear us. We need a plan."

I shook my head in a frenzy. "Sam, if we wait for the police, it might be too late. Preston's life is at stake."

"I'm not suggesting we wait for backup. I'm just saying, we can't go rushing in half-cocked and make things worse."

He was right. For all we knew, Alexis and Jameson had guns, knives, or other weapons they might use on Preston. Or us. If we burst through the door like Benson and Stabler, we'd forfeit any element of surprise.

"So what should we do?"

He thought for a moment. "We have no line of sight here. I say we head to the back. There are a lot of windows back there. We can look inside and get an idea of what's happening. Then we can figure out next move."

I nodded. With any luck, we'd be hearing sirens by the time we got back there.

We stepped off the porch and into the soggy grass, squishing around the side of the house. Woody and Carl darted ahead of us. "Stay," I hissed. Neither of them paused.

The creatures skidded to a stop at the corner of the house. Sam and I crouched low and moved to the porch. The rain beat against the roof so loudly I knew it would mask the sound of our approach.

Carefully, I eased toward the patio, feeling Woody and Carl at my feet and Sam pressed close behind me. I listened hard, trying to make out any sounds from inside. But the same patter of rain that muffled our approach made it impossible for us to hear anything.

I had to take the plunge. I stepped over to the window and peeked inside.

43

When I caught a glimpse of the scene inside, my hand flew to my mouth. Fear washed away any residual lethargy from the nitrous oxide. I was painfully alert.

In the kitchen, Preston appeared just as he had in the photograph—sprawled on the floor, hands bound in front of him. A clear medical mask covered his mouth and nose, attached by plastic tubing to a small canister. A camera strap curled on the floor beside him like a snake.

Alexis sat cross-legged next to him. As I watched, Jameson entered the kitchen, rolling my desk chair ahead of him. He settled it near Preston and grabbed the limp man under the armpits. Alexis scrambled to her feet and held the chair steady as Jameson positioned Preston on it. Then Alexis stooped down and picked up the camera strap, handing it to her boyfriend.

His turn to do the deed.

Sam peered over my shoulder. The shock on his face gave way to determination. No time for concocting a plan. We had to act—now.

Everything seemed to happen at once. Above us, thunder rumbled. In its wake, I heard the faintest warble of sirens. Then Carl yowled and darted through the pet door into the house. Woody scrambled through in his wake. Just after,

Sam smashed his elbow through the glass door. Then he reached through the broken shards and turned the lock.

All of this happened as I pulled my keys from my pocket. But I guessed their way worked too.

As I rushed into the kitchen behind Sam, Carl flew through the air and landed on Jameson's back. The cat swiftly reached around the man's head and raked his claws across his cheek. Jameson screamed and fell to his knees, thrashing about to dislodge the furry beast. Alexis grabbed the scruff of Carl's neck and pulled him off Jameson. The cat squirmed from her grasp and skittered away.

Then Sam lunged toward Jameson and pushed him to the floor. I heard the crunch of cartilage as Sam threw a fist into Jameson's nose.

A banshee-like scream issued from Alexis's throat. She jumped on Sam's back and wrapped her arm around his neck in a choke hold. I sprinted across the floor and slammed against Alexis, knocking her off of him. She quickly regained her footing and launched herself at me.

Suddenly, Woody was between us, teeth bared. Alexis stopped in her tracks and held up a hand. "Woody, stay," she said in a soothing voice. "That's a good boy." She took another tentative step toward me.

Woody sprang at her and sunk his teeth into the taut muscle of her calf. I heard the ripping of flesh and saw the shock in her eyes. She cried out and grabbed at his jaws, trying to pry them apart. The dog tightened his grip, and I saw blood stream down her leg.

Jameson reared up to head butt Sam. But Sam grabbed him by the shoulders and smacked Jameson's head against the floor. With a single thump, Jameson was out cold.

I knew the two of us could handle Alexis now, so I placed a hand gently on Woody's back. "Good dog, Woody. That's enough now. Release." When he complied, Alexis curled around her injured leg, moaning. My normally sweet, pacifistic golden retriever stood over her for a full minute, as if daring her to move.

The siren's shriek came from directly in front of the house. I hurried down the hall and opened the bolt to the door. Raul hurtled past me with his gun drawn, entering the kitchen just as Hardesty and Tollison rushed in through the back. All three had their weapons pointed at Alexis and Jarrett, who was dazed but awake.

Sam sat on the floor with his back against the couch, breathing hard. Woody finally felt safe abandoning his guard dog duties and turned his attention to Carl. He hovered protectively over the cat.

Sam and the creatures appeared relatively uninjured, so I hurried over to Preston. I squatted beside him and yanked the mask off his face. "You're going to be all right," I said. "Just breathe. Breathe."

A minute later, Preston opened his eyes and blinked. Then he started to laugh. And laugh. And laugh some more. He chortled so hard he had to struggle for breath. Tears streamed down his cheeks. The cops, who were in the process of handcuffing Alexis and Jameson, looked at Preston apprehensively. "It's laughing gas," I told them. "It'll wear off soon enough."

Tollison grabbed his radio and called for an ambulance. Then he looked around the kitchen at the blood and the three injured people on the floor and amended the call. "Better make that two."

Raul holstered his gun and crouched beside me. I sighed, preparing for the inevitable lecture. Instead, he clasped his hands between his knees and shook his head. "Callahan Cassidy. Never a dull moment."

Over the next hour, more officers bustled into my house—the whole force, by the looks of it, and maybe even a couple of neighboring forces. Paramedics loaded Alexis and a stunned Jameson into an ambulance. Their injuries would be treated at the hospital, then they'd be moved to a holding cell. Frank, who'd arrived just after Raul, had headed off to the station to see to their accommodations.

Reluctantly, but with a giggle, Preston agreed to go to the hospital. I figured it was strictly precautionary. Like me, he'd be fine as soon as the gas vacated his bloodstream. One of the paramedics examined my head wound. He cleaned the laceration and told me it wouldn't require stitches. He suggested I accompany Preston in the ambulance in case I had a concussion, but I refused. Sam and Raul just looked at each other, finally realizing there was no use pressuring me into anything.

My phone showed several missed calls from my father, so I called to assure my parents I was fine. Dad offered to relieve the twins from their gallery guard duty. Then I texted Tonya, promising to fill her in on the details later.

After that, I sat next to Sam on the couch and surveyed the aftermath. Slivers of my back door lay scattered across the floor, so I agreed that Woody, Carl, and I would spend the night at Sam's. Raul assigned an officer to watch over my house until the door could be repaired in the morning. He said he'd post another officer at Sundance Studio until the glass there could be replaced. Joe, my door and glass guy, would be able to take an extended vacation courtesy of my insurance company.

The forensics crew, who probably weren't quite as fond of me as Joe, would process both scenes. We didn't anticipate any surprises, but Raul had to cross all his t's and dot all his i's in preparation for arraignments and indictments and eventual trials.

I sighed. "After all of this, Jameson Jarrett will just end up in prison again. And now he's taken someone else with him." At least this time, I reflected, it wasn't my fault. Not entirely, anyway. I still grappled with a dull pang of guilt, since it was my inaccurate story months ago that had toppled the first domino, leading to a cascading series of events: Brie's death, Dev's assault, Preston's kidnapping. But as I'd begun to learn, taking the blame—or the credit—for other people's actions was useless. Despite what my ego wanted me to believe, I didn't control the universe.

Anyway, those were thoughts best saved for my next therapy appointment. For now, the adrenaline spike had begun to fizzle, and exhaustion moved in behind it. When I yawned, Sam put an arm around me. I gazed up at him, marveling at how he'd leapt into action without an iota of hesitation. He'd taken on a twenty-something to save my former boss, a man he didn't even like. And aside from the swollen knuckles he'd used to rearrange Jameson's nose, he didn't bear so much as a scratch.

A wave of affection filled me. More than a wave—a tsunami. I reached up and brushed a strand of his hair back into place and tenderly kissed his cheek. He pulled me closer, and I rested my head on his shoulder.

Raul cleared his throat. "Beat it, you two. I'll get your statements tomorrow."

"Mmm," I said drowsily. "Not too early. But then again, not too late. Don't forget, tomorrow is festival day."

At the thought of the Fireweed Festival, I shot a look at the creatures. Maybe it was time to admit defeat and withdraw them from Sunday's pageant. After all, they'd displayed talents tonight that topped anything we could put on stage.

Then my jaw dropped open. I nudged Sam with my elbow and pointed. He followed my eyes and grinned broadly.

Positioned next to the hearth, Woody lifted up onto his haunches and raised a big front paw. Beside him, Carl rose on his back legs and swatted Woody's paw with his own. High-five, brother.

Maybe we stood a chance after all.

44

The soothing warmth of the sun massaged my scalp and shoulders. I lifted my face to greet its rays. Carl shifted on my lap, purring as I ran my finger down his spine. Stretched out across my feet, Woody snored softly.

I let my gaze travel across the crowd gathered in the park. It was Sunday afternoon, and the Fireweed Festival was winding down. Only the pet pageant remained, and the creatures were resting up for their performance. Since their impromptu display in my kitchen Wednesday night, Woody and Carl had repeated their high-five display on command at every request. My confidence soared. We were going to win, I just knew it.

I caught a whiff of Tonya's familiar scent—jasmine and sweet orange—just before she appeared and slid onto the folding chair to my left. I smiled at the sight of her. On a bad day, the woman was drop dead gorgeous. Today was not a bad day.

She wore an orange floral dress, strapless and flowing, split on the side to reveal a length of toned thigh. Her hair hung loose around her shoulders, wavy and voluminous, commanding attention. Her brown eyes sparkled—but not nearly as vividly as the huge diamond that flashed on her ring finger.

I lifted my hand to my forehead, as if shielding my eyes. "Put that thing away. You're going to blind someone."

She laughed and admired the ring. "I'm still not used to it. I mean, I'm engaged. Who saw that coming?"

I put my arm around her shoulders and squeezed. "You deserve every ounce of happiness you get. And David—well, he's the luckiest man I know."

"Speaking of lucky men, here I am." Sam scooted into the chair on my right. The sun caught the red highlights streaking through his hair. He kissed me, and a wave of heat rushed through me that had nothing to do with the sun.

I studied his face for signs of stress. Elyse had mentioned that she planned to talk to him this morning about foregoing the dorm this fall and staying in Rock Creek Village. The news about Alexis had rattled her but left her resolved to do what she felt was best for her.

"How's Elyse?" I ventured.

"We talked, if that's what you're getting at. She told me you already know about all this." He rubbed his chin. "I'm not sure how her mother will react, but ultimately, it's Elyse's decision. Truthfully, I'm relieved. I wasn't looking forward to having her that far away."

I nodded, wondering how my life might have been different if I'd chosen to stay in the village instead of going to Texas for college. But as happy as I felt now, why dwell on the road not taken?

Sam squeezed my leg. "I stopped by the gallery to walk over with you, but you'd already closed up shop."

"We sold out of Fireweed Festival stock," I said proudly. "Ethan and I sat in the booth and took online orders for an hour afterward. Lots of demand."

Tonya clapped her hands, more to watch the ring sparkle than to celebrate me, I suspected. "That's fantastic. Your mystery shoppers really boosted business."

I grinned. Turned out Bradley and Tim, the handsome couple who had purchased five of my best photos, were social influencers with quite the celebrity status. Neither

Ethan nor myself were into that kind of thing, so we hadn't recognized them. But when the couple got home and mounted the photos on the walls of their lavish cabin, viewers took notice. Sundance Studio vaulted to a minor celebrity status of its own—one I realized would flash and fade, as such trends did. But until then, we'd ride the wave.

With all this work ahead and Alexis—well, gone—I'd need a new assistant. Maybe now that Elyse was staying in town…? Or perhaps the twins?

Sam spotted a friend across the park and went to say hello. Tonya pulled a floppy hat over her hair and leaned back in her chair. "Did you see the special edition of *The Gazette* this morning?"

"I did. Excellent story, even better than the one in *The Sentinel*. Contest-worthy, if you ask me."

She fanned herself in mock humility—using the ring hand, naturally. "Aw, shucks. I had access to top insider sources, you know."

I smiled, but I wasn't showering her with false praise—Tonya's story was outstanding. Clear, concise, accurate. And extensive. She'd packaged the main story with two lengthy sidebars, one covering Alexis's background and one devoted to Jameson's history. Most of the details I already knew, either from my own research or from transcripts of Raul's interrogations. But seeing it all laid out in black and white made things real.

It wasn't the first time I'd been face to face with psychopaths, but I sure hoped it was the last.

"I'm already gathering information for next week's follow-up stories. Raul told me he'd transferred the two of them to Chilula County to face first degree murder charges."

"I heard. I don't think Jameson will be wriggling out of this one."

Woody woke up then and got to his feet, indulging in one of those doggie stretches that starts at the nose and travels all the way to the tip of the tail. He licked my knee, but saved the bulk of his affection for Tonya.

As he rested his head in her lap, she scratched his ears. "Speaking of insider sources, what happened with Preston Garrison? Did he get fired? Promoted?"

I wasn't supposed to talk about it, but I filled her in on what I knew, anyway. It'd all come out soon. Might as well be Tonya that broke the story.

Nicole Harrison-White had sent her personal plane to retrieve Preston, Dev, Melanie, Gary, and Sanderson, the lawyer. Preston and I had barely gotten a chance to say goodbye before they were whisked out of town. Word of Preston's affair with Nicole had leaked out, and I suspected it was Preston who had done the leaking. If so, it was a savvy move. Nicole could hardly fire the man now, not without being accused of sexual harassment herself. It looked like he would get his promotion after all. And I knew he'd make a solid editor-in-chief, in spite of his less-than-ideal personal life.

Dev ended up with a concussion and twelve stitches in his scalp, but we all knew it could've been a lot worse. He'd tendered his resignation to Preston on the plane back to D.C., and Melanie had decided to take a leave of absence. Dev told me the two of them were going to give my lifestyle a try. They were currently scouting locations.

As I ended my summary, there was a burst of activity on the makeshift stage across the park. Carl woke up from his nap and glared at the people making all the racket. Woody appeared quite Zen, his eyes half closed under Tonya's touch. No performance anxiety for my creatures. Ice water flowed through their veins.

From the corner of my eye, I saw Sophie Demler approach, appearing as confident and brash as ever. "Callahan Cassidy, you and I need to talk. I've decided to launch a podcast, and you're going to be my first guest. Bradley and Tim's visit might have kickstarted your gallery…" she paused to stretch her hands across the sky, "…but *Sophie's Starlight* will send it into the stratosphere."

Tonya and I looked at each other and smirked. "You

have to give her credit," Tonya murmured.

"She's got gumption," I agreed.

Sophie beamed expectantly. Then Mrs. Finney marched toward us, carrying two cardboard coffee cups. "Shoo, Sophie," she said. "We need to prepare for the pet pageant. You're disturbing the aura."

Sophie pursed her lips and glared. Mrs. Finney stared back, unblinking. Finally, Sophie broke eye contact and stomped away.

Mrs. Finney placed one cup in my hand and the other in Tonya's. Then she reached into the pocket of her purple muumuu and extracted chunky treats for the creatures. Woody delicately lifted the offering from Mrs. Finney's fingertips. After a quick sniff at his treat, I swear Carl rolled his eyes. Mrs. Finney chuckled and tossed the second treat to Woody as well.

I lifted my cup and read the newest axiom: "When the storm ends, the sun always reappears."

This one I understood. "Very fitting," I said. Mrs. Finney nodded sagely.

Willie stepped onto the stage and flipped through his notecards. So far, word of the key theft seemed to have been contained. With villagers none the wiser, his cherished role as Chamber president remained intact.

A glance at my watch told me it was five minutes until showtime. I took a moment to scout the competition. The main contenders, I figured, were the labrador in a tophat, the serene-looking border collie, and the ferret wearing a kimono.

I reached into my bag and took out the creatures' outfits. Simple sweaters, navy blue to set off the gold of their fur, knitted by Maggie Cassidy. No razzle dazzle here—our goal was classy and sophisticated.

My parents walked toward us, Mom pausing to show her friends the medal hanging around her neck. Cradling Carl in one arm, I stood and hugged my mother with the other. "Congratulations! First place! Told you so."

"That's my wife." Dad's face crinkled with pride.

"Oh, go on, you guys," Mom said, looking pleased. "Anyway, it seems likely I won't be the only champion in the family." She squatted, and Woody nuzzled her cheek. I handed over his sweater, and she secured it onto his furry body. Then she turned to Carl, who didn't even squirm as she outfitted him as well. "Now for the final touch." With a flourish, she reached into her bag and pulled out two pet-sized headbands topped with enormous felt sunflowers.

So much for classy and sophisticated.

"There we are," she said, cooing at the creatures. Woody smiled and wagged, seemingly proud of his headgear. But I noticed a certain look in Carl's eyes that didn't bode well.

Sam rejoined us just as Willie tapped the microphone. David strolled across the grass, looking suave with his gelled black hair. He dropped into the chair next to Tonya, and the two of them gazed adoringly into each other's eyes. If I hadn't been so happy for them, I might have considered it gag-worthy. But I had to admit, from all outward appearances, they made the perfect couple.

Reverberation from the microphone echoed across the park. Willie's assistant gave him a little shove, and he took a step back. "Ladies and gentlemen," he said. "We hope you've had a wonderful weekend at the Fireweed Festival. As predicted, it has been a phenomenal experience, complete with—" he gestured to the sky "—the most perfect weather we could hope for."

Despite the irony of his statement, I smiled. He was right, after all. The storm that had terrorized us Wednesday night had blown away by Thursday morning, leaving us four days of blue skies and bright sunshine.

"What better way to conclude the Fireweed Festival than with our annual pet pageant? We will begin with the procession across the stage. Contestants, please take your places at the stairs."

I took a breath, surprised at my sudden nervousness. A week ago, I would have said this was an exercise in futility.

Now, after witnessing the creatures' high-five performance, I really believed Woody and Carl might end the day with medals of their own. I felt like a total stage mom.

I toted Carl toward the stage, and Woody pranced along beside us. Brimming with confidence, we lined up with the other contestants. I looked back to my group in the audience and saw that Jessica and Summer had joined them, along with Ethan. I smiled and waved at our personal cheerleading squad, and they roared their approval.

Then the ferret took one look at Carl in his sunflower headgear and made a clucking noise that sounded remarkably like laughter. Carl hissed and batted my arm, just hard enough that I eased my grip. He wriggled from my grasp and pounced on the ferret, sending buttons flying from the kimono. The ferret swatted Carl, Carl swatted the ferret, and the ferret's owner screamed and rushed into the fray. Then the labrador bounded into the fracas, his tophat sliding across his eyes.

The serene border collie sat to the side of the melee, panting contentedly as he observed. Woody trotted over and sat beside him. On stage, Willie tore at his hair. His assistant fanned him with a piece of paper.

I chewed my thumbnail, my cheeks burning with shame. The pet pageant was a fiasco, and we were responsible.

Then I turned to look at my people. Sam winked. Ethan put his fingers in his mouth and emitted a sharp whistle. Jessica and Summer threw their heads back in laughter, and Tonya blew me a kiss. I scanned the rest of the audience. A few people looked worried as Carl and the ferret bickered, but most of them seemed to be having a great time.

I turned my face back to the sun. Woody walked over to me and pressed his silky body against my calf. As the ferret transferred his irritation to the befuddled labrador, Carl strolled over to join us, watching the circus with an air of disdain, as if he hadn't started the whole thing.

And then I felt it, as deeply as I'd ever felt anything.

Life simply couldn't get any better.

Coming soon:

Frozen in Motion

Callie Cassidy Mysteries Book 3

Subscribe to the newsletter for updates

www.lorirobertsherbst.com

About the Author

Lori Roberts Herbst lives in Dallas, Texas, but spends a lot of time when she should be writing staring out the window and wishing she owned a home in the Colorado mountains, too. She is a wife, mother, grandmother (gasp!), former journalism teacher, former counselor, and cozy mystery author. Lori serves as secretary of the Sisters in Crime North Dallas chapter and is a proud member of the SinC Guppies and the Mystery Writers of America. You can (and should!) follow Lori on Facebook and Instagram.

Subscribe to her newsletter at www.lorirobertsherbst.com for updates and giveaways.

CPSIA information can be obtained
at www.ICGtesting.com
Printed in the USA
LVHW050131020522
717667LV00004B/211